Inspired by Grace

By Jeanna Ellsworth

Check out Jeanna Ellsworth's blog and other books by Hey Lady
Publications: https://www.heyladypublications.com
Follow Jeanna Ellsworth on Twitter: @ellsworthjeanna
Like her on Facebook:
https://www.facebook.com/Jeanna.Ellsworth
Like the book's Facebook page:
www.facebook.com/InspiredByGraceTheNovel
Connect by email: Jeanna.ellsworth@yahoo.com

This book is a work of fiction and any resemblances to actual
events or persons, living or dead, are purely coincidental, because
this work is a product of the author's imagination. The opinions
expressed in this manuscript are solely the opinions of the author.

Acknowledgements

First of all, I would like to thank the loyal readers who have supported me in my writing—always begging for more. To those along the way who encouraged me to step away from comfortable, familiar, dear Mr. Darcy and try my hand at an original work: you know who you are, and I thank you.

Secondly, I would like to thank my beta readers who saw this story in its raw form: Linda, KaraLynne, Christy, Donna, Kathy, and Patsy. Their questions and opinions led to extensive improvements, forcing me to answer questions I hadn't asked and showing me the holes I hadn't seen. Then I nervously sent it to my editor, Katrina Beckstrand, who over a long-distance run with her husband came up with some ideas on how to mend it. Her list of ideas and suggestions inspired five more chapters and about twenty-three thousand additional words. Just that little bit of guidance helped me fill in the missing parts and bridge the broken connections, leaving you with this completed novel that I am proud to present for your entertainment. Her hand may not have written it, but her head saw its potential. Thank you so very much!

Dedication

To Paige, my firstborn daughter, who has more character of heart and spirit than anyone I know. There is so much to love about you—and yes, to laugh at too. You handled everything life has thrown at you with grace, and I know you always will. You truly inspire me.

CHAPTER 1

October 1818

"So sorry, Your Grace," Gavin's valet apologized. "I shall be finished in just a moment."

"No, this is my fault, Winston. I should have been more careful with my tea," he sighed. "And please stop calling me 'Your Grace'; you have been my valet far longer than I have been titled."

Winston gave Gavin a brief, hesitant look and pursed his lips. Gavin could tell he was choosing to ignore the request. Winston was more than a valet; he was the closest thing Gavin had to a brother. Well, at least now he was.

It had been six months since his older brother Spencer died; six months since he had been called back from his navy ship and given the title of Duke of Huntsman. And it still felt just as foreign as the day he took it. All the formalities and soirees and dinner parties were exhausting. Every face and name blurred.

What he wouldn't give to have his brother back and to be at sea with his crew again! It was strange; he had enjoyed tossing to and fro with the waves as a captain. But now that his life had changed course, he felt unsteady, ill at ease with the surging demands placed upon him.

Winston finished retying the cravat. "There. You are ready, Your—" Winston picked up on Gavin's subtle glare and wisely caught himself just in time. "You're . . . welcome," the valet stammered.

Gavin muttered his thanks and turned on his heel. The click of his boots spoke of his anxiety, and the ache in his head built with each patterned clippity-clop as he nearly danced down the spiral staircase.

Why had his great-grandfather ever build such a tight staircase, one that literally wrapped around itself like a little girl's ringlet? Couldn't he have made better use of the foyer's space? After all, the room was expansive, almost as big as a ballroom. He would change that. Now that it was his house, he would change that.

There. His mother would be proud of him. He had just made his first decision that showed ownership of this blasted title and the wretched inheritance that he should never have received in the first place.

He was a second son. His parents had always been proud that they had an heir and a spare, as well as his younger sister. Well, now there was no spare. He was it. Spencer was dead, and so was his father.

Seeing the look on his mother's face as he came to the bottom of the stairs, he began imagining inventive excuses for his delay. But ultimately he opted for honesty. "Forgive me, Mother. I was not careful with the tea and stained my cravat. I am sorry to have kept you waiting."

His mother, Her Grace Patricia Kingston, Duchess of Huntsman, had no restraint when she felt her opinion needed to be shared, and she felt the need quite frequently. Gavin was in no mood for it and hardly gave her a glance as the butler handed him his top hat and jacket. Gavin opened the door of his London townhouse and motioned for his mother to proceed to the carriage. He ignored her mutterings about how the Tremontons were expecting a call twenty minutes ago.

He focused on ignoring everything around him—his mother, his title, the *ton*, and the rest of it. He did not wish to go to the Tremontons anymore than he wished for a needle in the eye. Their daughter, Sylvia, was relentless, and if the rumors were true, she had her sights set on gaining a title—his blasted new title in particular. Women were practically throwing themselves at him now that he was no longer the spare.

Six months ago he wouldn't have minded. Back then, he couldn't wait to make port. There had been Francis, in Liverpool—a dazzling blonde who enjoyed moonlit walks. And Patricia, off the coast of Scotland, who could outdrink even him. Amberly was a little too frisky for his taste, but it hadn't stopped him from seeking her out whenever the ship docked in Falmouth. Women in every port knew him as Captain Kingston, a man who laughed and flirted with anyone in a skirt. He wasn't a rake—he'd never done more than steal a few kisses—but it had been fun. He'd intentionally courted women who didn't want to settle down any more than he did. And not one of them had known who his father was. *How things have changed since those days!*

The clouds were thick this afternoon, and rain was just starting to fall. His mother glared at him as she headed toward the carriage. He took a deep breath and geared up for the lecture he was sure to receive once the carriage door closed. Placing the top hat low on his head, and keeping with his habit, he clippity-clopped down the townhouse's front steps while swinging his coat around in one motion and sliding his arms around so that the tight-fitting garment was snugly in place.

In less time than it took to blink, he had descended the stairs, pulled on his jacket, and somehow ran into a woman at the base. The woman screamed out in surprise, and he instinctively reached out, but the weight of her fall unbalanced him, and he tripped. Having achieved such efficient, forward propulsion from racing down the stairs, he had no choice but to somersault over her right into the street, landing under the belly of the horse.

In the presence of a woman—and, of course, his mother—he quickly held back a few choice words that came to his mind, but he needn't have bothered.

"Dragon's alive!" the woman cursed.

He chuckled slightly at her choice of blasphemy. He could think of several more colorful ones. He was a sailor after all. He rolled over and scooted out from under the horse, now doubly curious to see whom he had run into.

The first thing he noticed were the angry flames shooting out of her eyes. *Well, lucky for me this rain will save me from getting singed.* He couldn't stop chuckling. The woman's simple, dark gray dress was filthy. If his attire looked anything like her dress, he might be spared from going to the Tremontons' after all. He would certainly need to change first.

"And what, pray tell, is so funny about running down a lady?" The fire wasn't only in her eyes; every word was punctuated with emphasis.

He stood up and sobered himself quickly, reminding himself that he was at fault for running her down. "Forgive me," he apologized. "I was in a hurry and failed to take notice of where I was going. Let me help you up." He offered his hand and looked at the woman a little closer. Beautiful strawberry-blonde hair was just noticeable under her bonnet. And her eyes were the bluest he had seen in a long while, despite their angry flames.

She did not reach to take his hand. Instead, she looked away.

"Truly, I am sorry, miss. I did not mean to be so clumsy. My mind was preoccupied. Please, allow me to help you."

She whipped her head back to him, and something in her look made him laugh again. She was so beautiful when she frowned! Her pert lips deepened in their expression,.

"Being stubborn will not help you. Here, take my hand. I offer it as any gentleman would."

"And do gentlemen often run down ladies? If so, I shall stay clear of them."

Her temper, which had seemed so humorous a minute ago, was now starting to grate on his nerves. He had offered several times to help her up, and yet she had not moved. His reply came out with a bit of sarcasm: "Only when we are preoccupied. If you see any other absentminded gentlemen, take care, or they might sweep you off your feet. But is that not what every young girl wishes?"

"I am no young girl."

"You cannot be more than eighteen."

"And what kind of gentleman asks a lady her age? Do tell me, sir, are you a real gentleman, or do you just dress the part?"

He dipped his chin and bit his tongue, forcing himself to hold in the rebuttal. By now his mother had been handed out of the carriage and a footman was holding an umbrella over her. He noticed a book and another umbrella on the ground next to the woman.

He retrieved the items and passed the book to his mother, who took it wordlessly—*thank God.* He held the umbrella over the woman's head and offered his hand one more time. If she didn't take it now, he was determined to leave her there, rain or not. Obviously the woman had been preoccupied with her book; he had not been the only one at fault. "Look, miss, you can accept my hand, or you can wallow in the street. It is entirely your choice." He knew his tone was harsher than necessary.

The woman sucked in a ragged breath and then suddenly coughed, as if she were embarrassed by the original sound and attempting to hide it. It reminded him of times when he had caught his mother on the brink of tears and she had fought to regain control with sheer grit. The woman cleared her throat, and with control he knew she did not feel, she announced, "I truly cannot get up."

The duchess walked over to her and inquired, "Are you hurt?"

Blast it! Why hadn't I asked? He looked, and sure enough, she was cradling her left ankle with one hand.

"I believe I have rolled my ankle. I do not think I can stand."

Gavin's mother sent him daggers and then tipped her head toward the townhouse in one quick, subtle motion. He took a deep breath and handed the umbrella over to the footman.

"Hold on tight, miss." Without so much of a hint of a warning, he scooped her up and walked the six steps up to the townhouse. She tried to protest, but he just rolled his eyes. Her arms now clung to him as if she did not trust him to carry her. The driver had raced ahead of him and opened the front door. She was light as a feather and smelled of fresh linen and something else. Cinnamon? What a strange mixture! It was so pleasant that he took a few more deep breaths before placing her on the parlor chaise.

He heard his mother directing the household for warm blankets, clean washcloths, and hot tea. The absence of the woman in his arms was strangely painful. Now that they were out of the rain, he could see her more clearly. She had the tiniest dimple in her chin. As she said thank you to the servants, her voice sparked something in him. A memory? Something in her mannerisms was oddly recognizable.

He stepped back as the servants started to hover around her. Why did she look familiar?

The housekeeper started to wash the splatters of dirt off her face and then gasped. "You're Grace!" she exclaimed.

"Yes," Gavin, the duchess, and the woman answered simultaneously. Confusion swept over all three faces.

The injured woman looked closely at the housekeeper, and suddenly her pouty lips turned into the brightest smile while dimples formed on both sides of her face. "Mrs. Bearl!" she cried. "Oh, look at you!"

"Look at you! All grown up! I can hardly beli—" Mrs. Bearl exclaimed.

"Mrs. Bearl," Gavin interrupted the reunion, "do you know this woman?" He was all curiosity now.

Mrs. Bearl embraced the woman and brushed the ringlets away from her face. "Of course I do! Grace Ingrid Genevieve Iverson, what has your family been up to?"

Gavin's jaw dropped, and he said, "Gigi? Is that really you?"

*****

Grace felt her cheeks flush with embarrassment. She had nearly lost herself to tears out on the street at the way that man had been laughing at her. The situation was even more humiliating now that she recognized him. But she was stronger than that.

"Yes, Your Grace, I am Grace Iverson. Based on your title, I assume you are Spencer."

A cold look replaced the happy surprise in the man's face. "No. Just Gavin, I am afraid. You remember my mother, of course. Welcome to Willsing Manor. I will see to getting the doctor."

She watched him walk purposefully toward the door. As his mother reached out to him, he shook off her hand.

The duchess walked over to her and gently touched her cheek. "Grace, my dear, how good it is to see you! Forgive me for not recognizing you out there in the rain. How long has it been?"

"I moved away when I was barely fourteen, Your Grace, so it has been ten years now."

"Ten years since your father died? I cannot believe it! Well, Gavin was correct; you certainly do not look older than eighteen. The years have been good to you."

Grace smiled politely. She could play this game. She had spent nearly a full season in town three years ago when she was one-and-twenty, so she had learned that people do not always mean what they say. She had let too many people into her heart only to be taught this powerful and painful lesson: people say one thing and do another. People may say they love you, but most hearts are not as loyal as hers. When she loved someone, she loved them forever. So, the only thing to do was not love anyone else.

"And how is your family?" the duchess inquired. "Your mother and sisters?"

"I am sorry to say, Your Grace, that my mother passed away three years ago, just as I came of age."

"Oh dear! I am so sorry. How terrible for you to be left to London society without a sponsor! Is that why your last name is still Iverson? Have you not found a match yet?"

The audacity of this woman! She had always been a little bold, but this was unbelievable. Although the duchess's guess had been correct. Grace had left the season early when her mother passed and had been living very quietly with her sister and her sister's husband in East Sussex for the last three years. She fumbled in her attempt to answer the duchess, "Your Grace . . . after my mother's death, I . . . ."

The older woman gently put her hand on hers. "I, too, have lost loved ones, my dear. My husband and Spencer have gone to the other side." The pain in the woman's eyes was fresh, unlike Grace's own that was years old. The duchess was wearing all black, a detail that had escaped Grace's notice until then. She chided herself for being so quick to judge. This woman had been like a second mother to her for years. She had known the Kingston family as well as her own back then.

"It is hard to lose those we love," Grace said. "How long has it been?"

"Oh, let us not talk about that now. I remember one afternoon, years before your family left Suffolk, when your mother and I swore an oath. We said that if anything ever happened to one of us, then the survivor would step in and help the other's children if they were ever in need. And from the quality of your muslin, dear, you are in need. I insist on sponsoring you this season! How splendid is that?"

Grace looked down uncomfortably and tried to think of an excuse, but she knew that if either of her sisters ever found out that she had refused such an offer from the duchess, she would never be forgiven. They had both found matches in their first season. Reluctantly she said, "I would like that very much. Although the duke may like it a bit less."

"Oh, nonsense! When can you move in?"

A loud crash was heard outside the door, and a distinct male voice let out an oath that even Grace had never used. But then again, Grace enjoyed thinking up ridiculous words to shock people while maintaining her ladylike behavior. Standard, unimaginative curses weren't really her style.

*****

Gavin placed a smile on his face, leaned his head into the parlor, and said, "The doctor is on his way. Mother, could I have a word?"

"Whatever happened? That was not my tea set, was it? Good gracious, Gavin! We just replaced it!"

"Mother, please, a word. You can chide me out here just as well as in there."

"Very well." His mother followed him out the door.

The servants had already started to clean up the spilled tea and broken china that lay scattered all over the foyer. Gavin guided his mother to a corner out of earshot. "My apologies, Mother. I took the tray from the servant and was just bringing in the tea when I thought I heard you invite Grace to stay here. Pray tell me you have not offered such a thing."

"Whyever not?"

"Well . . . ," he flustered, "as you are so fond of telling me, this is my home now. And I am a single gentleman."

"Nonsense, I live here too. There is nothing improper about it. She will be my pupil, and I shall find her a husband by the time the season is up. Mark my word."

Gavin felt his throat tighten ever so slightly with anxiety. "But," he stammered, "we know so little about her. What if she has a past that would taint us by association?" He had his own reasons for hesitating, but he had no intention of discussing them with his mother.

"Really, Gavin, how much more can our names be tainted? There are already enough rumors floating around about Spencer and your father that we cannot go unnoticed."

"Precisely. That is exactly why she cannot stay under my roof."

His mother pressed her lips together and placed her hand on his face and said, "It is done. I cannot take back the invitation, nor will I."

He groaned inwardly and prayed that at least Gigi had the sense to decline the offer.

CHAPTER 2

While the duchess was outside talking with Gavin, Grace inspected her ankle. She could move it with a bit of pain, so it probably was not broken. She pointed her toes and could feel its strength, but when she rotated it inward . . . She winced at precisely the wrong moment; Gavin had just come in and witnessed her flinch. Once again, she felt weak. She didn't like to feel weak. She quickly covered her ankle again and sat back against the pillow.

Grace gave what she hoped was a plausible smile and announced, "I have good news: I may not need a doctor."

Gavin chuckled, and the sound brought back flashes of childhood memories, recollections of his glorious laughter. Although, this laughter had a deep resonance to it that sent tingles up her spine. She looked at him and saw the excessive confidence that he had always carried, and she smiled more sincerely. Gavin was always so bright and carefree. He never let anything bother him, not even when she would prank him. If anything, he welcomed it.

One summer, she had snuck into his bedchamber and stole a pair of pantaloons and his best shirt. The gardener helped her fashion them into a scarecrow with a large, painted gourd for a head. She hung a sign around his neck—*Kiss me! I know you want to!*—and put him on the road that led to town. Young girls from all over the village dared each other to kiss the scarecrow. Gavin thought it was such a good joke that he refused to let anyone take it down.

There were rumors that Gavin would hide behind a tree and watch the girls reaching up on their tippy toes to kiss the gourd. If the girl were plain, he would jump out and scare her; but if she were handsome, he would insist on a *real* kiss. This only encouraged more girls to romance a painted vegetable to see which of the surprises they would obtain for their efforts. Once, she asked him if the rumors were true. With a glint in his eye, Gavin denied any involvement and suggested, "Try it and see for yourself!" But Grace was never brave enough to try.

That was how Gavin was. He didn't mind being the center of attention, and he didn't seem to mind being in trouble either. Some days he was more trouble than she could handle, but it didn't stop her from spending day after day with him.

Two years before he left for Eton, what started as a simple trick to frighten Grace's governess with crickets in her soup, escalated into a scheme of Gavin throwing up crickets during lunch. They spent all afternoon catching the insects. Gavin found that he could hold three in his mouth without gaging, but four made his stomach clench. How he handled even one was beyond Grace. Her role was simple but vital, as she needed to do all the talking until the time was right. Then Gavin moaned and wailed and retched the crickets into his soup bowl.

The governess screamed and resigned her position on the spot. She reconsidered only after the duchess secured vows from both youths that they would never eat live crickets again. Gavin said his vow with a faint smile, whispering to Grace that he hadn't actually eaten any and never intended to.

Grace found herself in the midst of trouble many more times until he left for school at Eton. And when he did, she found her days were dull and lifeless. He had been such a huge part of her life that his absence left a void.

When she heard that he was back that first summer, she was so excited to see him and hear how school had been that she could hardly finish her lessons. But no sooner had she ran out to meet him than she found him headed to her door to tell her about it. It had always been that way with them. They were the best of friends. Nothing stopped them from seeing each other.

Soon their parents gave up trying to separate them for their studies and hired a tutor to teach them both during the summer break. More often than not, they would find mischief, because that was the best part about Gavin; he was always getting into trouble. He had a knack for literally tripping into the muck and then laughing about it.

It wasn't until the summer before her father died, when she was fourteen and he was sixteen, that things started to change. As usual, they had shared a tutor, but this time they had shared a dancing master as well. It all started out so innocent. And then things changed.

Gavin's voice startled her back to Willsing Manor. "Grace? Are you sure you are well?"

She looked up at his worried brow. He had changed a great deal since that summer. He was quite handsome, none of the awkward pre-adulthood problems. His skin was clear, his jaw was strong and chiseled, and his sideburns were long and shaved in the latest fashion. His hair was a darker blonde, and his chestnut brown eyes . . . were different. They had always been so expressive when they were young, but now they seemed guarded.

"Yes, I think I can walk now. This happens to me all the time."

He let down his guard momentarily. The left side of his mouth turned up, and his right eyebrow arched. "A man runs into you and knocks you down all the time?" he asked.

She felt her heart flutter, and she quickly looked away, trying not to smile. *Gibblets! Did he have to be so handsome? Say something, Grace!*

"Indeed not, Your Grace. That was a first. I mean I roll my ankles all the time."

His eyes narrowed. The effect was instantaneous, like blowing out a candle. He had changed back again from his lighthearted, teasing self to a man who seemed to know his role. She wondered what his role was at the moment.

"Did I say something wrong, Your Grace?"

There was a moment of silence, and then he offered his hand in a cool manner and said, "Try to stand up. Hold onto me if you need to."

She didn't fail to notice that he had changed the subject, but she did as he asked. She gingerly placed both feet under her and felt him gently pull her up. From experience, she placed all her weight on the right leg and then eased into shifting her weight. She tried not to grimace, but he was too observant and wrapped a supporting arm around her waist, which only made her knees even more unsteady. She could nearly feel his breath next to her.

It was just like their dance lessons.

She looked up at him briefly and caught his watchful gaze. He smelled so heavenly! It was a mixture of sage and lemon, the same soap he had always used, but, in case she was in any doubt, the sandalwood addition confirmed that he was no longer an adolescent. She felt her palms and cheeks heat up, which was not good. He could always tell when she was getting emotional because her cheeks colored. Most of the time it was from anger or irritation with him, and she prayed he assumed the same reason now. She did not wish him to know what she was thinking.

Suddenly she knew her ankle would have to hold up her own weight regardless of whether or not it was capable. She stood up straight and said, "Thank you, Your Grace. I believe it is as I said; I shall be fine. I will just put on my boot again and be on my way. No need for a doctor."

He nodded but did not step away as she had hoped. Her cheeks colored again. Why wasn't he letting her go? She threw him a nervous glance, and he appeared to suddenly realize her meaning. Carefully stepping away, he let her bear her own weight. He seemed to be waiting for something; was he waiting to see her fail? She was not going to give him the satisfaction.

Gavin cleared his throat and eyed her boot, still sitting across the room where the maid had placed it. "Yes, of course, Grace," he said. "No doubt you have several prior engagements for this afternoon. Do not let me detain you any longer." He then exited with a smile and left her standing all alone in the parlor.

*****

After discussing a few unimportant sundries in the foyer with his butler, Gavin peeked back into the parlor and held back a smile. Determination was written across Grace's face, and she had every intention of reaching her boot. She lifted her chin and squared her shoulders and took a few faltering steps. *Still the same Grace, I see.*

It reminded him of when Spencer would pull her pigtails. No one was allowed to do that but Gavin. It was an unspoken ritual. Whenever she grew too stubborn or pigheaded, Gavin would pull on her pigtails and say, "A tail for the stubborn pig." But if Spencer dared try, Grace would wrestle him to the ground. She knew all sorts of ways to pin his arm behind him until Spencer yelled out, begging for mercy.

This is ridiculous, Grace! How he wished he could pull her pigtails now! She hobbled in her own feminine way over to her boot, but she was clearly in pain. Her every movement was cautious, and she held her breath with each step, letting out an audible sigh when the weight transferred to her good foot.

Why must she always have things her way? She never did like to lose, but this is hardly a competition.

Walking back toward her, he clicked his heels a little loudly, alerting her of his presence again. She pursed her lips together and straightened up as he approached, letting go of the settee she had been using as a support. As proudly as she could, she lifted her chin and said, "Perhaps I could use a doctor."

"Is this Gigi admitting she needs help?" Gavin folded his arms in front of him and leaned against the doorway, casually bending a knee as if he had all the time in the world to wait. He knew she was hurting, but he also knew what she was made of. None of the ladies he ever came across were made of the same stuff.

She flashed him an angry look and said, "I said no such thing. I can retrieve my boot without your help."

He walked over to the boot and handed it to her. "You only had to ask. Now, sit down before you fall, you stubborn girl."

"I am not a girl anymore."

His breath caught in his throat. He was all too aware of how she was no longer a girl, but it was entirely inappropriate to say that. He pulled himself together and said, "Yes. If I am to understand correctly, you are my mother's pupil now. Hardly a girl, for sure."

Gigi opened her mouth to speak, but their attention was turned to the door when his mother's voice echoed her disapproval. "Sit down, Grace, this instant! The doctor is here to examine you.

14

Gavin, how can you stand three feet from her without offering any kind of assistance?"

Knowing there would be no peace until he did as his mother told him, Gavin stepped forward and offered his arm for support. Grace took his arm and allowed him to assist her back to the chaise. She always did like his mother.

The duchess then directed the doctor into the room, and out of propriety, Gavin turned around while the man examined her ankle. It wasn't that he hadn't seen her feet before—they had waded in the river all summer long—but this was different. She was a grown woman now, no matter how close they had been as children.

She was different now. She seemed hardened. Not just stubborn, but compulsively independent. He wondered what had made her so stoic. Where was the witty young girl who had made him laugh since before he could remember? What had her life been like over the last ten years?

Mr. Hyde made his assessment and confirmed that the bone was not broken. He advised her to rest the foot as much as possible to avoid any further strain. Apparently there was no swelling yet, but it should be expected. She would be back to normal in a day or two.

Gavin assumed it was safe to turn his attention back to the doctor, and he was indeed correct. Gigi was covering her foot, and once again she had bright color rising in her cheeks. She thanked the doctor graciously, and Gavin seconded the sentiments, only to add that the patient would be well taken care of here at Willsing Manor. Gavin rang the bell, and the butler showed the doctor out.

The duchess inquired after the tea, and then she turned her attention back to Gigi.

"So, Grace, darling, where are you staying right now?"

"With my second-eldest sister, Sarah, and her husband. She lives here in London."

"And your other sister? Is she settled as well?"

"Yes, Your Grace. Tamara married almost immediately after Papa died and now has two children. I have been living with her for several years. I only came to London a few weeks ago to prepare for another season, but unfortunately Sarah took ill after my arrival. She is with child, and we are all very worried. We barely had enough time to get measured for a few new gowns before the doctor confined her to bed."

The duchess took a seat next to her and reached for her hand. "I am so terribly sorry. This is Sarah's first child?"

"This is the first one she carried this far. She is in her seventh month now. She and her husband are devastated over the illness, but she is following the doctor's orders religiously, and we all hope for the best. She sleeps a great deal now. During her naps I often feel the need to stretch my legs. I was just coming back from a walk this afternoon when—"

"—when my son ran into you," the duchess finished for her. "I, for one, am so glad he did. How delightful to see you again!"

Gavin stepped into the conversation and said, "I will write to your sister directly."

"No, if you could just take me home, that would be my preference. Even if your mother is sponsoring me, I will be much more comfortable—"

"Nonsense, Gigi. You heard the doctor," Gavin said. *I can be stubborn too.* "You will stay here." It just felt right to offer her his home. She was like family and always had been. Well, perhaps not always.

She seemed to be either staring him down or trying to determine how he really felt about her staying at Willsing Manor. Either was a real possibility, so he gave her the benefit of the doubt and confirmed what he hoped was the reason for the prolonged silence. "I would be honored to have you in my home. After all, we have a great deal to catch up on, Gigi. What better way than to take our meals together like we did all those years ago? Only this time, we will not be in the nursery with your dolls' tea set. Then again, your dolls' tea set might be useful if you still have it. I seem to have broken my mother's last set." He gave her a wink which earned him a smile in return.

It was a beautiful smile, which she had shown infrequently thus far, and it affected him more than he had anticipated. It sparked something inside him. Something that had been dormant for a while. Maybe it was a blessing that she had come back into his world. She was so full of life.

He had not even noticed that he was examining her again, but his mother's words broke the spell. "Willsing Manor will come alive with your presence, Grace. What a delightful time we will have! Eliza and I enjoyed her season so much."

"How is Eliza?"

"Splendid. She lives in Derbyshire with her husband, a very fine man, Sir Jonathan Jones. She still comes to town every now and again, but I miss having her around." The duchess beamed. "I must admit that I am nearly giddy to think that I shall have a hand in finding you a husband! Gavin and I will make sure that you have a successful season, right, Gavin?"

He snickered a little and said, "Mother, if you intend to make me a part of this, I cannot guarantee that she will find much success. I, myself, have only been back in society for a few months. Grace will probably make more connections by walking the streets with an umbrella and a book on a rainy day. Look what it did for her already." He was pleased that she recognized he was teasing her.

Grace replied with a laugh. "Indeed," she giggled, "I could very nearly start an advent calendar for my wedding day if the gleam in your mother's eye is any indication of the efforts she will make on my behalf."

Gavin tapped his finger on Grace's nose and said, "There she is. I wondered what you had done with my best friend."

*****

Grace forced herself to smile back at Gavin. She wanted to say that she had done nothing with his best friend. She wanted to say that *she* had always been around; it was *he* who had abandoned her. But she could not. The real truth was evident to her without her making conflict; life had simply gotten in the way.

There was nothing she could have done when her father suddenly died of influenza. Their estate in Suffolk was entailed away to her cousin, and there was little money. The small stipend awarded her mother was barely enough to start fresh, let alone to visit old friends. Travel was expensive, and her mother was determined to squirrel away every possible penny for her daughters' nearly nonexistent dowries. That meant that Grace could not go to see her best friend, Gavin; she learned to forget him as best as she could.

The duchess ushered in the tea, and they talked briefly of their plans for the next few weeks. Gavin kept looking at Grace. It was all she could do not to stare back at him. He seemed to switch from the boy she remembered to someone who resembled what she remembered of his father. She wondered what was weighing on him.

Finally, when it looked like the next two weeks were sufficiently planned, Grace asked politely if someone could send word to her sister, Sarah Shaulis of Foxtail Lane. Gavin jumped at the opportunity and slipped out of the parlor to do that very thing.

The duchess stood and took Grace's teacup from her and asked, "Tell me, Grace, how are you doing? You were never one to voice your needs or thoughts, but I can sense a deep sadness in you. I know how close you were to your father." The older lady sat down next to Grace and reached for her hand.

"I was close to my mother too. She meant the world to me. I have never found her equal. In every challenge we faced since my father's death, she rose to meet the situation as if the Prince Regent himself had asked it of her. No problem was too big to solve nor too small to be ignored. She was so determined. And she wanted nothing more than to see her daughters successfully and happily matched. I am afraid that I am the only one that failed her in that regard. My other sisters found matches in their first seasons. But I ended my season early because of her death."

"Oh dear, had you any potential matches? Were there any suitors paying you special attention? I may know if they are still available."

Grace tried to maintain eye contact but failed miserably. If she didn't look away now, the duchess would be sure to see her pain. "I thought so at the time. Things were looking very promising with one man. In fact, there was a lot of promising going around. Before I left, he promised to visit me and send me word through his sister. But the only news I received was the announcement of his engagement to an heiress two weeks later. It appears he had been courting her for several months."

"That was very wrong of him. Was there an actual understanding?"

"He said his only hope was that I would come to love him as much as he loved me. He said he wished to marry me."

The duchess took her hand and turned Grace's chin toward her. "My darling, he used you most abominably. But why did you not return the next year? Did you not say that was three years ago?"

She pulled her chin away then and looked toward the window. Unfortunately she saw Gavin standing in the doorway with a pained expression on his face.

He took a few steps forward and asked, "Who was he?"

Pride stiffened her spine as if someone had dropped ice down her gown. How much had he heard? She took the only road that she knew. She let out a laugh that probably sounded a bit forced and said, "You need not protect me. If you remember correctly, it is I who protected you far too often. I tore many gowns wrestling your older brother off you. And I believe I still can claim to be Queen of the Boulder on Chester Pond. No one ever defeated me."

His words were quiet, but distinct: "Grace Ingrid Genevieve Iverson, no one ever will. I swear it."

CHAPTER 3

The evening had gone smoothly enough after Gavin and his mother stopped probing Grace about her first season. Her sister Sarah had sent over a trunk of Grace's things and a note approving of the duchess's arrangements.

Gavin had made good on his promise to dine with her. The three of them ate a simple meal together in the parlor, so that Grace could rest comfortably on the sofa, and conversation was light and came easily. Grace had nearly forgotten that ten years had passed. When it was time to retire, Gavin kindly asked if he could assist her to her chamber. Her ankle was already feeling much better, so she declined any help. But after watching her take a few staggering steps, Gavin rolled his eyes and, once again without asking, lifted her easily into his arms and hiked the spiral staircase to the second floor. It affected her no less than the first time, and she enjoyed the closeness of his person. She had wrapped her arm around his neck and clung to his shoulder only to find a firmness and fullness that she hadn't anticipated. He was no longer a lanky sixteen-year-old.

Now as the dawn broke, she was alerted to the fact that a maid had nearly finished lighting the fire. As the young woman tried to sneak out the door, Grace whispered, "Thank you."

The maid startled a bit. "Sorry, miss, I tried not to wake you. I will be quieter tomorrow."

"No, you did not wake me. I did not sleep well."

"Sorry to hear that, miss. Can I fetch you anything?"

She considered her ankle. It throbbed only a little, and Grace had no intention of staying in bed all day.

"Would you mind assisting me to freshen up?" she asked. "I am not entirely confident that I can do it on my own quite yet. I would appreciate your help."

"Yes, miss."

Grace pushed off the covers. The maid had already found her slippers and was bending to place them on her feet. There was just the slightest swelling on the outside of her ankle but no bruising. That was a good sign. She wondered if Gavin would carry her downstairs again. Being that close to him had such a powerful affect on her mind and body. She wanted to both pull away and embrace him tightly at the same time.

With her slippers on, Grace eased off the bed and the maid helped her up. She was pleased to find the pain was tolerable. With a cautious step, she made her way across the room toward the washbasin.

"You are doing well, Miss Iverson."

"Yes, I think I can manage on my own now. Thank you."

"Very well. Should I send up your lady's maid?"

"My lady's maid?"

"Yes, miss. The duchess has appointed Charlotte to attend to you while you are here. She is ever so happy to be a lady's maid again. Ever since Miss Eliza married Sir Jonathan, she has not been able to magnify her talents. Shall I send her in?"

"Yes, please do." Grace had never had her own lady's maid. She'd been too young to have one before her father died. And funds were far too tight to employ one afterwards. Even when she had lived with Tamara, Grace simply went without, except for a few special occasions when her sister's maid attended her. It was pleasant to consider that she would have someone to prepare her hair and clothing for the duchess's growing list of dinner parties and balls.

Grace gingerly moved about the room and tried to do her morning toilette but sat down again after a few minutes when her ankle began to ache. Soon she heard the knock on her door.

"Enter."

A maid about her own age came in and curtsied. "You must be Charlotte," Grace said.

"Yes, Miss Iverson. I hope that I can meet your expectations." Charlotte then began detailing her vast experience in coordinating jewelry and accessories, creating intricate braids, and crafting floral embellishments. When she moved on to mending and altering gowns, Grace interrupted.

"Charlotte, I have no doubt in your abilities. I am very grateful for your service and look forward to seeing all these talents, but please, you need not apply for the position. If the duchess feels you are capable, then I do too. I am afraid it will not be hard to impress me."

A smile came to Charlotte's face, and she curtsied. "I shall not disappoint, I assure you, miss. Would you like a bath before you break your fast?"

"I most certainly would, thank you."

Grace soaked even longer than usual and pondered all that had occurred the day before. She spent far too much time thinking about a certain man and how he had awakened every sense in her body that seemed to have withered and wilted in the last ten years. Could this really be happening to her? Was she really going to have her best friend back?

From his lighthearted laughter, to his protective declaration that no one would ever defeat her, to the playful tap on her nose as he said "There she is. I wondered what you had done with my best friend"; it all was so endearing. She could feel her heart pound in her chest as if it had stopped all those years ago and his kindness had restarted it. In truth, she had never trusted anyone since being ripped from his presence. Sometimes even the pain of losing her father did not compare to the heartbreak of not knowing whether she would ever see him again.

Every year she had hoped to receive word that the Kingstons were coming to visit, but no word ever came. Her mother never spoke of them again. Grace wondered why but never dared to ask. It was clear that Grace no longer moved in the same circles as the children of the Duke and Duchess of Huntsman.

Soon she stopped hoping and valiantly fought the memories every time they rose unbidden. In quiet moments, she would allow herself to remember the times when they had raced across the hayfields until they reached the far corner that connected their lands. It was tradition to meet there every morning after breakfast and select a challenge for the day.

Sometimes the challenge was to see who could skip a rock in Chester Pond the most times. Other times it was who could walk the fence the farthest without falling off. And sometimes it was a challenge to the death.

Grace laughed at their fearsome name for this particular challenge. It was really only a game of trust. One person would ask questions while the other would be forced to climb the treehouse rope ladder. Every truthful answer would earn the climber permission to ascend one rung. If the climber reached the top, he or she won and was allowed to climb down safely. But if the questioner suspected any dishonesty, the climber was forced to close his or her eyes, let go of the rope, and "fall to certain death".

But Grace never worried about falling, because she had no doubt that her best friend would be there to catch her. She often ruminated on this game during her lonely ten years without him; somewhere, in the deepest part of her heart, she hoped that he would still catch her.

And as the trials started coming, some right after another, she would tell herself that this was just another game of challenge to the death. It took courage to move up a rung, knowing that the higher she went, the more danger lurked if she were to let go. So, she buckled down and trusted in no one but herself. In truth, she leaned far too much on her own strength during the last few years.

And now she was living under Gavin's roof. She had dreamed all night of those dance lessons, the last one in particular. Did he still remember it? Did he remember the promises they made? She forced the forbidden thought far from her mind but not before she was fully engulfed in goose bumps.

Charlotte startled her out of her mental ruminations. "I am sorry, Miss Iverson, the water must be getting cold. Are you chilled?"

"I suppose I must be." She climbed out of the tub and thought, *I am not sure I want him to remember that last lesson.* Surely it would only bring him embarrassment. He was no longer the second son. He was the Duke of Huntsman. She let out a sigh and reminded herself that a duke marries one of his own. He may have been her best friend once, but a friend was all she could hope for now. That was enough for her.

*****

Gavin had seen Grace's lady's maid heading upstairs. He instructed Charlotte to alert him when Grace was ready to leave her room. He didn't want to miss an opportunity to be near her again. It was strange—he could not explain it—but he felt pulled to her. Maybe it was her cinnamon scent. Had she always smelled so intoxicating? Surely he would have remembered that.

But that wasn't the only change. She had her same eyes, blue as bluebells in rain or shine, but something lurking behind them suggested the years had been difficult. Her smile, the one that used to be such a permanent fixture on her face—except when she was determined to win—had dampened. All of these changes made him even more curious about her.

He pondered on Grace Ingrid Genevieve Iverson, or Gigi, as he always called her, while he sat in the foyer, keeping a watchful eye on the spiral staircase for her appearance. It seemed to take forever; the newspaper he had brought to occupy his time was quickly read from cover to cover.

When over an hour had passed, he was considering knocking on her door. And then he heard the quietest of whimpers from the top of the stairs.

There she was, with her strawberry-blonde hair pulled up in such a tempting way, and when she caught him looking up at her, she gave him a smile. He took the stairs two at a time and was nearly to the top when his boot caught and he had to catch himself from falling.

She giggled and said, "Falling at my feet again? I see nothing has changed. You are still just as clumsy as ever."

He stood up straight and took the last few steps gracefully and then bowed to her. "You bring it out in me, Gigi. I had nearly taken society by storm with my evolution from boy to gentleman, but I see you still see only the boy."

She colored slightly at his teasing and then cocked her head to the side. "Ah, but the boy is always the making of a man," she replied. "You cannot start with the ingredients of rice pudding and expect to get raspberry tarts."

"Indeed, but you are mistaken on one count," he countered with a smile. "I have never been made of rice nor pudding. I am all white sauce and pheasant—far more refined."

"I see you still have more confidence than height. And just look at you—over six feet tall! Dare I ask how horridly exaggerated your self-worth is now, Your Grace?"

He flinched slightly at the reference to his title and decided that it was time to have a little discussion about that with her. But first, and with a move that he deemed entirely graceful, he swept her off her feet and into his arms. It was selfish, he knew, but she couldn't say no. And once her ankle was healed, there was no telling when he would be this close to her again. The cinnamon was strong enough to detect but not so overpowering as to offend. *All the better. Too many women drench themselves in perfume.*

She squealed in delight. "If you drop me, Gavin," she shrieked, "I swear I will throttle you. You know how I hate to lose."

"Feel free to try. I have a good hundred pounds on you now. I am no longer some lanky, skinny thing with feet too big for walking."

He carried her down the stairs, enjoying every moment of it until she said, "Speaking of big feet, it seems you have some big shoes to fill."

He cleared his throat and silently headed into the dining room. After he set her on her feet, she said, "Thank you, Your Grace. Did I say something wrong?"

He looked away from her as he said, "You can start by calling me what you have always called me. I am not particularly fond of my new title." *There! I said it.*

He chanced a look at her and caught sight of her reaching for him. Her soft hand rested on his face, which sent his heart flying completely out of control. "Of course," she murmured. "I would be happy to call you 'muttonhead' or 'bacon-brained'." And then she giggled.

He burst out laughing and kissed her beautiful hand. "You always have to win."

She smiled at him and replied, "No. It just usually happens that way."

"I forgot; you have to have the last word too."

"I see we will get along splendidly. I will always be right, and you will always be Gavin."

Breakfast was casual and comfortable now that "Your Grace" was out of the way. As soon as his mother came into the room, she asked Grace if her ankle was feeling better; once again Gavin chided himself for not thinking of it first.

"Yes, it is much better," she replied to the duchess. "Another day and it shall be as good as new."

The conversation veered toward dinner plans for Thursday. It sounded like the entire *ton* would be invited.

"Gavin," his mother asked, "which of your bachelor friends would you like to introduce Grace to first?"

He was stopped short by this reminder that Gigi was here under his roof to find a husband. He was suddenly uncomfortable in his own skin and didn't know why. Of course he should help by introducing her to his friends. He saw her hopeful eyes on him, and he interpreted it as if she truly desired his help.

Trying to appear confident, he declared, "That depends on what Grace wants. There is Harrison, who struggles with stuttering but is loyal and devoted if his obsessive relationship with his horses is any indication. Then there is Jeffers; do not let his port belly get in your way of getting close, Grace. And Patrick Underton may be right; he has no spine, so Grace could dictate which breeches he is to wear every day."

His mother waved her hand dismissively. "Never mind," the duchess declared, "I know who your friends are, and I shall make the introductions myself. Shame on you for teasing her so mercilessly! Now, Grace, do not let my boy scare you off. He knows many eligible bachelors who would love to get to know you."

Gavin frowned at the thought and found he'd suddenly lost his appetite. As he bowed and took his leave, he heard Grace say, "I would be happy to meet any of his friends. I shall challenge every one of them to a foot race. Is that not how gentlemen are sized up? Whoever is the biggest and bravest wins the lady's heart?"

He turned his head back around and caught her looking at him in earnest. He turned silently and went to his study.

He tugged his arms out of his confining coat as quickly as possible and tried to focus on the morning post. But his thoughts kept drifting back to what she had said. He wondered what she was referring to. It was true that whenever his cousins or friends had visited, Gavin had always introduced them to her. There had probably been a race or two, but what did she mean that "the biggest and bravest" would win the lady's heart? Could she possibly be referring to that late August afternoon ten years ago?

He pushed the post aside and leaned back in his chair. He interlocked his fingers behind his head and let himself drift off to that summer afternoon.

"I shall be leaving for Eton again in two days. I wish I could squeeze your annoying little body into my trunk and pack you along with me. You would make it so much more fun."

"As your father has said so many times, you pay too much attention to me," Grace told him. "I would only distract you."

"No, Gigi, you know that is not true. Why else has he allowed us to share tutors? He knows you bring out the best in me."

She laughed and said, "Well, around me you do trip slightly less often. It must be admitted as an improvement."

"You sound like my father," Gavin sighed. "And I trip much less nowadays. I have never tripped during our dance lessons."

"Yes, I suppose you are commanding of your person during our lessons. But every other time I can safely count on whipping the breeches off you because of your lanky, skinny legs."

He chuckled at her and tapped his finger on her nose. "Think what you must. I shall never win a debate with you. But I am glad to hear you consider me graceful on the dance floor."

"I never said you were graceful. I said you were commanding."

"That is the same as being graceful."

"No, it is not. Graceful means to move smoothly with clean, imperceptible movements."

He knew he had her now. "Ah, but with you in my arms, I am full of Grace. Therefore, by definition, I am Grace-full."

She gave him a small smile and said, "You will always be full of grace in that sense."

"Did you just admit defeat?" he teased.

Grace said proudly, "I did not, and I shall not. I was only saying that I will always be your friend."

He didn't know why—perhaps it was the rare success in a debate that gave him the confidence—but he paused and then said, "Someday, Gigi, there will be someone who will take you away from me. He will be bigger and braver than me. I shall fight him off with a stick, but he will stake claim on your heart, and he will no longer let us be best friends. What we have cannot last forever."

"You sound like you are saying goodbye."

"No, I am just being realistic. Your father will arrange a smart match for you once you have your coming out, and you will be the happiest debutante in London's upper ten thousand. I shall demand to be best man at your wedding, of course, but at some point, what we have shared these many years will no longer be."

"How will I know he will make me happy?"

"He will be big and brave. He will be everything you have ever wanted."

"Promise?"

"I promise. You will see. Keep your eyes wide open."

"What if I never find him? What if I end up a spinster?"

He tapped his finger on her nose and lightly said, "Then I will marry you."

She laughed and said, "Us? Marry? Never." Her tone had been somewhat forced, as if she lacked confidence in her own declaration. It filled him with the slightest amount of hope. But what if she had meant it? What if she could never see him differently? The hope disappeared.

She quickly turned and headed home. She left him standing there hearing her words echo in his heart. He would never be more than a friend.

CHAPTER 4

Gavin was startled from his thoughts by a knock, which sent his already quickened heart galloping. He called out, "Enter," and began to shuffle papers on his desk to make it look as if he hadn't been daydreaming.

"Gavin?" Her feminine voice brought his heart up to his throat, and he looked toward her. She had stopped a few feet inside the door. Her strawberry-blonde hair picked up the sun from the window, and her eyes looked concerned.

He stood and bowed, then forced himself to stop staring at her smooth, pale, ivory skin. It was beginning to be rich with color again. "Yes, Gigi?"

"I hope I did not say something wrong at breakfast. You seemed upset when you left."

He smiled at her. "Not at all," he insisted. "My mother enjoys monopolizing conversations, and I could see my presence was no longer required. You do not need my help finding a match. She knows far more about such things than I do."

"All right, if you say so." She was turning to go, but he sensed she was still uncomfortable about something.

He called after her, "Do you still play chess?"

She turned back around, lifted her chin, and replied, "I do not play chess; I win chess."

He smiled at her and said, "I have not been beaten in years. Now, do tell me if you still require to be black."

"Of course I do. I like to give my opponents the illusion that they start out ahead." She tilted her head in an adorable way that said, "Defy me if you dare". He dared.

He couldn't help but smile. "I remember. Shall we?" He motioned to the side table, and she hobbled fairly smoothly over to a chair. Her ankle was already much better.

He quickly reached for his boxed set and handed it to her. For a moment, he was mesmerized watching her slender fingers quickly set up the pieces.

He walked around to the other side of the table and reached behind him, out of habit, to flip up his tailcoat before sitting down—only to remember he had taken off the confining garment. He laughed and sat down.

Grace looked up at him and asked, "What is so funny?"

He chuckled again. "I just realized that I am not properly clothed to entertain a lady, but then I remembered I am perfectly clothed to spend time with Gigi, my friend."

*****

"You have never cared much for propriety," Grace replied. "But I assure you, I am a lady now, regardless of whether or not you wish to acknowledge it."

He shifted his position a little and said, "I did not mean to imply that you are not a lady, Grace. Of course you are. But if I were to treat you like an eligible lady from the *ton*, I could not be alone with you now. I could not have carried you upstairs last night. The fact that we are best friends means I get to do all of that and more."

Grace tried not to smile. It was true; they had been in all sorts of improper circumstances. "So, are you saying that I have already been compromised?" she said with as serious face as she could muster, "Thank you for the warning. I shall attempt to keep intact what is left of my reputation."

He laughed again, his chest and waistcoat straining to burst. "Well then, Gigi, it is a good thing you are just my friend, for I would hate to give rise to any more rumors about me. My family's reputation is already quite solidly set as less-than-reputable these days." Then he leaned forward with a flirtatious grin and added,

"When word gets out that you are staying here in my house, people are bound to make assumptions about the two of us, Gigi. You know little of my reputation."

She looked him straight in the eye and challenged him in more ways than one. "Make your move."

"I believe I shall." He moved his pawn. "So, tell me, Gigi; we have talked a great deal about our time growing up together but very little of the last ten years. You seem different."

She made her move without flinching at his words. "And I doubt you are still the same person I grew up with."

"True. I am not even the same person I was six months ago."

He moved again and motioned for her to continue. Talking to him was not a chore. That much had not changed. She moved another pawn, freeing up her bishop. "How so?" she asked.

He brought his hand to his chin. "Well, it is not me who has changed," he said, "so much as everyone else. People have different expectations of me now that I am titled. I would still much rather be Gavin Kingston, nothing more than the second son, instead of 'His Grace, the Duke of Huntsman'."

"But you were always titled. Why is 'Your Grace' so much worse than 'Lord Gavin'?"

He had been studying the board and looked up at her briefly, his eyes flashing momentarily with sadness. He moved his knight then leaned back and said, "Because every time I hear *that* title, I am reminded that my father and only brother are dead."

For a moment, neither said anything. "I am so sorry, Gavin," Grace murmured. He nodded wordlessly, and they played in silence. She sensed that he was not ready to discuss their deaths, so she directed the conversation elsewhere.

"I was very close to my parents," Grace began, "my mother especially. Her death was very hard on me. You did not get to see her fighting spirit. When Father died, a whole new woman emerged. She was no longer timid or afraid. She was forced to support herself and three daughters on a fraction of her income. My father left us a small lump sum and an annual payment of just a few hundred pounds. Luckily, he also bequeathed the country home in East Sussex, although it was rather run down. My mother put thousands of pounds into repairing it, and then we lived there with just a maid, a cook, and a manservant."

"Sounds like it was rather hard for you."

She made a move that took his knight. "In some ways, it was good for me. I no longer lived the leisurely life of a gentleman's daughter. I had to work and clean and even help cook. I had to do everything I could; we all did. My days were not spent embroidering or endlessly arranging flowers. Instead, I knelt in the garden and dug for potatoes. No kid gloves needed there."

He smiled at her and said, "I have never known Gigi to wear kid gloves."

"Yes, you did. When we danced, the dancing master made us both wear gloves."

"Not the last time."

Her heart started racing, and she worried he would see it bouncing in her chest. "No, not the last time."

Once again they played for a few minutes silently.

He made a move and said, "Check."

For a moment, she was convinced he had seen right through her, that he had somehow witnessed her thoughts drifting back again to that last lesson. Then she realized he was referring to the game. She moved out of check. Out of habit, she reacted defensively, turning the topic back to him. "Your father and Spencer died six months ago?" she probed.

She looked up to see his reaction. He seemed to be studying the board intensely. It was as if he had not heard her at all until, finally, he made a move and then leaned back and replied, "Yes. It was a carriage accident. At least, that is what you will hear in public. The truth is far more painful."

Grace observed how she could win in two moves with her rook. She was not one prone to pity, but she moved her knight instead; she didn't want the game to end yet.

Gavin's thoughts seemed to pour out of him as if he were desperate to share. "Spencer was a rogue," he began, "no doubt about it; even that term seemed too soft a description. He had a good heart, but knowing that the title and estate would pass to him, no matter his course in life, was simply too much freedom for him. Do you remember how Spencer and Father fought about his inattention to his studies and his lack of interest in the estate?"

"Yes."

Gavin moved his rook again and took one of hers. Surprisingly, she found she didn't mind. She quickly made her next move and gave her whole attention to the man who sat in front of her. "The life of leisure was the only thing that mattered to Spencer," he continued. "And me. I always mattered to him. He often travelled to meet me at port, even when I was only docked for the day. His friends were my friends. In truth, besides my shipmates, he was the only true friend I ever had. He never neglected me, never excluded me, even at Eton. So, even though I did not agree with his incognitas or the hired prime articles who accompanied him wherever he went, his lifestyle never cut up my peace."

"So, he was a womanizer?"

"A selective womanizer. Those who made their living that way, mistresses for hire or ladies of the night—yes, he used them. But he always treated ladies of the *ton* with respect. As far as I know, he never ruined any of them. Am I making you uneasy? Sometimes I forget that you are a lady and not just my friend. Perhaps I should not be discussing this with you."

With anyone else, she would have been uneasy, but not with Gavin. They had always been completely honest with each other. She trusted him. "The only thing that makes me uneasy is that you forget I am a lady. I do not mind being called your friend, but things are different than they were ten years ago."

"Yes, I am well aware that you are a lady now. It would be impossible to forget." He shifted in his chair and refocused on the chessboard. He seemed to have a bit of color in his cheeks, but she couldn't imagine why. Was she being too honest? He made his move and continued. "One day Spencer was accused by the Earl of Longmont of compromising his daughter."

She took his bishop in her move and asked, "Did he?"

"He swears he did not, and he refused to marry her. The earl challenged Spencer to a duel. He immediately told my parents, which is how I learned about it. My father agreed to serve as second, confident that he could prevent the duel from actually happening. But my father always thought too much of his title. On the morning of the duel, while my father tried to reason with him, the earl lost his temper and shot him in the chest. The duel had not even begun. The surgeon did what he could, but he could not save him.

"The earl fled in his carriage amid the commotion," Gavin continued. "When my father died, Spencer took off after him. They tell me he was driving like a Corinthian in pursuit. The carriage turned and lost control, throwing him. His injuries were extensive. He did not last to see the next dawn."

Grace reached over and placed her hand on his. "I am so sorry. To lose both of them in the same day in such horrid accidents must have been a shock."

He looked down at her hand, squeezed it once, and then pulled his hand back, withdrawing it to his own territory. There was a bit of silence as he made his next move and then weakly said, "The death of my father was no accident. I still intend to find the Earl of Longmont and hang him for murder. He has not been seen since that morning. Rumors are that he fled to Italy. His daughter was indeed compromised, but I swear to you that it was not Spencer. If Spencer said he did not do it, then he did not do it." Although the words sounded like a grand mission, his tone spoke of how futile his hopes were.

She worried if reaching for his hand had been inappropriate. She took a breath and looked away from his beautiful brown eyes, which were threatening to swallow her whole. They had a power and passion in them that were unfamiliar in Gavin's face.

She made her move quickly, but as soon as she let go of the piece, she realized she had left the rook exposed and endangered her queen. How could she have been so careless? She determined to concentrate harder in order to get his king. His skill was markedly improved from ten years ago. Her queen would probably be taken if she did not find a way to escape the trap he had set.

He indeed took her last rook and then looked up at her suspiciously with one eyebrow raised. With a smile, he interlaced his fingers in front of him.

"Perhaps I have been distracted from the game," Grace admitted. "I was thinking only of you."

"Thinking only of me? A penny for your thoughts!" he asked with a confidence that was not there moments ago.

She suddenly realized how that sounded. "Certainly not," she said. "You already think too highly of yourself as it is."

He grinned wide enough to make her blush with heat. "Yes, many people cannot help but sacrifice their queen when I speak—I believe the Prince Regent was tempted to do so once. Tell me, Gigi, do you just like sad stories or have I really captured your queen with my skill and charm?"

"My queen is not yours yet." Her face colored even more but this time with a bit of anger because he was mocking her. Her only option was to sacrifice a knight to save her queen. "You may have my knight."

"Is that a promise?"

His pompous smirk needed to be rubbed off soon. "What do you mean by that?"

"You just told me I could have your night. I say we practice those dance lessons in the ballroom. If I am going to find you a husband, I need to know what skills I have to work with. I would hate to think that your training is limited to those lessons from ten years ago."

"Very well, you may have my night. My one aching left foot is up to it if your two left feet are."

"Touché!" He made one move and stood up.

"Where are you going?" Grace asked.

"That is checkmate. You were so worried about losing your queen that you neglected your king."

CHAPTER 5

Grace stared at the chessboard, worry etched in every corner of her face. Gavin felt a twinge of guilt for winning.

"Do not be a sore loser, Gigi. Surely you have grown out of that by now." Gavin watched her flush even redder. "I am sorry," he added. "It was unfair for me to distract you."

He had always softened the blow when she lost, as he knew just how painful it was for her to admit defeat. Grace was the kind of girl who excelled at everything she put her mind to. She never held herself back from a challenge. It didn't matter that she was a girl and two years younger and in a dress. No matter the challenge, she fought with a spirit of endurance and self-sacrifice that only Grace had.

Just as he was about to offer a rematch, there was a familiar, patterned triple-knock on the study door. He turned to find his friend, Kenneth Silence, letting himself in, closely followed by a frustrated Mr. Robison.

Silence and the poor butler, Mr. Robison, were engaged in a long-standing war. It was Robison's job to announce guests before they entered, but Silence, determined to announce himself, always managed to weasel his way ahead.

"Silence, Your Grace," Robison called out, rushing into the room.

Silence's laughter rolled, and he replied, "Robison, I am impressed! Not many servants would dare hush their masters so boldly."

"Your Grace, I would never attempt such a thing," Robison quickly added. "Mr. Silence is here, as you can see. Shall I bring in refreshments?"

Gavin chuckled and said, "Yes, please do."

"And bring some sherry," Silence requested. "I see there is a lady here, and if she has spent any time at all with Kingston, she is surely in dire need of fortification."

"I do not require sherry," Grace replied.

"No?" Silence asked. "Have you given up the drink like Kingston?"

Gavin cleared his throat and stood up. "Grace," he said, "I would like to introduce you to Spencer's close friend, Mr. Kenneth Silence. Silence, this is Miss Grace Iverson."

She stood and curtsied, "It is a pleasure to meet you, Mr. Silence."

"Please, call me Silence. Everyone else does."

Grace smiled back, far too wide for Gavin's taste. "But then what shall I say when I need you to stop talking?" she asked. "Must I really stutter, 'Silence, Silence!'?"

Is she flirting with him? Gavin wondered.

Silence laughed, bowed deeply, and kissed her hand. "The pleasure is entirely mine, Miss Iverson. Now, how is it that we have not met before? I know I would have sought an introduction to such a handsome lady if I had seen her. Kingston, how is it you have hidden this gem from me? Do tell me she is a cousin. Hopefully a distant one who has no chance of passing on your ugly features or your innate lack of humor. Oh, come now, Kingston, you must wipe that frown off your face; it limits your attractiveness even further."

Gavin turned to Robison and said, "Please bring tea, thank you." He then turned toward Grace and saw that charming smile again being bestowed upon Silence and felt the need for a drink for the first time in three months.

"Now, Miss Iverson," Silence began, "do not tell me that you too have given up drink like Kingston."

Grace's questioning look forced an explanation from Gavin. "I was a captain," Gavin conceded, "so, of course I drank. We all drank as if we had hollow legs. There are few sailors, if any, who do not mute the hardships of sea with a bit of spirits. But I have recently sworn it off."

"I see," Grace replied. "Well, to be honest, I rather detest the stuff myself. I do not like feeling like I am not in control of myself."

Grace smiled at Gavin, and he felt his heart begin to relax again. *How on earth will I introduce her to anyone if I don't even want to share her smiles with Silence?*

Grace turned back toward Gavin's friend and said, "I was sorry to hear about Spencer, Silence. I spent many summers tagging along behind him. I grew up in Suffolk with the Kingstons and have very fond memories of him."

"Then we have something in common," Silence said, "for there are few people who still hold Spencer in high regard. Gavin and I have been through it all together. We both saw Spencer walking the tightrope he called life and knew that sooner or later gravity would win. His untimely death was a terrible blow, but Gavin helped me through it. Unfortunately, Kingston tried for a while to *drink* his way through it, and that proved unsustainable. But in the end, he gave up the drink. I admire him for it, although it took him banishing all the alcohol from Willsing Manor and the rest of us enduring a few days of him in high dudgeon. He has not touched alcohol now in . . . how many months?"

"Three," Gavin answered. "So, stop trying to order Robison to bring you sherry. You know there is not a drop of it in the house."

"Indeed. But it never hurts to try. That is my life's motto, which brings me back to you, Miss Iverson. Has anyone ever told you how beautif—"

Gavin quickly cleared his throat and pronounced, "Silence, Silence!" Everyone laughed.

"Well, Miss Iverson," Silence chuckled, "thanks to you, I will never know whether Kingston is trying to quiet me or whether Harrison's stuttering has become contagious. Speaking of which, Kingston, I am here to pass along a message: Harrison's mare is ready if you wish to breed Zeus with her."

"Is that all you needed?" Gavin was hoping he would just leave. He found himself feeling quite protective of his time with Grace.

"Kicking me out without tea? It is bad enough that you did not offer any port, but at least let me cool my saddle." Without waiting for a reply from Gavin, Silence kissed Grace's hand again and sat down on the sofa, motioning for her to join him. "Now, Miss Iverson, do not let Kingston's coolness interfere with our short acquaintance. Please, sit down, and we shall hear what Kingston and his brother were like as children. No, wait, I have a better idea. Let us play a game. I shall act out something, and you tell me which brother it resembles."

Grace smiled again and said, "Only if I get a turn."

Silence's eyebrows rose. "Indeed!" he declared. "I would be delighted to see you act!"

Grace sat down and, reluctantly, so did Gavin. He would have preferred to be alone, or at least alone with Grace. He sighed. The morning was not turning out as he would have liked. First, he had remembered that terrible day ten years ago when he realized Grace considered him only a friend, and then he had recounted the grisly details of everything that happened six months ago. Undoubtedly the worst memories of his life. Now, it seemed he had to watch Silence flirt with Grace while they mocked him in his own house.

But it really wasn't so bad; he had spent the last hour entirely in Gigi's presence. He would endure far worse to spend time with her. He took a seat that allowed him to observe her without being obvious.

She had matured physically, and her gown accentuated her form in a modest way. Yesterday, he had initially thought she was only eighteen, but the more he studied her, the more he saw a maturity of spirit and mind that was almost incongruent with her tiny waist and petite arms.

Silence went first and pretended to swing a cricket stick; Grace guessed Spencer right away. The tea came and each took a moment to enjoy it before the game continued.

Gavin let his mind drift back. When he was young, he thought he knew what he wanted: a permanent playmate who would make him laugh and never tire of his jokes. But almost overnight he started seeing Grace in a different way. He suddenly noticed characteristics that were desirable, even irreplaceable. He had not found anyone else like her since. Soon, Gigi stood out in his mind as the paradigm that he measured every other lady against.

Of course, she had some rough spots, just like anyone else. She had always been quick with her rebuttals, for instance; but truthfully, he did not mind being wrong. If anything, he liked seeing Grace aglow with success in debate. She prided herself on her wit and logic. She never argued unless she felt sure she could win, and she only fought the battles that needed to be fought. When he realized this about his best friend, their fights very nearly ended altogether. But sometimes, when he missed seeing the fire in her eyes, he egged her on just for fun.

Gavin started to pay attention half-heartedly to what was happening in the room. Silence pretended to place something on the study floor and then mimed tripping over it. Gavin and Grace both laughed and knew he was referring to Gavin's knack for tripping. Then it was Grace's turn again. Instead of being offended by her mockery, he realized he was pleased to have an excuse to watch her so closely.

She mimed someone walking along a fence, then falling off and crying over an injury. Gavin knew right away it was himself, the day he broke his foot, but didn't say anything. Grace wailed and cried mock tears until her laughter exploded and the act was up. She quickly jumped up and curtsied to their applause.

Gavin found the image of Grace crying unnerving. She had always kept such tight control over her emotions. He remembered the day his dog, Macie, had been run over by a carriage. Grace had loved that dog even more than Gavin. But she had refused to let her tears fall in front of him.

She had responded to the dog's death in a slightly exaggerated way, insisting that they dig the grave themselves. It started to rain halfway through, and her dress was soon covered in mud. But Gigi kept silently digging with a passion. It was as if she were racing her tears. The harder she worked, the longer her tears stayed away. When she finished, she lovingly wrapped the dog in her own shawl and lowered the body into the grave along with one of her watercolor paintings of Macie.

Gavin had learned much about Grace that day. No matter how much pain she was feeling, she did not like to show emotion. Other ladies might talk about their problems, maybe even dramatically cry into their pillow for days and refuse to come to meals, but Gigi was different. Not until she patted the last bit of dirt on top of the fresh grave did she let her tears fall. He said nothing at the time to acknowledge them, but the muddy streaks on her cheeks were irrefutable.

All that work and loyalty for a dog that was not even hers! That is when he grasped that she loved deeper than anyone he knew. It was true what they say—"Still waters run deep". That night, Gavin had asked his mother if he could share his Latin tutor with Grace. He knew he wanted to spend as much time as possible with her.

While at Eton, he secretly sent letters to Grace through his sister, Eliza. Grace did the same in reverse. Their parents never found out.

The next summer, when studying History and Latin was not enough time together, he approached his mother about sharing a dancing master as well. He only had a month left of summer, and he was desperate to spend more time with her before he left. He knew he had approached the right parent when his mother readily agreed.

He did not dare ask his father, who felt that Gavin spent far too much time with Gigi as it was. There had been several arguments over the years about it. "Gavin," his father would say, "you are the son of a duke, and that Iverson girl is not worth the mud on your boots. Be careful not to track dirt into the house."

Gavin was only allowed to continue spending time with her because he assured his father that he felt nothing but friendship for Gigi.

When the dancing master, Mr. Moser, was hired without the duke's approval, Gavin's father became suspicious again. Truthfully, Gavin had already been given several lessons while at Eton and hardly needed more practice. But the duchess had come to Gavin's rescue and defended the arrangement. Eton only allowed the boys to dance with other boys, she had said, so it would be good for Gavin to practice dancing with a female partner.

This seemed to satisfy the duke. If there was one thing that Gavin understood about his father, it was that the way his family was presented to society mattered a great deal. It was all about the show. So long as they performed their roles, no one would be the wiser to the conflicts at home. Gavin wondered if one of the reasons his father disapproved of Grace was because she was around often enough to see scenes where the show was not so well rehearsed.

So, the summer he turned sixteen and she turned fourteen, they had two lessons a week. As each Tuesday and Friday afternoon approached, his heart would take flight. Nothing could dampen his spirits before or after a lesson. They were the highlight of the summer.

The dance lessons were the last memories he had of her until yesterday. When he returned to Eton, the letters had suddenly stopped coming. His sister, Eliza, didn't understand it either. Gavin worried about her so much that his grades began to suffer. When he learned her father had died, he assumed that was the reason for her silence. He had begged his parents to let him come home, but his father refused. He never heard from Grace again.

He kept reviewing that last dance lesson and all that was said and all that had happened. Why had she stopped writing? Surely she could have used a friend during that time. Was she so afraid of showing emotion that she would refuse his friendship? Or had he been too forward in the last dance lesson? Should he have kept his peace? There were so many questions left unanswered around that time.

Gavin hadn't realized he had been staring at Gigi until she spoke to him.

"Gavin, what is it? You look worried. Is something wrong?"

Gavin forced a smile onto his face and said, "No, I just realized I have a few things to attend to. I must excuse myself. I shall see you, Silence, at the dinner on Thursday. I am sure my mother has included you in her list of eligible bachelors who may compete to sweep Grace off her feet and end her season with a bang."

Silence scoffed. "Is that so? But I can already tell Miss Iverson is too smart to be swept up by me. I am afraid the duchess does not know me well enough."

Gavin was pleased that Silence seemed slightly wary of the idea. "Well, although the accuracy of my mother's judgment may be debatable, you made the list. But I warn you, Gigi is staying under my roof and therefore is my charge."

Silence raised his eyebrow suspiciously at the nickname he used. "Gigi?"

Grace laughed and explained, "When I was five, I loved my full name so much that I would introduce myself to everyone as Grace Ingrid Genevieve Iverson. Gavin was two years older and learning to write his letters. His tutor would make him write short notes to his mother and father for practice. One day he decided he wanted to write me a letter. He was determined to write my full name, but his skill was not good enough to write, 'Grace Ingrid Genevieve Iverson'. So his tutor suggested that he write just the initials, G-I-G-I. He rarely called me anything else. Honestly, it is strange to hear him call me 'Grace' again."

Silence said, "Well, Miss Grace Ingrid Genevieve Iverson, I look forward to seeing you again on Thursday."

"The pleasure will be all mine."

Gavin tried to control his emotions, but his words still came out clipped. "I will show you out, Silence."

Silence gave him a look that meant he understood. He politely bowed and followed Gavin out of the study. But once they had closed the door behind them, leaving Grace inside, Silence grabbed his arm and said, "Out with it! Who is she? And how long have you admired her?"

*****

Grace needed to stretch her ankle a bit and thought a walk in the gardens would be good—just a short one. She finished her tea and walked toward the door but paused when she heard Gavin's voice on the other side. It had a deep, velvety, baritone quality; its smoothness flowed over her with a reassuring nature. She leaned her back against the door and listened. She was surprised to realize they were talking about her.

"I already told you," Gavin said. "She is Grace Iverson. We grew up together."

"Yes," Silence replied, "but I have never seen you jealous over a woman before. Who is she really?"

She heard Gavin sigh. "My best friend."

"But I have been your friend for five years, and I have never heard of Miss Iverson before. How can she be your best friend?"

"I should say she *was* my best friend. Now I do not know what to call her. My mother has taken her in for the season and hopes to find a match for her."

"Where is her family?"

"Both her parents have passed away. Yesterday was the first contact we have had in ten years. When my mother found out she was in town without a proper sponsor, she invited her to stay here."

"But you feel something for her. I see it. Is it wise to have her under your roof? In the same house?"

"I would rather not discuss this, Silence."

"It will cause talk, Kingston. Marilyn from the Red Dragon asked where you were last night. Apparently you had plans to 'show her the stars', but you never showed up. And word is getting around that you failed to materialize at Sylvia Trementon's tea yesterday. Listen, I am not saying everyone will pick up on your regard, but even Miss Iverson noticed you were staring at her."

Grace didn't realize she was holding her breath. Did he really feel some regard for her?

"Silence, Silence," Gavin retorted.

She heard them both chuckle quietly.

Then she heard Silence ask a question. "Do you really admire her?"

She leaned her ear against the door and listened with all her might, but Gavin's voice was too low. She could only make out a few words: " . . . friend . . . responsibility . . . now . . . no more . . ."

"Very well, Kingston," Silence sighed. "If that is your wish, I shall not mention it again."

"Thank you." She heard their footsteps walk away.

After a moment of shock, Grace walked over to the table and began gathering the teacups. The silver tea tray was highly polished, so reflective that she could see herself in it. She turned around to make sure no one was watching and gingerly held the tray up to her face.

Her hair was ornately styled, twisted, and braided, nothing like her normal, simple bun. Her stubborn curls, usually spilling out everywhere, were each carefully pinned in place. The pearl-studded, flower hairpin was on loan from the duchess. *It is probably worth more than a month's food*, Grace mused. Her mint green dress was perfectly pressed, not a single wrinkle in sight, and even the old tea stain on the shoulder had been cleaned by Charlotte last night without Grace knowing.

What am I doing? This isn't me. I don't wear silver flowers and pearls in my hair. I don't have a lady's maid. This arrangement, this life, was getting out of hand. She sensed she was setting herself up for disappointment. How could she stay here under Gavin's roof when she still harbored feelings of familiarity for her best friend? Feelings that bordered on infatuation and, possibly even, love?

She saw the light rouge that Charlotte had painted onto her cheeks and wondered what exactly Gavin had said so quietly. Did he admire her? The thought brought a deeper color to her cheeks. She surprised herself when she thought, *I hope so*. But one of the decipherable words he had said was "friend". *Is that all I am to him?*

CHAPTER 6

Grace kept off her ankle as much as possible the rest of the day in preparation for that evening's dancing plans with Gavin. Her foot was almost back to normal now. Only quick movements made her cringe. As Gavin escorted her into the music room that night, her nerves were a mixture of anticipation, elation, and hope. The pianoforte stood in its corner along with a harp. She could see that the chairs and other furniture had been pushed to the walls, turning the large room into a rather impressive dance floor. Even the rugs had been rolled up and moved to the side. She was surprised to see no one else in the room.

"Gavin, who is going to play for us?"

He grinned as if he knew a secret. "Follow me."

He led her to a beautiful table that held a wooden box. It was intricately inlaid with different colors of wood. As she came closer, she saw beautiful scenes in the design—a man with his eyes closed, passionately playing a perfectly shaped violin; a sumptuously ornate treble clef; and a couple waltzing in a close embrace. The artistic talent required to piece together these masterpieces was awe-inspiring.

She couldn't help but trace her fingers over the smooth images to feel the perfectly matched wood seams for herself. "Gavin, this is beautiful. What a work of art! Why do you not display this more prominently?"

"Because it belongs in the music room."

She glanced up at him and asked, "Why?"

"It is a music box."

"What is a music box?"

He smiled handsomely, winked at her, and teased, "I thought that your genius would have figured it out by now. A music box is a box that plays music."

"By itself?"

Without answering, he lifted the lid and showed her the inside, where she saw a bumpy metal tube and several pegs and wheels. It reminded her of the inside of a clock. Then he began winding a knob on the back. Gradually the gears started moving, and a beautiful, tinkling music filled the room. She watched in awe as the metal cylinder slowly rotated, striking the prongs in patterned precision to create musical notes.

"Where did you get this? I have never heard of such a treasure." Her wonder was noticeable even to her. She looked up at him and saw how pleased he was with himself.

"I knew you would enjoy it. When I was traveling after university, I found myself in Switzerland. I noticed a small store with pocket watches in the window, and I just so happened to have broken mine in a very classic Gavinism."

She couldn't help but giggle. "You tripped and broke your pocket watch?"

Gavin laughed as well. "Yes," he admitted. "But I will have to tell you that story another time, because at the moment, I do not wish to relive it. My pride was far more injured than the watch."

Being with him and laughing together was just like it used to be. "You cannot start a story like that and not finish it!"

"Let us just say that I had help from a sheet of ice and my chin got a good look at some excellent Swiss cobblestones. The result was that I needed a new pocket watch. Anyway, I found this little shop, and there, inside, was this wooden box playing this song. I did not know a word of German, but between the shopkeeper's broken English and what little French I knew, he showed me how it worked. See, this cylinder is powered by a spring, and the music is a result of the revolving cylinder's teeth striking these metal pins. It fascinated me to no end." He took a deep breath, but instead of coming out strong, his voice was deep and soft as he said this last part: "All I knew was that I wanted it so that someday I could show it to you."

She turned her gaze to him. What did he mean? Her nature was too direct not to ask him outright. "Show it to *me*?"

He reached for her cheek and tenderly brushed the back of his fingers against her face. "Yes. You. Everything I have done is usually with thoughts of you."

Her face burned under his touch, but it was the vibrato in his velvety voice that unraveled her. His words came out so comforting, and she had not known how badly she needed to hear that he had thought of her over the last ten years.

The reality of what he said started to sink in, and all at once, she burst into tears. *He did not forget me!*

As the tears started to fall from her cheeks, she was afraid that she had misunderstood him. She forced herself to clarify. "Do you mean you did not forget about me?"

"How could I forget about you? You were everything to me. Every good thing in my life had you in it. Every memory that I care to remember is about you. There was no one who meant more to me than you. You were my world."

Her tears fell with new fervor, and for once, she did not feel self-conscious about them. They were happy tears—healing tears. The years of heartache and loneliness had built a cavern between her and the world. And as he reached to pull her into his arms, closing the gap between them, she was keenly aware of the physical and metaphorical closure. There was no canyon separating his heart from hers. She knew at that moment, as he guided her tearful face to his chest, that the only thing that had changed between them was the passing of time. She wrapped her arms around his chest and held him as if she had never been held before.

And as she cried, the music played on. Slowly he shifted weight from one foot to the other, rocking both their bodies. He asked, "What made you think I forgot about you?"

She laid her ear next to his heart and listened to the rhythm while feeling his body move her to the beat of the music. She lifted her head to look at him only to find he was looking down at her, making their faces just an inch or two apart. For a moment, she thought he was going to kiss her. She managed to say, with the same breath that seemed caught in her throat, "You stopped writing."

He stopped swaying and stepped back, holding her by the shoulders.

"What do you mean, Grace?" Gavin asked with a perplexed look on his face.

"After the danc—" She blushed, flustered for a moment, before continuing, "I mean, after you went back to Eton. You stopped writing to me."

"But I wrote you twice a week for a year."

"You did? But I never received anything."

"When did my letters stop?"

"After you returned to school. I was so sure you would at least write to me when my father died, but you did not."

"Oh, Gigi, I did write! I wanted to come home that very day! If you only knew how crushed I was that my parents refused to let me leave school. I tried to hire a post chase, but by the time I arranged it, my mother told me you were gone. I did not know where you were."

"But I told you in my letters. I sent them all to Eliza. You did not receive them?" Grace's head was spinning. None of it made any sense.

"Just one," Gavin said. "But it did not mention the dance lesson or what happened afterwards. I assumed you did not wish to discuss it, so I wrote back to you that very day and apologized. Then all of a sudden the letters stopped. I thought you stopped writing because you were angry at me. Are you saying you did not get my apology?"

The revelation that he had written her so long and so frequently confused her a great deal. "Eliza never sent me any letters once you went off to school. You wrote every week?"

"Of course I did! How could I leave you wondering what I really felt? You were my best friend, and we had crossed some imaginary line between best friends and . . . well, something else."

She smiled at his lack of description for what happened. "Well, I agree that we crossed the line into that 'something else', but I still wanted our friendship to continue. Why did your sister not send you my letters? What if . . . what if your parents found out that Eliza was trafficking letters between us? Your father—"

He finished her sentence, "—would have stopped it immediately if he knew." He seemed to be pensive for a moment, and she took a moment to ponder what had said.

Grace was so grateful to know that he hadn't abandoned her, that he still cared for her, but something was still aching inside. He had expressed how important she was to him—as a friend. Was that all she was to him? For just a moment, it felt like something else, but then the feeling had vanished. What did he say he had written in his letter? An apology? For the dance lesson?

The music stopped and so did her heart. *He regretted it.*

She walked to the music box and did what she had seen him do, twisting the knob on the back to buy herself more time to think. He felt remorse for that last dance lesson. He had not meant to cross into that "something else"; it had been an accident, a mistake.

Her fingers continued to turn the knob as she debated in her heart how she felt about that. She had already decided that as long as she had her best friend back, friendship was enough. As the music began, she realized it was playing the very same song they had danced to at their last lesson. She was taken back to that moment.

Grace thought Gavin had improved a great deal over the four weeks of dance lessons. In fact, she had to admit he had never been so graceful. The music made him elegant. They had gotten to the point where the dance master, Mr. Moser, would play at the piano and call out corrections rather than call out the steps. At times, Grace forgot they were rehearsing and imagined herself at a real ball. Although, in a classic Gavinism, Gavin had lost one of his gloves in the mud that afternoon. Mr. Moser grudgingly permitted them to dance with bare hands, just this one time.

"Lord Gavin, lighter on the ball of your toes. Miss Iverson, chin up," Mr. Moser instructed from across the room.

Grace did as she was told, and the dance brought them together again. Gavin quickly whispered, "Gigi, I need to speak with you. I leave in two days, and I cannot go without telling you what I meant when I said I would marry you."

Her heart started racing. When he had first said that someone big and brave would take her away from him, she had grown cold in her heart. No love could ever be worth having to give up her best friend. She was not sure she wanted to discuss it, but this was Gavin; she held nothing back from him. "There is nothing to explain," Grace whispered. "I have decided I shall never marry if it means having to give you up."

"No, that is not what I meant. Someday you will fall in love. Real love. Not the kind of silly love that your sister reads in her ladies' novels. You are simply too special for men not to see your worth."

She whispered back so that Mr. Moser did not hear, "Truly, it is all right. I have a plan. I shall be the governess to your children. We will still be able to see each other every day."

Gavin's response was far too quick. "I do not want that."

At first his words hurt, but then he explained, "I do want to see you every day, but I cannot employ you. I care too much for you. Gigi, I love you. When I said I would marry you, I meant it. Not to save you from being a spinster, but because you are the only one my heart wants. I thought I was content to be just best friends. I thought that was enough. But I am more convinced than ever that it is not."

Grace nearly tripped in her steps, and she heard Mr. Moser call out, "Focus, Miss Iverson. Now take his hand and promenade down. Quick-step, kick, slow-step. That is right."

Grace turned to look at Gavin. "You want to marry me?"

"I think it is the only option I have. I cannot give you up; you are far too dear to me. I cannot imagine greeting you as Mrs. Monroe or Mrs. White. You will always be my Gigi. Mine. I am too selfish to let someone else claim you."

Just then his mother came into the room, and Mr. Moser stopped playing to speak with her. Gavin halted and turned toward Grace. The moment was more than she could have asked for. "Gavin, we are too young to know whether the kind of love we have for each other will really cement a lasting marriage. Marriage should be based on friendship, but it needs more than just that."

Mr. Moser interrupted their discussion and called out, "The duchess needs to speak with me for a moment. You may relax until I return." Both Gavin and Grace watched them leave. The *discussion was all too private as it was, but now there was something tangible in the air.*

Gavin took her hand and asked, "Tell me, Grace. What else does a marriage need?"

Grace may have been only fourteen, but she was pretty confident in her ideas. "To make a marriage work, there has to be that 'something else'. A man needs to love a woman enough to make her insides melt. He needs to be able to make her knees go weak with a single kiss, and—"

But before she could finish describing what she had read about, he took her face in both his hands and placed his lips on hers to silence her. It was no small act. Without conscious thought, her lips responded in kind, and she felt her mind lose all coherent thought. It was as if time had slowed down, and she could feel each and every heartbeat as a distinct thump in her chest. LUB-DUB. LUB-DUB. The sound got louder and louder as her lips caressed his, making her very insides melt and her knees go weak.

He pulled away, and she opened her eyes to see his chestnut brown orbs shining down at her. The corners of his mouth pulled up, and he said, "Is that what is missing between us?"

He still had his hands on each side of her face. He held her so close that his breath cooled her heated, swollen, wet lips. She reached up and kissed him again. This time, he let go of her face and pulled her into his arms, but before the kiss could get heated, they heard Mr. Moser's voice and they both jumped away.

"Miss Iverson! I think you should be getting home. Now."

She looked over at Gavin. He was not even pink. She was blushing from the tip of her toes to her ears, and he had the confidence to act as if being found kissing a girl happened every day! Gavin grinned and said, "I will walk you home."

"No," Mr. Moser quickly said, "I think I will accompany Miss Iverson home. Lord Gavin, I think you should redirect yourself. Perhaps something physically diverting."

Gavin then reached for Grace's hand and kissed it. "What a beautiful way to end our dance lessons. Have a wonderful day, Miss Iverson."

It was the first time he had ever called her "Miss Iverson", instead of "Gigi" or the occasional "Grace". He seemed to have matured in the last few minutes. Where she once knew a boy, now she saw a young man who would someday soon be a grown gentleman. A gentleman who had just made her insides melt.

She let him kiss her hand, and she curtsied. Gavin had kissed her hand before, of course—acting out Romeo and Juliet or some other play—but this time the kiss lingered; his lips pressed in a way that meant something more.

She knew it, and she knew that he knew it. They had just crossed from best friends into "something else."

*****

Gavin sensed that Grace was pondering what to say as she stood by the music box with her back to him. He thought he had expressed himself well enough. He had told her how important she was to him, and she had dissolved into a ball of tears in his arms. *Happy tears, right?* He thought so. He hoped so. After all, he had been hopelessly in love with her for the last eleven years. Listening to the song they had danced to playing from the music box, he recalled that kiss from long ago. The memory had not faded in the slightest; it had kept him warm during the cold nights at sea.

Every woman he had ever met had been measured against Grace and found lacking. Perhaps that is why he used to prance around with a different girl every week. One lady might have her charm, but none of her spirit and flare. Another, her drive and determination, but no compassion. Some were sweet, but not clever; others were clever, but not sweet. And so the search went on year after year.

Grace rewound the music box, and the song began again. He felt like he should say something. What was she feeling? What exactly had caused her tears? Ten years ago, before their kiss, she had said they didn't have that "something else". Did she feel "something else" when he kissed her back then? Did she feel it now?

After that kiss, he had been sent to Eton a day early. They never even got a chance to say goodbye. All these years, he had wondered what she felt about him crossing that line.

"Grace?"

She turned to him and smiled. "This is the last song we danced to," she replied. "I remember Mr. Moser had to play this part slower because it was the hardest part of the dance."

"Now you understand why I had to show you this music box," Gavin said.

"I do. It was the last time we were together. You left early for school, and we never even got a chance to say goodbye. Month after month went by, and there was no word from Eliza. She never even answered the letters that I directed to her. I found that rather odd."

Gavin agreed. "I know that if Eliza had received letters from you, she would have found a way to get them to me. She knew how important you were to me. Do you think that Mr. Moser told our parents what happened?"

"It would certainly explain why you were rushed off to Eton the next morning. Do you think that the letters were intercepted?"

"It is the only explanation. You know how my father felt about you. As long as you were simply a playmate, there was little harm in us spending time together. But if Mr. Moser told him about that last dance lesson, then my father would have done anything to keep me away from you. Unfortunately he is not around to ask anymore."

"Your mother is."

Gavin nodded but there was something more pressing on his mind than trying to discover the mystery of the missing letters. Gavin had declared himself ten years ago. He had told her he wanted to be more than friends. And he had just told her tonight that she meant the world to him, but she still did not say how she felt. It would be easy to leave it unspoken, but after ten years of not knowing, he was not going to waste another minute.

"Gigi, please, I have to say something. That day I kissed you . . . I was selfish and impulsive. I am so sorry. I know it was wrong of me. I am worried that I painted over all those years of friendship with a brush of my lips. Is there any way you can forgive me?" Grace's reaction confused him, and he faltered for a moment. But he had to know if she loved him too. "Grace, what I am trying to say is, can we ever be—"

"Of course, we can be friends," she replied flatly. "And I will always forgive my best friend." Her stiff spine and thin lips made it clear she was angry with him. But why?

He was a moment too long in responding, and she turned to leave the room. He quickly reached after her and took her elbow, pulling her to him.

"Dance with me," he asked.

She glared at him. "Why?" she asked tersely. "So you can apologize for it later?"

Awareness dawned on him, and he realized where he had gone wrong. There was only one way to make it right. He wordlessly placed her left hand up by his neck. Then he took her right hand. He stepped closer to her and moved his hand to her waist. It was the position of the waltz.

As the music played, he twirled her around the room in the three-step pattern. The waltz was a new style of dancing, one they hadn't practiced in their dance lessons. He relished holding her in such an intimate embrace.

She began to protest when the music stopped, but he shushed her and kept dancing. There was plenty of music playing inside his heart. *If she won't let me say how much I love her, I will show her.* Gavin let his mind work through his confusion, and things started to become very clear. No doubt, it was because she was in his arms.

One thing he knew was that just as he had tripped her the day before on the street, his bungled apology tonight had stung her and tripped her emotionally. He hadn't meant to hurt her—he was trying to explain that he was still in love with her—but he could see her emotional walls going up again, brick by brick. If he pushed her too far, if she felt threatened, she would pack up her trunk and be gone by the morning.

Grace had never been good at expressing her emotions, but he had learned a few things about her over the years. The key to understanding Grace was really listening to her, not just paying heed to her words.

She did *not* say that she loved him too. She did *not* say that he was more than a best friend. She did *not* say that she enjoyed the kiss ten years ago, but every indication was that she had welcomed it. Her deep blue eyes looked up at him without any hesitation.

If the key to understanding what Gigi felt was dependent on something deeper than words, then he still had a good chance of winning her heart. It would have to take some finesse, perhaps even some grace. He was not known for his gracefulness, but with her in his arms right now, dancing without a note of music, the breadth of what was left unspoken was blatantly obvious. Grace loved him. And he just had to help her see it. He suddenly felt very inspired.

Being graceful was never more important.

He took a bold step forward, dipped her deeply, and looked straight into her surprised eyes. "Do you trust me?"

She did *not* say yes, but he saw her eyes soften. She took a deep breath and looked straight back at him. He knew what that meant.

So he kissed her.

CHAPTER 7

Gavin couldn't have helped himself even if he'd tried. He had kissed her on impulse, to gauge her response. But he hadn't realized his body was aching to show her how he had missed her. That ache was ten years old.

With one arm wrapped around her petite waist, in a dip so deep that she was nearly horizontal, he pressed his lips to hers, urging her to kiss him in return. At first, there was nothing but surprise and stiffness, but that was impressively—and reassuringly—short lived. After a moment, it was he who struggled for breath. She gave every indication that she enjoyed it—from the fluidity and urgency he felt from her lips, to the way she clung to his shoulder. It was so much more than that first, young kiss they had shared at the dance lesson. He knew he had his answer. She loved him too, even if she did not know it yet.

He slowed the kisses and gave one last feather-light kiss, softly brushing her lips with his. They both opened their eyes at the same time. All the anger from before had been replaced by a look of desire and surrender that he had never seen in Grace before.

He pulled her up to a standing position and waited for her to say something. It seemed to take forever for her to find words. She stepped away but still didn't say anything. The suspense was killing him.

Finally she grinned and said, "Well, Gavin, that was . . . something else."

He couldn't help but grin at her word choice. He was about to answer with something smart when someone interrupted them from across the room.

"Pardon me, Your Grace," called out a footman. "Your mother sent me to ask if you require her services at the pianoforte." His smirk made it clear that he had seen the kiss.

Grace blushed a deep scarlet and turned away.

"No, not tonight, Tim," Gavin quickly called out to the servant.

"Yes, Your Grace," Tim responded, leaving with a bow.

Grace's hands began to shake ever so slightly. She nervously smoothed her already flawless dress. "I believe my ankle has had all the dancing it can handle," she announced.

"Of course. Perhaps we can continue our lessons another day. We still have many things to discuss—"

"Perhaps," she responded with barely audible words. "But I believe I have a reputation to uphold." Her face was a riot of color and emotion. Where just moments ago her eyes had been drunk with desire, now they flared with embarrassment. *But not anger, I hope,* he mused.

She loved him. He just needed more time to persuade her of that fact.

*****

Grace left the ballroom and passed the footman in the foyer. She strained to avoid looking at him but felt his eyes following her. He made no effort to hide what he had witnessed. How could Gavin have kissed her like that?

She tried to think of a place to hide for the next few hours. It was far too early to retire.

The duchess was arranging the flowers in the entryway. Grace walked by as quickly and silently as she could, but the duchess noticed her right away.

"Are you finished dancing already, Grace?"

"Yes, I am afraid my foot could not take much more. Thank you for offering to play for us."

"You look flushed. My son did not make you exert yourself too much, did he?"

"No, Your Grace. He was . . . very accommodating. If you will excuse me, I wish to get a book from the library."

"Of course. How is your ankle?"

She took a deep breath. All she wanted to do was retreat to her own world. She couldn't make heads or tails of what had just happened in the music room. She knew it was not difficult for people to read emotion in her face, especially when it was aglow with a heat that was spreading to her ears. She could hardly look the duchess in the face just now, knowing that she knew about the last dance lesson.

What must she think of me? The world Grace had just begun to painfully reconstruct with hope, friendship, and fond remembrance had suddenly transformed into nothing but unease and embarrassment. She could have sworn that the duchess saw her swollen lips and the racing pulse of her neck.

Without thinking, she reached up and touched her neck. *Foolish girl! Of course she cannot see your pulse!* Unable to form a complete thought, and not even sure of what had been asked of her, she gave half a curtsy and retreated to the library.

Once she was there, she collapsed into the sofa, thankful that the sturdy furniture seemed unbothered by the weight of her anxiety. Even more worrisome was the unfamiliar sensation of her heart flapping around in her chest in complete disorder. Grace strove for predictability and control; this was not how she liked to do things.

He did not abandon me! He kept writing for over a year! Her heart somersaulted against her ribs with the hope that somewhere, somehow, those letters may have survived. She would have to find a way to ask the duchess. How, she did not know, as that would involve asking the duchess about the last dance lesson. It would be mortifying. But all the evidence suggested that Gavin's parents already knew. They had whisked their son off to school early to keep him away from Grace.

But none of what happened ten years ago was nearly as important as what happened moments ago.

She still felt the warmth of his lips on hers. His kiss was so powerful; it had awakened every sleeping hope inside her. At first, she had been surprised, but that feeling only lasted a moment. She had never been kissed by a man. Her only experience had been the dance lesson ten years ago. And this kiss was different. It could only be described as an igniting. Just as a torch is prepared with oil-soaked cloth, so her heart had been prepared for the reunion of his touch.

She closed her eyes and relished in the fresh memory of his strong arms engulfing every inch of her. He had literally swept her off her feet for the second time in two days. She needed to get some control over her emotions, and quickly! She squeezed her eyes shut tightly and quietly mouthed her self-soothing mantra: *Perform everything with grace.* Deep breath. *Perform everything with grace.* Deep breath.

Just then she heard a rustle of papers. She sat bolt upright. "Who is there?"

"Only me, Miss Iverson," Winston replied. "I am sorry to disturb you. I was just returning some books that His Grace has finished. I can come back another time."

Relieved that it was not the duchess or Gavin and grateful for the distraction, she calmly stood and smiled. "It is no bother," she said. "I am thinking about selecting some books myself. May I ask what Gavin has enjoyed recently?"

"Of course, miss." Winston held out the three books in his hand.

"*Persuasion*? Is that not written by a woman?"

"Yes, miss. It is about a man who went to sea after being refused, only to return after making his fortune. I hear it is rather good."

It intrigued her quite a bit. "So, it is about a sailor?"

"Yes. His Grace tells me it is a very hopeful romance, one where an old love has to stand the test of time. The duke said he understood what Captain Wentworth felt when he said he was 'half agony, half hope'. He finished it just last night."

Grace looked up at Gavin's valet. He was quite a bit older than Gavin, perhaps almost five-and-thirty. His temples showed a bit of graying at the hairline, but it made him rather regal looking. Something about the man seemed innately trustworthy. And Gavin probably shared all his little secrets with his man, especially now that he no longer had a brother to confide in.

She decided to take a risk. "May I ask you a question, Mr. Winston?"

"Of course, miss."

She took a moment to pause and craft just the right wording. "The duke, he is changed since I last saw him ten years ago. What has he done over the years besides go off to sea?"

Winston smiled and said, "I have served His Grace for almost seven years, ever since he came back from his grand tour. We sailed all around the world together. Captain Kingston was known for good humor in ports from here to Siam."

"I see. Did he make many friends on his voyages?"

"Oh yes," Winston agreed, "His Grace made friends wherever he went, miss."

She had a sinking feeling that he meant something more than "friends", and her honest nature clarified before her heart could restrain it. "*Lady* friends, you mean?"

Winston raised his eyebrow a bit but masked it quickly. The look was so fleeting that she could almost convince herself she had imagined it. It was the subtlest of gestures, but it had a profound impact on Grace's heart. *So, Gavin has had many women in his life.*

She steeled herself for the valet's response. "The duke was a different man then, miss," Winston explained. "He enjoyed meeting people, and he was always well-liked—"

"Yes, I think I can imagine."

"No, miss, not like that. I did not mean to imply anything improper."

She paused in surprise. "But he was like his brother, right? I know Spencer enjoyed the ladies."

"No, miss. Spencer liked the ladies because of what he could get from them. I would say that the duke was quite different from his brother. His Grace, I believe, was looking for something as he went from lady to lady."

"What do you mean? What was he looking for?"

Winston looked at her intensely for an extended moment. It was clear he was deliberating on how honestly to answer her question. "Well, I think that His Grace has had a very clear idea of his ideal woman for many, many years. I believe he was looking for someone like her."

Grace's heart grew heavy. *My goodness! "Many, many years"? How many ladies did that involve?* Hearing that he was a ladies' man was not new information. But it stirred feelings of inadequacy like never before. Would she be discarded with all the others when she did not measure up to this perfect woman he sought? Was she any different from the other "friends" he had over the years?

"Do you mean to say he has been looking for someone in particular all this time?" she asked.

"No, he *was* looking for someone." The emphasis was not lost on Grace.

She swallowed hard. "But not anymore?" she asked.

Winston took a deep breath. "Miss Iverson, I cannot betray His Grace's confidence." He pursed his lips and carefully considered his words before continuing. "But it is no secret that His Grace detests his title. He is afraid it defines who he is, and he has a strong distrust of the women now. He believes they will say or do anything to become the Duchess of Huntsman."

"Are you saying he no longer wishes to marry?"

Grace watched the valet closely. "The duke is under a great deal of pressure to marry," Winston replied, "as anyone who has ever spent a day under the same roof as his mother knows. But the idea of marriage with anyone but this ideal woman is now distasteful to him in the highest degree. He—"

She had schooled her features for as long as she was capable. "Of course. Thank you, Winston," she interrupted. She looked down at her hands. There were so many emotions and thoughts fluttering her treacherous heart.

There was silence for a moment as Winston hesitated. "Miss Iverson?"

"Yes?"

"I would never presume to speak for His Grace, but I know the duke was very much looking forward to dancing with you tonight. I have begun to see a bit of the man I knew in the earlier years, more light hearted and spontaneous, since you came. He seems less burdened. You are good for him."

A blush started to spread across her face. "He was certainly spontaneous," Grace murmured. Winston held back a smile, which only embarrassed Grace further. "Do you mind if I hold onto *Persuasion*?" she asked.

He handed her the book. "Not at all, miss." Then Winston bowed and left.

She took the book and sat down. She was not truly in the mood to read at the moment, but she opened the book and acted the part as she contemplated all she had heard.

So, he has enjoyed his fair share of attention from the ladies? The news wasn't altogether surprising. His lips certainly seemed experienced. She had always known that about Gavin. But she had always felt a bit of pride in knowing that she was special to him. He had said as much in the music room. *"You were everything to me. Every good thing in my life had you in it."* Did he mean it? Was she still that special someone after all these years?

Perhaps, but Winston had made it clear that Gavin did not want to marry. At least, not anymore.

Then what did he want? Only to steal the hearts of vulnerable ladies?

Surely he did not wish her to be his mistress . . . The thought hung in the air around her head, confusing her.

No. She could not believe he was so calloused as to intentionally hurt her or damage her reputation. To believe that he was a rake rankled. The Gavin she knew had always protected her in every way possible. Even as children, whenever their misdeeds were discovered, Gavin had always claimed responsibility and had usually received the worst of the punishment. He was chivalrous in that way. And he still had a very strong sense of right and wrong. He would never intentionally ruin a woman's reputation. She felt secure in this thought.

Her heart bounced powerfully in her chest. The organ was not behaving as it should. If she wasn't careful, she would find herself giving away its loyalty to a man who . . . who no longer wished to marry. But, surprisingly, she realized she didn't care. The beating in her chest had found resonance years ago with Gavin. She still loved him. There was no doubt about it now. His kiss had simply rekindled those emotions she had strived to keep under lock and key for ten years.

She had loved him so deeply. And she had truly felt he loved her the same way. But then circumstances had changed, and it all ended so suddenly.

The first year they were apart, she told herself he was busy studying for his Cambridge entrance exams. And when the next summer brought no Kingston visitors, she assumed he was traveling with his parents to Italy, like they had talked of doing. But two more years passed, and she knew he had already entered university and was being introduced to all sorts of new people. When it was time for him to begin his grand tour of the continent, she prayed that he would seek her out and ask her to go with him.

Of course her mother would never have allowed her to accept such an invitation, but in her heart she traveled with him. She studied French and Italian and geography, just to feel close to him. She kept putting off her first season in hopes that he would seek her out, but when she was one-and-twenty, her mother insisted that she make her debut.

Remembering it reminded her of his silly game, challenge to the death, and each increasingly dangerous step. Making her debut had been the most difficult rung of the ladder yet. Either Gavin would be there in London, waiting to catch her, or she would have to try to find that big, brave man he had promised. And when Gavin hadn't arrived, she had thought she might make do with Mr. Broadbent. She had tried to convince herself that he was as good as Gavin. She had trusted him and nervously climbed another rung of the ladder. But then her mother died and Broadbent betrayed her. She had fallen to her death.

And no one caught her.

After that, she secluded herself at Tamara's home for three years. She stopped confiding in her sisters and refused to reenter society. It was only when Sarah begged her, for Mother's sake, that Grace began to consider attempting another season. It took several months of correspondence and the news of Sarah's coming baby for her to finally agree. And, truthfully, she had been only too relieved to cancel the plans when Sarah took ill.

Sarah didn't need Grace in London—she had servants and a hired nurse—but Grace had been pleased to have a reason to stay in town. Simply being in London increased her chances of hearing about the Kingstons. Grace hoped that she might at least see the announcement when Gavin married.

Well, I am definitely hearing about the Kingstons now, she mused, *although not all the news is welcome. But does it matter if he doesn't wish to marry? Does it matter that he once had "friends" in every port?*

No.

He was her best friend.

She would take whatever he would give. And he had given her a special memory. Some moments of the last hour had been trying, certainly, but it had been worth it. She wouldn't trade the memory of that kiss for anything. If he wanted a best friend, she would be that person. Short of sacrificing her reputation, she would walk arm in arm with him as long as he would let her.

She pondered the events of the last hour for several more minutes until she heard someone enter the room. From the clippity-clop click of his heals, she knew who it was. She closed her eyes and repeated her mantra in her heart and mind. *Perform everything with grace.*

*****

Gavin could not believe his good luck. There she was, sitting on the sofa in the library. He had assumed Grace had disappeared for the night.

What was she feeling? What did she think of the kiss? Did she understand now that he had loved her all these years? Did she know how vital she was to his happiness? There was only one way to find out.

"Grace, can we talk about what happened in the music room?"

She opened her eyes and looked up at him. They were steel blue in the candlelight. She sat up straighter, closed her book, and set it aside.

"Yes, about that. I just had a very interesting conversation with Winston. I believe he was trying to warn me about you."

The firmness of her eyes was reflected in her manners. But a small playfulness and ease was there as well. He could not be sure, but he thought she was teasing him.

"Really?" he said with a laugh. "Well, valets do not know their masters as well as they sometimes think," Gavin asserted. In response, she raised her eyebrow and grinned silently back at him. "Let me guess," he said, slightly more nervous now, "Winston told you that I have decided to never marry? That I have heartlessly crushed the hopes of young debutantes all over London?"

This time both eyebrows rose in surprise. *Hmmm . . . I might have just revealed more than Winston did.* She smiled at him mischievously. *What on earth did Winston tell her?* Reading Grace had never been this difficult.

Gavin continued cautiously, "I see that was not what he told you. Might I enquire as to what new information my servant disclosed to you?"

"Oh, I did not say the information was new. Part of me has always known. He just reminded me of some of your traits." A teasing look flashed in her eyes.

"Come on, Grace, tell me. You are killing me."

"Let us just say it is no secret that you have more dance experience than I do. He also let me borrow your book," she said, picking up *Persuasion* again. "I hear it is rather good."

He smiled cautiously. "Yes, it is rather entertaining. You will like Anne Elliot. Her heart is always loyal to Captain Wentworth, even refusing other offers that came her way. She always held out hope for him to return."

"So, this Captain Wentworth, he returned to ask for her hand?"

"No. It was a chance meeting that brought them together again."

"I think I would very much like to read this story. What drew you to it?"

He couldn't help but smile. "Hmm . . . perhaps it was the sea captain who had lost his first love. Or maybe it was Anne's quiet strength in spite of the fact that she had lost her home, her mother, and even her social standing and was nearly on the shelf when she finally learned to follow her heart."

Just as expected, color infused her cheeks. She seemed to falter just for a moment. Then she stood up straight and said, "Well, I look forward to reading it if it is as good as you say. I bid you goodnight. Thank you, Gavin, for adding a bit of entertainment to this evening. It was . . . something else." She stood and curtsied. He stood and bowed and watched her leave with the book in hand.

Well, that did not go as badly as it could have. Knowing Grace, that was as close as they would come today to discussing the kiss. But he had already discovered the answer to one question this evening. There would be time enough for more detailed research in the future.

CHAPTER 8

Now that the ankle was healed, the duchess swooped into action, commandeering Grace's every waking moment. The next two days were a whirlwind of shopping adventures and social calls. Lady Anaheim was amiable, as were Mrs. Kensington and her daughters, but the Tremontons were very inquisitive and nearly rude, especially the daughter, Sylvia.

The dresses Grace had ordered two weeks ago with her sister were now ready for the final fitting. The duchess approved of Grace's selection and commissioned more gowns of varying styles, some more revealing than others. Several of them were made as rush orders, especially the ball gown. Her Grace insisted on paying, which meant she had the final say on every detail. Knowing how stubborn the duchess was, Grace wisely chose not to fight a battle she knew she wouldn't win.

All in all, the duchess commissioned three additional ball gowns, four day dresses, and five evening dresses. They spent an entire afternoon in milliners' shops, purchasing accessories for eighteen new dresses. It was a staggering number; never in her entire life had Grace owned so many clothes. It took the footman five trips just to transport everything from the carriage up to Charlotte for final approval.

Charlotte was invaluable. She had discreetly added lace to the décolletage of two gowns to make Grace more comfortable, making a special trip to the lace shops on Market Street to find the perfect piece. She even dyed the delicate fabric a pale peach color to match the dress Grace was wearing to tonight's dinner.

Now, as Charlotte finished her hair, Grace found herself thinking about the kiss in the music room two days ago. She remembered how Gavin had guided her effortlessly around the room in silence as if the music had never stopped. *Perhaps the music hadn't stopped,* she thought. *Lord knows my heart was beating loudly enough to create an audible beat.* She ruminated a bit longer on it and felt her cheeks grow warm again. She couldn't help herself; it happened every time she thought about him.

Charlotte looked at her in the mirror and asked, "Now, Miss Iverson, what has gotten you to glow so brightly? I know your radiance tonight has nothing to do with my skill."

"Of course it is. Look at this dress! When I picked it out two weeks ago, it was plain as day. But the pearls and lace you added have made it so beautiful! I do not remember a time when I felt so lovely."

"Well, we could not have your first dinner back into society be anything less than breathtaking." She patted Grace's curls once or twice before announcing, "Finished. I do declare not a single bachelor in sight of you will fail to seek an introduction."

"Thank you, Charlotte. You are a miracle worker. A master at everything."

"No need to thank me. 'Tis easy when I have perfect material to begin with. But I do enjoy hearing all the details. You can repay me by telling me all about dinner later. Now go. The duchess will have my hide if you are late."

Grace stood and looked in the mirror one last time at her pale peach dress. She had never felt more beautiful. As she reached the spiral staircase, she could hear a number of voices coming from the parlor. The butler, Mr. Robison, bowed respectfully and directed her in.

Grace faltered for a moment upon seeing the crowd. The duchess must have invited twenty people! Just as she caught sight of Gavin, the duchess gracefully glided over to her and cried, "There you are!" She took Grace's arm and started to guide her from group to group. The Tremontons were there, with Sylvia clinging possessively to Gavin. He smiled and winked imperceptibly when they caught sight of each other. She colored, thinking about the music room again.

Heathen's milk! Why do I have to blush every time I see him? She smiled back at him, hoping that the color in her cheeks and her fluttering heart were not obvious to everyone. Sylvia Tremonton pulled on his arm and led him away.

The duchess began the introductions. William Ellis was handsome and made good conversation. Abigail Woods looked to be younger than Grace. Her brother, Mr. Fredrick Woods, wore a black dress coat with silver threads subtly woven into the fabric to create an elegant sheen. His fob was a bit over the top as well, with three dramatic loops. Each button was decorated with tiny white gems. *He must think very highly of his tailor*, Grace mused with a smile. When he finally stopped talking about himself and his country estate in Kent, the duchess continued presenting her to the others in the room.

The faces and names began to blur after the first dozen introductions, but she brightened at being introduced to a Mr. Harrison, who had a distinct smell of worn, aged leather and spoke with a stutter. She knew at once that this was Gavin's friend who raised horses. They talked easily enough, and he even asked if he could escort her to dinner when the time came. Grace consented.

The door opened, and a familiar face walked into the room. Grace followed the duchess to greet Gavin's sister, Eliza, whom Grace had not seen for ten years. She was dressed in the latest fashion and paraded in with a proud air of confidence. Not a single curl was out of place.

"Eliza, dear!" the duchess called out, "I am so glad you were able to join us tonight. You remember Grace Iverson. Grace, this is my daughter, Lady Eliza Jones."

Eliza said, "Of course I remember Grace! How good it is to see you again! Forgive me for being nearly late, Mother, but the children were not easily settled tonight. Alexander has been having nightmares and is far more work than my nursery maid can handle."

The duchess smiled and replied, "Of course, dear. A mother's touch is always the key. No doubt he was privy to a song or two as well."

Eliza smiled and confessed, "Yes, perhaps more than a few. I may not be able to sing tonight."

"Nonsense! You will be the finale. So, drink plenty of lemonade during dinner. Would you be so kind as to occupy Grace for a minute? I see Mrs. Bearl waiting for me. I do hope it is not another problem with the meal."

Eliza turned to Grace and took her arm. "Come, take a turn with me. I am quite familiar with most of the guests tonight. And let me say, I was so sorry to hear of your mother's death. You poor thing!"

Eliza was only a year younger than Grace, but she and Grace had never been very close. Eliza was more feminine and careful in playtime than Grace, and her only competitive streak was to look better than anyone else in the room. She enjoyed the spotlight and society. Her birthday parties had always been extravagant and themed, and the entire neighborhood always hoped to be invited. It was no surprise to learn that she had found a spectacular match in her first season at eighteen and already had two children at the age of three-and-twenty.

Grace did not particularly wish to discuss the death of her mother and father at a dinner party, so she quickly changed the subject. Picking a person at random, she asked, "Eliza, who is the dark-haired gentleman speaking with Mr. Silence?"

"Ah, yes, good eye. I shall introduce you. Let us head in that direction."

As they approached, Silence called out, "Miss Iverson, you are looking quite fetching tonight in that peach gown. It complements your ivory skin tones very handsomely. But I am quite disappointed that my lovely partner in crime has not sent me any covert communication tonight on how we shall embarrass Kingston. Fifteen minutes together in the same room and not even one wink!"

Grace smiled but was quick with her reply. "I have never known a man who needed less help to embarrass himself than the Duke of Huntsman." It felt odd to refer to her best friend by his formal name.

The dark-haired gentleman to the side of Silence chuckled and replied, "I see you know His Grace well."

Eliza interrupted them and said, "Mr. Lewis, allow me to introduce Miss Grace Iverson. She is a dear friend of the family and could probably burn your ears with stories of us, but I understand that she will be sentenced to dancing with Gavin's two left feet if she discloses anything of real value to the gossip magazines." Although Eliza seemed to be joking, there was also an undercurrent of warning as well. It seemed that Lady Eliza had inherited more than just her golden locks from her father.

"I know nothing save that Lady Eliza can eat more strawberry Italian ice on a hot summer day than both myself and the duke combined," Grace replied. "It is a pleasure to meet you, Mr. Lewis."

"The pleasure is all mine. I understand that there will be music and singing after dinner. Will we have the pleasure of hearing from both of you ladies?" Grace was only partly listening, because she was busy glancing over Silence's shoulder to see Gavin. She hadn't had much time to take in how handsome he looked. It wasn't until Mr. Lewis repeated his question that she realized Silence had caught her watching Gavin. He was grinning knowingly at her.

Mr. Lewis asked again, "I asked, will we have the chance to hear both of you sing tonight?"

Eliza quickly answered for both of them. "Of course! My mother would not allow me to decline, and Miss Iverson is quite accomplished."

Grace tried not to flinch. She hadn't been asked to sing anything by the duchess. She suddenly felt quite ill. "Pardon me, Mr. Lewis, Mr. Silence, Lady Eliza, but I see that I am being hailed by His Grace." She hadn't really been summoned, but it was the first excuse that came to her mind.

Gavin was watching her approach and excused himself from the conversation that he had been participating in. He met her halfway and could tell she was distressed. "What is it, Gigi? If Lewis said anything—"

"No, he was very nice."

"Was it Silence?"

"No, nothing like that. I believe your mother might be under the impression that I will be singing tonight. I have not prepared anything to perform."

"What about *Red Is the Color of My True Love's Hair?*"

She rolled her eyes at his dismissal of her concerns. "The song is called *Black Is the Color of My True Love's Hair.*"

Gavin was grinning from ear to ear. "Is it now? You might be right. I could have sworn that red was the color of my true love's hair."

"I shall not argue with you, because this is a ridiculous thing to debate. Of course the color is black. I am being serious; what will I sing?"

He took her hand and casually wrapped it around his arm. It was the first time he had touched her since their kiss in the music room. She had successfully avoided him for the last two days, although not entirely on purpose; his mother had kept her quite preoccupied. Feeling his touch again excited her and calmed her at the same time. His presence reminded her to breathe. He counseled her in a quiet, reassuring voice, "We used to sing all the time growing up. Surely there are a few songs you know."

She hesitated. "Well, there is one song that I sing when I am feeling lonely. Do you still play the pianoforte, Gavin?"

"Yes. My mother insisted I continue lessons. Do you need me to play something?"

"How much time do we have before dinner?"

"Based on my mother's consultation with Mrs. Bearl in the dining room, not much longer. Ten at the most."

"Can you meet me in the music room?"

"Right now?"

"Please?"

"Of course. You go ahead, and I shall follow shortly. Silence is eyeing me suspiciously. I will have him delay Mother if she tries to escort everyone in before we return."

"I must retrieve the music from my room. I will hurry."

*****

Gavin arrived in the music room first, but Grace was right behind him. "That music book looks rather thick. We are not practicing an entire opera, are we?"

She laughed. He was glad that he could get her to smile. "No, just one song. A rather old folk song."

He took the book from her and sat at the pianoforte bench. "Which song?"

When she didn't answer right away, he looked up to her and gave her a puzzled look. "Grace? Which song? We only have a few minutes."

She took a deep breath and answered, "*The True Lover's Farewell*. It is the third song."

"I have never heard of it."

"Like I said, it is rather old."

He flipped to the third song and saw that it was fairly easy to play. He put his hands on the keys and started. It was a sweet melody. He finished the introduction and waited for Grace to begin, but nothing happened. He stopped playing and looked up at her. "What is wrong?"

"I do not know if I can do this."

He saw how flushed she was. He knew she struggled with performing in front of strangers. He scooted over and patted the seat next to him, and she appeared to welcome the opportunity to sit beside him.

"Grace, you can do this. I believe in you. Let us remember that it is highly unlikely that you will stutter or miss a note. You should be more worried about the likelihood that I will trip on my way to the pianoforte." A tiny smile crept across her face. "Right now the only person you are performing for is me. Just me. Your best friend. That is all. And when it comes time to perform, you just keep imagining that you are just singing for me. Let us try again, all right?" He put his arm around her shoulders and gave her a gentle squeeze. She nodded and sat up straighter.

He returned to the music and played the introduction again, and this time she started singing.

Her voice was like watching liquid silver being poured into elegant chandelier molds; it was so smooth that he wanted to reach out and touch it. It was no longer the voice of a fourteen-year-old, and she certainly was not singing playground rhymes.

> *O fare you well, I must be gone*
> *And leave you for a while;*
> *But wherever I go, I will return,*
> *If I go ten thousand mile, my dear,*
> *If I go ten thousand mile.*

Her voice filled his heart with purpose, and he played to complement the variations she made to the melody. He noticed she liked to crescendo a bit in the middle of the verse and then trail off and hold the note longer than the music dictated, so he made the adjustments for the next verse.

> *Ten thousand miles it is so far*
> *To leave me here alone,*
> *Whilst I may lie, lament, and cry,*
> *And you will not hear my moan, my dear,*
> *And you will not hear my moan.*

It wasn't hard to see why she was so moved by these particular lyrics. It reminded him of her tears in the music room and how she had thought he had forgotten her. All these years she had held out hope of meeting him again someday. It nearly broke his heart to think of it. No wonder she sang it when she felt lonely. He could only imagine the pain she had gone through.

> *The crow that is so black, my dear,*
> *Shall change his color white;*
> *And if ever I prove false to thee,*
> *The day shall turn to night, my dear,*
> *The day shall turn to night.*

He continued to play and listen to her sweet voice, but the beauty of the song was nothing compared to the beauty that sat next to him. He could tell the song was nearing the end. He tried to focus on what she needed from him as he accompanied her. He noticed that every time it repeated the last line of the verse, she very nearly whispered it, so he played softer to match the emotion she expressed.

> *O don't you see that mil-white dove*
> *A-sitting on yonder tree,*
> *Lamenting for her own true love,*
> *As I lament for thee, my dear,*
> *As I lament for thee.*

The river never will run dry,
Nor the rocks melt with the sun;
And I'll never prove false to the girl I love
Till all these things be done, my dear,
Till all these things be done.

There was a distinct crack in Grace's voice as she sang the last line. He looked over to her, and their eyes met. Her blue eyes begged him to reassure her. He felt inspired to do more than that. He took her hand and brought it up to his lips and kissed every knuckle softly.

"My dearest Grace, I have no words. Believe me when I say, you inspire me. Have no fear tonight when it is time to sing. I will be right beside you listening to your every word as if you were singing to me."

She looked away briefly, and for a moment, Gavin thought she was about to admit that she was singing to him, that she loved him just as much as he loved her.

But instead, Grace seemed to collect herself and said, "It is a beautiful song, is it not?"

"You are the one that made it beautiful. Sing it as you just did, and you will leave everyone speechless."

She stood up from the bench. "Thank you, Gavin. We should return before we are missed."

Looking directly up at her, he said, "That is impossible."

"We have only been gone a few minutes."

He patted the bench and said, "But I miss you already."

"You are such a flirt."

He grinned at her and winked. "And you love me for it."

She looked at him and gave a subtle smile as she left. "Your self-worth is entirely too exaggerated. Think what you must."

Oh, I will, he jokingly thought. *God give me patience before I devour her beautiful lips again with my own!* There was no doubt he had felt moved by the words and meaning of the song, but, in truth, he was nearly driven to distraction just sitting next to her on the tiny piano bench. At least when she sang for everyone she would be standing. He wouldn't feel the warmth of her body or be distracted by her breath rushing past his ear.

He shook his head in disbelief. This snail's pace of her heart's awakening might very well be the death of him. *Be patient,* he reminded himself. *It's only been four days since you ran into her.* And instead of jokingly praying for patience, he humbly bowed his head and earnestly prayed to be the kind of man she deserved: kind, patient, considerate, and, above all else, a friend. He felt his heart beat hard at the last words of his prayer. She needed him to be a friend—the kind of friend that never failed her, the kind of friend that would stand by her and hope for her every happiness. He closed the prayer and realized that it was the first time he had prayed since his father and brother died.

Listening to her sing, he had been touched by how much *she* needed *him*, but now it dawned on him just how desperately *he* needed *her*. He was beginning to wonder if what he felt all these years had been love. It was nothing compared to what he felt for her now.

CHAPTER 9

Grace thought she had slipped into the parlor unnoticed until she saw Silence sidle up behind her. "Strange, do you not think," he murmured, "that the guest of honor and the host should disappear and reappear at the same time?"

She turned around to see the grin that she could hear in his voice. "I do not know what you mean. A hairpin come loose, and I needed to replace it. Are you saying that Gavin left at the same time?"

He grinned wider. "No need to be sly with me, Miss Iverson. But I am not the only one watching you tonight. I just thought I would remind you of that."

"Thank you. I am well aware that far too many eyes are on me."

She glanced around the room and saw Gavin looking back at her sweetly; she couldn't help but smile back.

Silence sipped his tea, hiding his smile, and added, "I see some eyes are more welcome than others."

Grace took a deep breath and managed to control her embarrassment from making itself known in her cheeks. Being a fair-skinned ginger made hiding one's emotions difficult, but she was not about to let others, not even Gavin's close friends, be misled. "Silence, Silence," she replied. "I assure you, the familiarity you may think you see is entirely proper. Gavin has been my friend, and nothing more, for many years. He told me as such only a few minutes ago."

"Oh, I see! While he was assisting you with your hairpin?" Grace felt a blush warm her face. She didn't think it was possible for Silence to smile wider, but he did. "My apologies, Miss Iverson," he said. "I see from the color in your cheeks that I have either angered or embarrassed you; neither was my intention."

Luckily Mr. Harrison joined them just then. Silence bowed and left grinning. Mr. Harrison did not say much, just the usual pleasantries. It gave her time to put Gavin and Mr. Silence's words behind her. It dawned on her why Mr. Harrison had come to stand by her when the duchess reentered the room and the butler announced dinner.

Mr. Harrison offered his arm. "I sh-sha-shall be happy to escort you to din-dinner."

"Thank you, Mr. Harrison."

It was no surprise that her seat was in the middle of the table. Mr. Harrison was to her left, making her think that his confidence in escorting her to dinner was perhaps due to some prior knowledge of the seating arrangements. Seated next to Silence, on Grace's right, was Sylvia Tremonton—who looked very displeased to discover Gavin had been seated as far away as possible from her. Grace couldn't help but gloat a little. But her satisfaction was short-lived; Grace would have liked to been seated closer to the duke herself. As it was, conversation with Gavin would be impossible.

Across from Grace was the flamboyant Mr. Woods, a dandy if she had ever seen one. The two guests seated on either side of him were both unfamiliar to her. The blonde-haired gentleman to his left was strikingly handsome and kept flashing her bold, flirtatious looks. The lady to Mr. Woods's right was clearly married if the extravagant ring on her left hand was any indication.

As each course was brought out, Grace tried to participate in the conversation. But she spent most of her time answering questions about her ties to the Kingstons. Luckily many of the guests had already heard the story of Gavin knocking her down in the street, so she only had to fill in the details. It wasn't hard to elicit laughter when she described how His Grace had somersaulted over her and landed directly under the belly of a horse. She had to admit that it did make a good story. The more she talked about how Gavin hadn't changed since his youth, the more she felt at ease.

By the time the roast duck and lobster tails were served, she had learned that the handsome man next to Mr. Woods was Mr. Patrick Under. If she remembered right, Gavin had described him as a spineless man who would let Grace direct the very breeches he wore each day. After a whole meal with him, she added "noncommittal" to that description. He seemed to agree with every opinion shared, even that the creamed peas and onions had just the right amount of pepper—a ridiculous comment she had said to test his compliant nature as she could taste no pepper in them at all. Mr. Under was just as Gavin had described him. He wouldn't do for her at all.

Mr. Harrison, on the other hand, improved upon further acquaintance. His stutter bothered her less than she thought it would. For the remainder of the meal, she focused on getting to know him more. He did not deliberate his replies excessively long when asked a question, and he seemed to truly listen to her answers. There were times she found herself laughing outright at his wit. She could see why Gavin called him a friend.

Miss Tremonton as good as ignored her during dinner—and the feeling was mutual—but Sylvia was all ears whenever someone inquired about Grace's connection to Gavin. Then Miss Tremonton was only too eager to join in. Her pointed questions on that topic could only be described as underhanded barbs. It was evident that in Sylvia Tremonton's judgment, Grace did not stand a chance to . . . *to what? What was I about to say? Win Gavin's heart?* It wasn't even remotely possible.

Unfortunately every conversation topic seemed to lead her thoughts back to Gavin—a subject that was far too tender an area to dally with. He had welcomed her into his home to help her find a husband. Clearly he wasn't interested himself in filling that role. *But what about his promise to marry me if I end up a spinster?* Her heart filled with hope for an instant. But she was hardly a spinster yet. And she could never accept a man who made her an offer only out of duty.

Sometimes a tiny thought tickled her mind, reminding her about that kiss in the music room. One moment she would let her heart hope for a future with him, and the next moment she was listing off all the reasons why he saw her only as a friend. None of it was very reassuring.

She kept thinking back to the kiss. She knew him too well to believe he was a rake like his brother, Spencer, but he was too smooth in his compliments to believe he was as inexperienced as she was. His expert, urgent lips verified that fact. His kiss and his words had felt calculated, overly-confident. Every time, her thoughts led her to the same conclusion—that he had kissed many women in just the same manner. Perhaps he was even comparing her inexperience to theirs. And every time she reached that conclusion, she needed some serious self-soothing. It bothered her that she had let herself get her hopes up. She knew better. She knew better than to trust anyone again.

As the guests stood to begin the typical separation of sexes after dinner, she chided herself for deliberating on Gavin's kiss like that. It was a topic she usually successfully avoided thinking about; doing so while at an important dinner was remarkably unwise. Mr. Woods had already circled the table and was offering to help her up. She accepted his attention graciously. But as he pulled out her chair, his quizzing glass dropped from his face and hit her in the side of her neck. It took all of her self-control not to giggle; she couldn't stop her lips from forming a smile.

He mistook her smile as genuine interest and proudly accompanied her to the music room, where the ladies were already gathering. The sight of him strutting around like a peacock was rather funny, and her grin widened even more. She sobered up a moment too late when she realized he was bending down to kiss her hand, as if her smile was an indication that the half-hour separation would be torturous. The idea of hanging on his arm like an ornament for the rest of her life was unbearable. He would never do either.

She managed a brief curtsy to relay her thanks. Gavin was ushering all the men toward the library, and for some reason, he looked pensive and withdrawn. But at the last minute, before he closed the music room door, he glanced her way and gave a subtle wink to reassure her.

Almost immediately the ladies began discussing the gentlemen, debating who had looked the most dashing. It was not surprising that Mr. Woods's name came up, but Grace was stunned that they shamelessly ranked each man's appearance against one another.

Soon a formal vote was cast on which man was to receive the title of "the Shiner". "The Shiner", Grace was informed, was the lucky man deemed by the single ladies to have "outshined every other man in attendance" in both gentlemanly grace and attractiveness that evening.

Grace listened quietly to the ridiculous rules. It was hard to believe the ladies cared so much about such superficialities as fashionable clothes and a stylish demeanor. She shook her head and jokingly whispered to Eliza, "I assume your brother has never won, correct?" Unfortunately, there had been a lull in the room's conversation buzz, and more than Eliza heard the comment.

Miss Tremonton replied, "Actually, Miss Iverson, His Grace has been voted 'the Shiner' at many balls. It must be difficult for you to judge these matters, you being so new to cultured society. But I have had the chance to dance with him, as many of these ladies have—although perhaps me more than any other in this room—and he is the finest dance partner I know. There is no equal to him. Just because he dropped his fork at dinner tonight does not mean that he lacks all grace."

Grace anxiously glanced at the hostess. But instead of disappointment, Grace saw something in the duchess's eyes that gave her confidence to speak her mind. "Forgive me, Miss Tremonton," Grace replied. "I had not noticed he dropped his fork." It felt satisfying, but as soon as she said it, she regretted it. She was no simpleton, and Miss Tremonton was not someone she wished to make an enemy of.

Grace quickly stood and walked across the room, welcoming a private discussion with Miss Woods. She minimally attended the conversation and did not care in the slightest that the topic revolved around Miss Woods's brother. Grace was forced to admit that yes, his blue eyes were very handsome and yes, his dark curls did indeed fall across his forehead in a very attractive manner.

See, Grace? You can be attracted to more than blonde curls and chestnut-brown eyes. Unfortunately, this only brought back to her mind the image of Gavin's eyes as he asked, "Do you trust me?" She repressed the urge to groan aloud. She glanced at the clock and hoped that there were only a few more minutes to pass in this tedious manner.

Relief could not have come sooner or been more welcome. As the men trickled in, the ladies seemed to float from one seat to the other in a calculated way. It was like a game of chess. Sylvia moved toward Gavin, leaving a wake of disappointed ladies. Miss Woods moved toward Mr. Lewis. Two or three were waving fans and batting their eyes at Mr. Silence. The only person left was Mr. Harrison. Grace had always considered herself the queen in the game of chess, one who could move in any direction. Although she would have liked to find safety with Gavin, the property claim being signaled by Miss Tremonton's eyes and her death grip on his arm was unmistakable. Grace sighed and gave an encouraging look to Mr. Harrison.

As he approached, he said, "I see you have sur-survived the separation of the sexes."

"Just barely," Grace replied with a smile.

"Well, I am glad to h-h-h-hear it. I understand a certain title is given to the most handsome gentleman. Dare I ask who is the lu-luck-lucky winner this evening?"

She laughed outright, leaned toward him, and whispered, "Mr. Lewis is the lucky gentleman. It appears you know more about the ways of London's ladies than I do! You must tell me all about it. I admit I am rather astounded that such petty games are played as if the title meant something!"

He chuckled, "Ah, but it does, Miss Iverson. When the title passes to someone new, all the ladies' attentions are diverted to the lucky winner. Wh-what gentleman, besides Kingston, does not wish to receive the prized attention of the most el-elig-eligible deb-deb-debutants?"

This intrigued her. She led him a few paces away to ensure privacy and asked, "His Grace does not wish for the title?"

"Now, there is a ques-question that has two answers. I am sure you know K-K-Kingston's feeling about titles."

"Yes, I know he does not relish being a duke."

"Nor does he relish the attention of ladies who see him only for his title. So, if the title of d-du-duke is too much, imagine if he were to re-re-receive the title of 'the Shiner' too."

Grace thought she understood. But something wasn't consistent. "But Gavin has always enjoyed female attention—"

Mr. Harrison did not stutter with his next statement. "And he still does."

What did he mean? She forced herself to ask, "Then why does he shy away from it now? Why does he no longer wish to marry?"

"Miss Iverson, that is a long, complicated story. Might I interest you in a ride tomorrow morning to discuss it? It would be a pl-pleas-pleasure to take my new chestnut mares around town with you at my side."

"I would enjoy that very much."

"Not mo-mo-more than I." She thought it was sweet that his cheeks colored slightly. Maybe Mr. Harrison was more agreeable company than she realized. She had truly enjoyed having dinner with him.

The duchess encouraged all the guests to take their seats, and the music performances started. When it was her time to perform, Gavin played flawlessly. She did just as he had suggested; she thought of the only man she ever thought of when she sang that song. She couldn't quite forget the many eyes that were on her, but she was pleased to discover that it was easier to sing for a crowd than to sing an intimate performance for Gavin. When they had practiced, she had felt her heart slipping little by little. She had nearly told him how much she loved him. She would have to be more careful.

He may have thought that kiss was just like any other kiss from any other woman. But to her, it had sealed her fate. She would never marry. The two of them had that much in common now.

CHAPTER 10

Gavin was trying very hard not to stare at Harrison and Grace from across the room. There seemed to be a growing regard between them, and he did not like it. Harrison was a fine man and a good friend. But he wasn't right for Grace. For one thing, he stuttered. Knowing Grace, that didn't bother her in the slightest; that rankled him even more.

"Excuse me, Your Grace," murmured his butler. "There is a pressing matter with one of the footmen."

It irritated him that the man insisted on using the blasted title in front of guests. Robison usually obliged him with a simple "Kingston". But Gavin was somewhat glad to have an excuse to leave the room prematurely. "Bring him to my study," he directed.

Robison nodded and left.

Gavin was the first to arrive in the study. With the late hour, he had to light the sconces along the wall. Slowly, the shadows disappeared, and he looked around. Someone had already righted the furniture from his chess game with Grace and returned the chess set to the shelf.

She had listened so keenly when he told her of the duel. In fact, there was one moment that he thought she was about to put him in check, but she had retreated. For a girl who hated losing, it must have cost her a great deal to pass up an easy win. But Gavin wasn't surprised. Her compassion, not competitiveness, had always been her dominant trait.

Spencer never truly understood that about Grace. Sure, he played with her, but he only saw her fighting spirit. He never saw the girl who would sacrifice her own happiness to make others happy. Grace believed in the goodness of others. She had an ability to be passionate about whatever they were passionate about, to rejoice in their successes and accomplishments. Maybe that was why she made Gavin feel like he could take on the world.

There was a knock at the door, and Gavin waved them in. Robison entered with Tim, a footman hired about four months ago, and Helena, a young housemaid who had joined the staff only a week ago. Helena's eyes were deep red and swollen from crying. Her shoulders hung as if her head were far too heavy to hold up. She made no effort to look in his direction.

Tim, on the other hand, looked like he was prepared to do battle. His eyes were hard, and he walked with fists clenched at his side. As Gavin looked at him, Tim lifted his chin a bit more.

"What seems to be the problem, Robison?" Gavin asked.

Robison finished closing the door and returned to Gavin's side. "Sir, Timothy here has been fraternizing with this young maid. He was found kissing her, which of course is against the rules."

Gavin's eyebrows rose in surprise, and Helena burst into fresh tears. Tim interjected, "If I may say something, Your Grace?"

Gavin leaned back against the front of his desk and crossed his ankles. "Go ahead."

"First of all, sir, I was unaware that I am not to converse with the maids. Second of all, Helena is of age. She should be able to make her own decisions. Thirdly, how else am I to find a woman if I serve six and half days a week at Willsing Manor? Fourth, it was never my intention to compromise her. I am ready to marry her if she will have me."

Gavin saw Helena look up at Tim briefly. A bright flush came to her cheeks, and then she returned her gaze to the ground. Tim continued, "Fifth, if kissing someone is so terribly bad, I want someone who never snuck one before to tell me that."

Robison and Helena gasped, and Gavin coughed to hide his chuckle. *Well, I guess that answers the question of exactly how much he saw in the music room.* Gavin cleared his throat and tried to sober his countenance.

"Thank you, Tim. I would like to hear from Helena now."

The maid's eyes shot up to him with a look of sheer panic. Her mouth parted and hung there motionless as if she could not form any words. He raised his eyebrow expectantly and waited. "I am terribly sorry, Your Grace," she flustered. "It was only one kiss on the cheek. I didn't enjoy it none."

Gavin tried not to notice the look of pain on Tim's face. Clearly the footman's devotion was sincere.

Tim stepped forward and declared, "Helena didn't do anything wrong, sir. It was all me. This is my fault."

Gavin shushed Tim and addressed the maid again, "Helena, please do not be distressed. I do not blame you in this matter. Is there anything else you wish to say?" Helena shook her head frantically. "Do you wish to pursue something further with Tim? It appears he is quite ready to defend your honor."

"I am," Tim declared. "I love her. I want to marry her."

Helena gasped, and her hand went to cover up her slow smile that was forming.

"And how do you feel about that, Helena?" Gavin asked.

"Sir, I don't know. I . . . could I have some time to decide?"

"Of course. I know how important this job is to you and your sister. But if you want to leave service and marry Tim, I will be the first to congratulate you. The choice is yours. Confer with Mrs. Bearl, and let me know what you decide. Until then, you and Tim are not to have any contact. Do you understand?" Helena shyly nodded. "Then you may go."

"Yes, Your Grace." Helena curtsied and nearly ran from the room.

Once she was gone, Gavin turned his attention to Tim. "Do not disappoint me, young man. If I hear of you going near her again, I will have no choice but to let you go." Tim clenched his hands into fists at his side but made no reply. "If you truly care for Helena like you say you do, you must keep her reputation intact," Gavin added.

Tim paused briefly before lifting his chin even higher and then said curtly, "Like you kept Miss Iverson's reputation intact, sir?"

"Mr. Gardner!" Robison bellowed. "I should fire you on the spot for that! Never, ever, refer to the master or his guests that way!"

"He kissed her! What is the difference between me kissing Helena on the cheek and him smothering Miss Iverson with his affection?"

Gavin held up his hand to silence Robison's rebuttal. "Tim," he said, slowly standing up, "I have a duty to protect the ladies of this house from opportunists and rakes. Believe me when I say, I will do whatever it takes to keep them safe." He walked toward Tim until they were nose to nose. "Now, you are to have no more contact with Helena until you hear from Robison." Then, in a deadly serious tone, he warned, "And if I ever hear you speak of Miss Iverson that way again, I will fire you myself."

"Exactly my sentiments," Robison affirmed. "You should be ashamed of yourself, Tim. The truth of the matter is, your selfish actions have endangered Helena's position here. Any other household would have dismissed you both without references. The duke has shown you mercy, and you have repaid him quite ill for it."

Tim looked much more contrite, and he bowed his head. "Forgive me, Your Grace. I meant no disrespect. My mother always said I have a bit of a temper."

Gavin frowned and dismissed both men. As soon as they were gone, he collapsed into a chair. These kinds of decisions were so taxing. He was sure Tim meant no harm; it was only a youthful romance. But a girl had been compromised all the same. Helena was an orphan with no one to protect her. She could only be sixteen or seventeen, and her younger sister was dependent on her income. It was doubtful Tim could support himself, a young wife, and the girl on his footman's wages. He felt uneasy about the situation. Hopefully Mrs. Bearl would know what to do.

For now, he had to return to the dinner and watch gentlemen fall in love with Grace. Suddenly his cravat was entirely too tight.

*****

After the dinner, Gavin retired to his room with little more than a forced goodnight to his mother and Grace. He had already taken off his cravat by the time Winston attended to him. The dinner should not have been so difficult. Grace had seemed to enjoy herself. Isn't that what he wanted?

Winston, sensing his agitation, asked, "Did the night not go well for your Grace?"

"Blast it, Winston! Stop calling me 'Your Grace'!"

"Sorry, sir." Winston paused, then added with a grin, "Perhaps you misunderstood my question. I did not ask whether *your* night had gone well. I asked if it went well for your *Grace*."

"Ah, smooth recovery, Winston," Gavin chuckled. "My apologies. To be honest, I do not know what to make of the night. Grace seemed to enjoy Mr. Harrison's attentions. I like the fellow, of course, but did she have to smile so much around him? And Mr. Woods was practically beaming when he won a smile or two from her. She really did smile a lot. I am going to have to talk to Mother about seating us closer together next time. I could not hear a thing that was said that far down."

Sensing there was more to the story, Winston prodded, "But . . .?"

Gavin sat down on the chair and sighed, "But she looked happy. Happy with someone other than me."

"Is that not what you want? For her to be happy?"

"Not with someone other than me."

Winston started to remove Gavin's boots and seemed to be pondering his next statement. Gavin hadn't told anyone about the kiss in the music room, but his valet knew all about his feelings for Grace. For the past seven years, he had heard Gavin compare every woman he met to her. Winston was more than just a servant. Gavin had always considered him a confidant—one that just happened to have a good eye for fashion and a real talent for getting out stains.

Once both the boots were off, Winston stood and said, "Might I offer you some advice, sir?" Gavin nodded. "You told me two days ago how much you both need each other. From my experience with Mrs. Winston, to need someone is to love someone. To love someone is to need them in your life. If she needs you to be a friend, then be that friend. And if she needs you to be more, she will let you know."

"Clearly you do not know Grace that well. She would never let anyone know that she needed something. That would be dangerously close to admitting a weakness. I am not sure that possibility is in her makeup," Gavin sighed. "I want her to be happy, but with me."

"Sir—if I may be so bold—if you are still preoccupied with only your own needs, are you sure you deserve a lady like her?"

His statement was certainly very bold for a servant, but Winston was the closest thing he had to a brother. Gavin's shock was replaced quickly by humility. "I do not know," Gavin murmured. "I want to. I recognize that she deserves the best."

Gavin paused. "Winston," he continued, "It might help me understand her needs better if you told me about your conversation with her in the library—"

"Sir, I told you," Winston interrupted. "I cannot divulge what a lady says in confidence."

"Yes, I know, but I just need a clue . . ." Gavin could see the grin Winston was trying to hold back.

"Back to thinking about your own needs again, I see," Winston teased. "If you truly want to understand her, I recommend talking to *her* instead of badgering *me*."

Gavin sighed and leaned back in his chair. "Very good counsel, Winston. I suppose you are right as usual."

"As you say, sir," Winston chuckled. He looked Gavin in the eye and said, "If you listen closely, she will show you what she needs."

"I hope so. Because God knows I need her."

*****

The next morning, Gavin was prepared. If needing someone was loving someone, he was determined to be exactly what Grace needed.

He wasn't naturally an early riser, but Winston had promised to wake him as soon as Charlotte was called for. The plan worked perfectly; he finished shaving and exited his room just as Grace was exiting hers. She hadn't noticed him yet, so he had a chance to observe her unseen. She had adorable, giant ringlets at the base of her neck today—one was slung over her shoulder, and the other bounced temptingly with each step. Unable to resist, he reached out and twirled the ringlet in his fingers, only to startle her.

"Oh, Gavin! You scared me!"

"You should have known it was me."

"And you should have known better than to surprise me!"

"You always say you do not like surprises, but I know you better than that. You adore surprises. Speaking of which, this is for you." He handed her a yellow rose with the faintest of red tips.

She smiled brightly at him and took it. "Thank you, Gavin. The smell is heavenly. You are so thoughtful."

"Well, I wanted to be the first one to give you flowers after your marvelous debut last night. I had Winston put the rest of the bunch on the breakfast table." With a deep breath, he added, "You look lovely this morning."

She blushed slightly and said, "Thank you."

He offered his arm, and they continued to the breakfast room. "I want you to know something, Gigi. I would never lie to you."

"Which is wise of you, because I know you well enough to detect a falsehood."

"Yes, indeed. But do you also know that Mr. Harrison, Mr. Woods, and Mr. Lewis were all very interested in you last night?"

"Oh, I doubt that very much. I am a nobody, Gavin. There is no need to puff me up."

"No, you are a beautiful somebody. Do not doubt yourself. I would not be surprised if half of the gentlemen at last night's dinner call on you today, which brings me around to my point: If you are truly interested in any of these gentlemen, I would like to help. You are too stubborn to ask, so I am officially offering my services. I will never let someone take my place, but I want you to be happy. I want you to find that big, brave man. "

"Oh, Gavin, no one could ever take your place! I am grateful to have you as a friend."

It stung a little to hear her call him a friend; he wanted to be so much more. He wanted to be the only man in her life. He thought it wouldn't be too terribly wrong to say it. "As I said, I will not lie to you. If it were up to me, I would be the only man in your life. But I recognize that you need more than a friend. You need someone to marry, have lots of babies with, and grow old with. As much as it pains me to think you might fall in love and not need me anymore, I am your best friend. I want to give you whatever you need from me."

Her eyes filled with tenderness as she looked up at him. "You will always be more than a friend to me," she whispered.

He felt his heart lift. *More than a friend!* He wanted to reach out and kiss her right there, but just as he took a step closer, his mother entered. It was as good as dousing a flame. He stepped back and asked, "So, Gigi, I understand Harrison is taking you on a carriage ride today. When will he collect you?" The heaviness of the conversation lifted significantly, and Grace seemed grateful for the change of topic.

"I am not sure. He did not give me a specific time."

"Well, if I know Harrison, he has already brushed every horse he owns and is now wandering his stables, trying to calm his nerves. You will have to carry a good deal of the conversation."

"Oh, no, he was very good company last night. He hardly stuttered at all as the evening went on."

Gavin frowned. "Really?" He had been counting on Harrison to exhibit at least one poor quality.

They continued in this manner while his mother filled her plate and sat down to the table. They were both so consumed by their conversation that they didn't realize she was waiting for them to join her until she cleared her throat. Gavin sheepishly pulled out a chair for Grace, and they took their seats.

"So, you enjoy Harrison's company?" He couldn't help but be curious.

"Yes, very much. I am quite interested in the untold stories he has about you."

"About me?"

"Yes, that is why he is calling on me. He plans to tell me the long, complicated story about why you detest your title and have decided to never marry."

"I never said I would never marry."

His mother chimed in, "Yes, you did, Gavin. Numerous times."

"Mother, it is simply that I do not want to marry someone who knows nothing about the real me."

"Yes, my dear, but how will anyone get to know the *real you* if you continue to avoid everyone? You worry that people see you only as the Duke of Huntsman, but what have you done since being titled to distinguish yourself?"

He didn't want to discuss this. He had no interest in distinguishing himself as a duke. *How can my own mother not understand that I just want things to go back to the way they were?*

He turned to humor to lighten the mood. "There you are wrong, Mother. Just a few days ago, I made a very important decision. I decided that I will have the spiral staircase rebuilt. It wraps three times before it reaches the second floor. It is entirely too tight. One cannot even see whom is coming or going. The plan will be a waste of both time and money; surely a decision worthy of a duke!"

Grace hid a smile behind her napkin, but his mother was considerably less amused. "Gavin, if you think that is such a grand decision to make, then you mock the title. You are a duke! Do you not realize what influence you could have?"

He was no longer hungry. He excused himself from the table as politely as he could, but Grace followed him out. She reached out for his arm. "Do not be angry with her, Gavin," she said.

He folded his arms across his chest and looked at her. "Do not take her side, Grace. I need your support."

"You will always have it, Gavin," she reassured him. "I find I am no longer hungry. Would you take a walk with me? "

"But you might miss Harrison's call."

She shrugged. "We will only be gone a short time. Besides, your mother can entertain him until we return. Please?"

He reluctantly nodded, and she rushed to tell his mother that they were going to go for a brisk morning walk. He heard his mother say that she hoped Grace would talk some sense into him. Grace laughingly replied, "I am not a miracle worker!"

He followed her to the front door. Robison gathered her pelisse and bonnet, but Gavin had no intention of letting his butler perform an act that he would relish so much himself. Gavin helped Grace slide her arms into the pelisse, admiring her petite, tempting form. He lifted the two ringlets at the nape of her neck and got a whiff of her cinnamon scent. With her back to him, he closed his eyes and leaned in to take another breath through his nose. It had to be her hair. Whatever she washed it with smelled like cinnamon. Just as he was imagining bringing the ringlets up to his face and caressing his lips with them, Robison loudly cleared his throat.

Gavin opened his eyes and stepped away just in time before Grace turned around.

Friends do not smell each other's hair, Gavin! Get ahold of yourself! He hadn't realized how hard it would be to just be her friend, but he was beginning to get a taste of it, and it tasted like cinnamon.

*****

Grace had felt the slightest pressure as he lifted her hair out from under the pelisse. She was suddenly very grateful for the long sleeves that hid her goose bumps. She quickly put on her bonnet to hide that the hairs on the back of her neck that were standing straight up from his gentle touch.

Gavin offered his arm, and they exited together. There was still a bit of a chill in the late-October air; she could feel his warmth next to her.

They walked for a bit without talking. Then she asked, "Gavin, what was your father like?"

"You know what he was like."

"I do. But I want you to say it."

She heard him take a deep breath before he said, "Being a duke was the most important thing to him. Do you remember how he made me call him 'Your Grace' when we were in public?"

"Yes."

"His entire self-worth was wrapped up in his title. He was obsessed with power and respect. Every decision was handled as if it was a matter of the greatest importance. He was always in Parliament when it was in session. Before the king fell ill, he was quite influential. Growing up, he had been good friends with King George. But when the Prince Regent took over, I think my father grieved more for his own loss of influence than for the man he supposedly called 'friend'. Everything was a matter of status." He paused momentarily.

Grace said, "Go on."

"He was always grooming Spencer—or, more precisely, criticizing him. You remember. Spencer did not think like a duke; he did not carry himself like a duke; he did not talk like a duke. I remember thinking over and over again that I was so glad that I was not the heir. If Spencer could not do it, I would have been hopeless."

She sensed Gavin was finally getting around to what was really bothering him. She glanced up at him and gave him an encouraging look.

"Well, you know how I am," he sighed. "I trip; I drop things; I spill. How could I ever walk like a duke? I do not have an air of authority. My countenance does not demand respect as my father's did."

They walked in silence a few steps before Grace asked, "Can I tell you what I think?" Gavin nodded. "You worry that accepting your father's title will somehow turn you into him." He started to protest, but she shushed him. "No, Gavin, you do. You worry there is some mold that all dukes must conform to. But you are wrong. Perhaps you do not walk like your father, but you are still a duke. I always feel a certain amount of relief when I hear the clippity-clop of your boots coming down the stairs. Your confident stride does not elicit fear like your father's prideful gait; but it sparks something else. Something that I think your father always wanted but never really had."

Gavin stopped walking for a moment and looked at her. "What?"

"Respect. You said so yourself: he wanted the world to respect him. He used his title to claim that respect, but we both know he did not earn it from people. You, on the other hand, have the respect of every person you meet. The kindness you show people, no matter their status in society, is unprecedented. People love you."

"But I am the least graceful man I know, and everyone is forced to call me 'Your Grace'." She could hear the pain in his voice that came from something deep and well-developed, something that had been festering for six months like a growth in his heart.

"Gavin, perhaps you do not smoothly saunter," Grace said, "but you bring other qualities to the title. This mold that you imagine all dukes must conform to is rather ridiculous. No other role or title comes with such a delineation."

"What do you mean?"

"Consider the other roles of life. I was born as a sister and daughter. Someday I hope to inherit the role of wife and mother, and if I am lucky, I will live to take the role of grandmother. Should all sisters act a certain way? Should I pattern my behavior after Eliza? Or Sarah? Or Tamara? Or should I be myself?"

Gavin looked pensive as he pondered her words. They walked a while in silence. "Besides," she added, "there is more to grace than walking smoothly."

"What do you mean?" Gavin asked.

"Well, 'grace' has many definitions. Since my name is Grace, my mother made me learn its meanings long ago. For instance, you can *grace* someone with your presence. In that sense 'grace' means to honor someone. Or it can also mean being pleasant, poised, and polite."

"I suppose I am pleasant," Gavin admitted. "At least I try to be. Perhaps not poised, though."

"You are very pleasant," Grace said. Feeling a blush starting, she quickly moved the conversation along, "Consider the meaning in this sentence: 'That man has all the *grace* of the young at heart.' 'Grace' can mean charm as well."

He smiled quirkily and reached up to her face and caressed it with the back of his fingers. "Am I charming?"

His touch burned her cheeks, contrasting to the chill that was in the air. It literally made her insides melt. Even though he was trying to tease her, she could never give him anything less than complete honesty. "Quite charming, sometimes painfully so," she admitted. Then quickly changing the subject, she said, "What if I were to say, 'He had the *grace* not to disparage his mother publically'?" she asked. "What would 'grace' mean in that sentence?"

"I suppose it means a solid understanding of right and wrong," he replied.

She could see he was starting to understand. "Exactly! What if I said, 'She showed remarkable *grace* in handling the crisis'?"

"I suppose it can also mean dignity. I had no idea 'grace' had so many different meanings—honor, integrity, dignity, charm . . . How do you remember them all?" he teased her.

"It has taken me my whole life to understand my name. Fortunately my mother had the *grace* to start when I was a little girl," she smiled back.

"Ah ha!" he laughed. "I can think of another definition we have not discussed yet. What about 'grace' in a spiritual sense?"

"Well, I recommend you study that on your own. I believe we learn better when we are seeking answers. Things become engraved in our hearts when our minds are hungry and our hearts thirsty. Now, my fingers are getting chilled. Might I ask for your hand to cover mine?"

"You never need to ask." He covered her hand with his. He then winked at her and huskily asked, "How are your lips?"

The man has more confidence than the Prince Regent himself! And he enjoys embarrassing me far too much! "Toasty warm," was all the response she could muster.

He chuckled and tapped her nose with his finger, replaced his hand over hers, and turned back around to head home. "Now, I ask you, Gigi, how is it I have the ability to warm your cheeks with a simple wink and a single sentence?"

Indeed her cheeks were flushed. "It must be all of the charm and *grace* you never knew you had!"

She felt the moment was coming to a close, but there was one more thing she needed to say while he was listening so closely.

She looked up at him for emphasis. She wanted to make sure he was really listening. "One more thing. Sometimes 'grace' is a quality that gives something that 'little something special' which increases its value or worth." She took a moment and swallowed. "For example, I might say, 'As if being my best friend were not enough, Gavin has the *grace* to assure me that I will never be lonely again.' I do not care whether you ever take being the Duke of Huntsman seriously, but you should never fear being called Your Grace. It is the highest form of respect. Whether you believe it or not, you are graceful—at least to me."

His eyes softened as he looked down at her, and the sweetest smile appeared on his face. "I have not blushed in years. Thank you for saying that. I know it took great courage, and you have made my day."

CHAPTER 11

When Grace and Gavin returned from their walk, Robison was waiting for them. "Mr. Ellis, Mr. Lewis, and Mr. Harrison are in the parlor with the duchess," he announced.

"To see me?" Gavin teased. "How thoughtful of them!"

Robison cleared his throat and clarified what everyone already knew: "To see Miss Iverson, sir."

Grace turned to Gavin with a worried look on her face. "Which one was Mr. Ellis?" she asked.

Gavin tried to act natural, but his response was edged with a bit of sarcasm. "The handsome, intelligent chap who gave no indication that he would be calling today. He sat on my end of the table."

"Oh, yes, I remember meeting him. But I only spoke to him once the whole night. I cannot imagine why he feels so encouraged." Grace took a deep breath. "Gavin, how do I do this?" she asked anxiously. "I feel as if I must put on a show. What if I do something wrong?"

"Gigi, just be friendly. You could never fail at that." Gavin took her hand and squeezed it. "Do you want me to come with you?"

"Would you?"

"Of course. There is nowhere I would rather be than with you. Especially when three men are falling at your feet."

Gavin had been expecting a retaliation, so when Grace playfully took a swing at him, he easily dodged it. And when she sent him her most-irritated look, he didn't mind in the slightest.

Instead, he enjoyed the opportunity to admire her pouty, tempting lips.

"Now, Gigi," he teased, "with that pout on your lips, it almost looks as if you are puckering up for a kiss!"

Grace glanced at the butler with a rather embarrassed look, but Robison had the dignity to pretend he hadn't heard anything. Gavin leaned in and whispered, "Forgive me. As your best friend, I should know better than to embarrass you." Then he cleared his throat and proclaimed, "I believe it is time to help you choose your husband. Come, they have waited long enough."

The visitors stood as Gavin and Grace entered the parlor. For a moment, Grace appeared unsure about whom to acknowledge first. Each suitor had brought flowers. Mr. Harrison had bluebells, Lewis had daisies, and of course the flagrant Ellis had the largest batch of all. *Red roses! Rather bold of you, Ellis. At least I chose yellow to represent friendship.* Ellis was almost as much of a dandy as Mr. Woods. "Good morning, Mr. Harrison," Grace began. "I hope you do not mind taking tea before our ride."

Ah, perfect, Grace! Let Lewis and Ellis know you will take tea with them, but make it clear you had a previous engagement with Harrison. It was evident, despite her concerns, that Grace could handle the situation without him. But Gavin had no intention of leaving. He wasn't about to grant a suitor unrestricted access to the woman of his dreams—definitely not three of them at once.

Harrison replied, "It is rather ch-chilly outside. I have no problem delaying our ride until it is warmer."

Mr. Ellis laughed haughtily. "Harrison," he snickered, "most people go riding in Hyde Park in the early evening! I am sure that is when Miss Iverson was expecting you!"

Grace smiled and ignored the barb, "I am quite looking forward to our ride, Mr. Harrison. Thank you for the bluebells. My father used to tell me that my eyes are the color of bluebells. How very thoughtful of you! And thank you for the roses, Mr. Ellis. They are so beautiful. It is good to see you again, Mr. Lewis. I used to play with daisies as a child, and they always bring me pleasant memories. Thank you all for coming, but really, there was no need for any of you to bring me flowers."

She directed the servant to take the flowers to her chambers and proclaimed that it would be the best-smelling room in the neighborhood. Everyone took their seats, and the tea was brought in.

Gavin moved to take the tray but froze when he heard his mother gently clear her throat behind him. He forgot he had promised her to not carry her nice dishes anymore. He glanced at his mother and then at Grace, who had also seen his mother's subtle warning. He couldn't help but smile at Grace's poor attempts to hide her amusement. When no one was looking, Gavin winked at her.

The duchess directed the servant to place the tea in front of Grace. Grace's smile faded slightly. He knew what she was thinking. She was wishing that his mother would pour the tea herself, but Grace understood her role as debutant. Every move she made was to be scrutinized as if she were applying for a position in a shop.

Gavin sat back and thought, *Let the interview begin.*

For the next half hour, Grace was the epitome of genteel society. She politely smiled at each gentleman's efforts to engage her attention and gave enough encouragement to make each man feel like he was the favored one. The time passed quickly as he marveled at her ability to handle the situation. He thought to himself, *This is what real grace looks like.* Indeed, she had taught him more about grace in the last hour than he had learned in his entire life.

He didn't even flinch at being addressed as "Your Grace" during tea. He actually felt a bit of pride when Grace said it. For the first time, he felt content with his new title. He understood now that grace was more than being the opposite of clumsy. It meant being the bigger man in impossible situations, like Grace was doing right now as three—no, four—potential suitors sat in front of her.

When Mr. Lewis and Mr. Ellis were finally shown out by Robison, Gavin sighed in relief and slapped Harrison on the shoulder. "Good man, Harrison. You probably thought they would never leave! Take care of Grace for me. And do not spread any accusations you are not prepared to defend with fisticuffs." Harrison smiled and Gavin could see that he didn't take the threat seriously, which was somewhat disappointing.

As he watched them leave for their ride, Gavin couldn't help but ponder what was different today from last night. He had been jealous last night, yes—and he wasn't exactly thrilled at the sight of Grace walking off with Harrison just now—but it was more than that. Last night he had been filled with distrust, resentment, and anger—all familiar feelings these past six months.

Ever since he became the Duke of Huntsman, he had distrusted every kindness shown him. He assumed everyone was looking to improve their situation in life. Every look or flirtation made him want to turn and run in the other direction.

He had resented his brother for living the kind of life that made the Earl of Longmont suspect him. He had been angry at his father for believing himself important enough to single-handedly prevent a duel.

But something was different today. He was still the Duke of Huntsman. His brother and father were still gone. And he still missed his carefree days at sea. But today he felt content. For the first time in his life, someone had told him he was graceful. Grace had changed everything. She was an inspiration.

*****

Grace was better prepared to go out in the cool weather; this time she brought her gloves. As she exited with Mr. Harrison, she was overwhelmed by the phaeton in front of them. It was an impressive silver color with red decorative metalwork. It seemed rather flashy for the shy man standing next to her.

The matched chestnut mares harnessed to it were nothing less than stunning. "What beautiful horses!" Grace exclaimed. "Their legs are so shapely And they must be at least seventeen hands tall. Is that not large for mares?" Mr. Harrison did not say anything right away. When she turned to look at him, he was blushing. "Did I say something wrong?" she asked.

"No, n-not at all. Fo-for-forgive me. I was rather distracted and was just thinking how lovely you look in the sunlight. Your hair is beau-beautiful. And your father was right; your eyes do appear the color of bl-bl-blue-bluebells."

Gavin used to say they were blue as bluebells in rain or shine. She tried again to push him from her thoughts. "Thank you,"

Grace said. *He's blushing again! Oh my, he must be even more nervous than I am.* Grace focused on putting Harrison at ease. She gently put her hand on his arm and asked, "May I meet your horses?"

He led her to the front, and she rubbed their noses a little and combed her fingers through their mane.

"Your interest surprises me, Miss Iverson. Do you enjoy riding?" Harrison asked.

"I used to. I admit I have not had much opportunity during the last ten years. But I still appreciate their beauty."

"Yes, beauty is something that is universal."

"I highly doubt that. I think that beauty is in the eye of the beholder. What you may think is beautiful would not attract a bee."

"I-I-I think your b-beau-beauty would be con-con-considered striking by anyone," he stuttered.

"That was a very kind lie, but I do not need flattery. I think we can have an enjoyable time as friends."

"Yes, as friends." He paused to help her into the phaeton, and once settled and on their way to Hyde Park, he continued where they left off as if the thought had been at the tip of his tongue all along. "Friends like you and Kingston."

It took a moment to connect the two comments. "Yes," Grace said. "Gavin and I are very good friends."

"Really? I know how difficult it can be to articulate one's thoughts, Miss Iverson, but there is clearly more to your relationship than just friends." He glanced over to her before she could hide her embarrassment. "Come now, I find you very at-attractive, and I cannot deny that you are extremely stimulating to converse with, but I also know there is no chance for me when the d-du-duke means so much to you."

Grace looked down at her hands, and she fought the tears that were welling up in her eyes. She had not trusted a soul with her thoughts over the last few days, but for some reason, she felt safe with Mr. Harrison. He seemed trustworthy. As he patiently waited for her to reply, his silence filled her with confidence.

Finally she opened with what she hoped would not expose her too much: "I do find Gavin just as pleasurable as ever."

Mr. Harrison turned down a quiet path through the park, and she was pleased that he simply waited for her to expand her thoughts. He was so quiet, and his gentle nature elicited more trust than she had felt in a long while. But what would be the consequences of admitting her true feelings? She found herself biting her lip. Part of her warned that she should change the subject. But her curiosity at Mr. Harrison's perceptiveness overruled her lingering anxiety.

"Mr. Harrison, do you mind if I ask you a question?"

"Of course not."

"How did you know that Gavin means so much to me?"

"Let us be frank and call the el-elephant in the room what it is. You lo-lo-love him."

The deepest of blushes filled her cheeks, but she felt profoundly relieved to hear someone else say it. "I am afraid I have had strong feelings for him for some time. But he has very clearly stated that he wants to be my best friend and nothing more."

Mr. Harrison laughed slightly and asked, "He said that? Those exact words?"

"I am afraid so. He offered to help me find a husband. My disappointment was quite severe."

Harrison made a noise that showed he was pondering what she had said. "Did he say anything else?"

She slowly shook her head, remembering the acute pain of his words. "He said he wants to be my best friend. He wants to help me find someone who will make me happy."

"There has to b-b-be more."

"I told him no one could take his place. It was the truth, or at least as close as I could come to telling him the truth. Is talking like this hurting your feelings? I know this might be difficult if you had thoughts about our future."

"No need to worry about that. Clearly your heart is already engaged. I am not one to compete or fight for a lady. Perhaps that is why I am st-still a bach-bachelor. But back to what he said to you. What d-d-did he say after you said no one could take his place?"

She tried to remember. Her heart had been pounding so hard when she told Gavin no one could take his place that she could hardly recall his reply. Even now, trying to remember the discussion was bringing small beads of sweat to her brow. She took out her handkerchief and dabbed her face.

"Do you remember what he said?" Harrison prompted.

"He said, 'If it were up to me, I would be the only man in your life.'"

Mr. Harrison pulled on the reins and brought the phaeton to a stop. He then turned to look at Grace. His kind eyes pulled up at the corners as a slow smile formed on his lips. Harrison said, "What part of that is confusing?"

"I do not take your meaning. He has always been the only man in my life; he wants things to stay the same."

Mr. Harrison grinned slightly and patted her hand. He then took up the reins again and said, "I took you for an intelligent woman, Miss Iverson."

"There is no need to insult me," she retorted.

"You know as well as I that I did not intend to disparage you. Now, let us imagine that I said the same thing to you. If I said, 'Miss Iverson, I wish t-to be the only m-ma-man in your life,' what would you think?"

She hesitated and bit her lip. "I cannot say."

"Yes, you can, Miss Iverson. If I can say it with my st-stut-stuttering, you can too. What would you think?"

A tiny seed of hope was building inside her. "You do not think . . . no . . ."

"Yes."

"Really? You think he might wish to court me?"

"I think it is m-mo-more than that. I think he wishes to m-mar-marry you."

Grace looked dumbfounded at Mr. Harrison. He looked over and laughed and then returned his gaze to driving his team. "I see that this is a welcome thought," he chuckled.

"It is indeed. How do I tell him that I want to marry him too?"

"Now I am sure you are wise enough to answer that question. All I will say is that you should not do-doubt his intentions. The rest will all come n-nat-naturally to two people who value each other so much. If there is any way I can assist, let me know."

They drove home in silence as her mind started to grasp this new revelation. Gavin wished to marry her? Could that possibly be true? She started to examine everything he had said and done over the last few days. It was as if she had put on spectacles that allowed things to be seen with the right perspective—the chess game, the music box, the kiss.

The seed of hope was taking root. His apology in the music room had pained her—she had interpreted it as regret. Her pride had been injured, and she had tried to close herself off. But Gavin knew her too well. It was beginning to make sense. He kissed her because he wanted to know how she really felt. No wonder it seemed almost scientific or calculated in nature.

All the dizzy fluttering of her heart during the kiss was nothing compared to what she felt now. She could only imagine how she would feel when he kissed her for real! She surprised herself when she giggled out loud. Mr. Harrison smiled back at her and patted her hand.

As they pulled up to the front of Willsing Manor, Gavin immediately appeared on the steps. He must have been watching for their return. He seemed a little nervous. He hid the anxiety well with some humorous comment about how long they had been gone and how Harrison didn't have permission to whisk Grace away for the whole day. They all laughed about it, because it wasn't even time for noon luncheon.

Harrison smiled at Grace mischievously, kissed her hand, and said, "I wish you every happiness. If I can be of any use, please ask." As Gavin walked closer to them, Harrison dropped her hand and stepped back.

Grace replied to Harrison, "I have enjoyed this ride immensely. It was quite revealing. I hope we can do this again."

"It wo-would be my pleasure." Harrison bowed and turned to leave.

Gavin had taken possession of her arm by that point, and he was gently guiding her away. She looked up at him and smiled. His true feelings were clear in his eyes. She could see it now. How could she have been so blind? If she was going to put her trust in anyone, it would be him.

He guided her effortlessly up the stairs of the townhouse, and he did not trip or stumble at all. It felt right to wrap her arm around his. Each little look and mannerism helped build her confidence. She had never felt so inspired by His Grace.

CHAPTER 12

Gavin led Grace into the foyer. "Well, Gigi, how was your ride with Harrison?" Gavin forced himself to ask. He did not wish to hear it was good.

"It was good."

He tried not to groan.

To need someone is to love someone. Be the friend she needs you to be. Show an interest in her suitors. "How delightful," he muttered. Trying again to muster enthusiasm, he asked, "And what did you and Harrison talk about?" He braced himself for the answer.

"Actually we talk about your plans for marrying."

He heard the mirth in her voice, and he looked down at her. "Indeed? And what shall be the plan? Am I to marry an heiress? Or a genteel woman of no status whom I will elevate with my title? Ooo, I know: a princess who is locked away in a dungeon!"

Grace's laughter made him relax a great deal. He could always make her laugh, and it was very important to him. Grace finished taking off her bonnet and handed it along with her gloves to Robison. Grace announced, "Actually, Gavin, if you must know, I have resolved to find you a wife!"

"You have what?" Gavin asked. He heard Robison chuckle slightly as he walked away.

"You need a wife!" Grace said.

He scoffed and said, "You sound like my mother."

A most unwelcome voice interrupted their private moment in the entryway. His mother said, "Who sounds like me and how shall I thank them?"

Grace walked over to the duchess and kissed her cheek. "I apparently sounded like you when I told him he needs to find a wife."

"And so he does! If that is all it takes to sound like me, then I must be the most thoroughly imitated lady of the *ton*! And I so dearly wished to be original. But I shall accept being only average in exchange for more grandchildren. Gavin does not know what is good for him."

"Mother, please. Grace was only offering her matchmaking skills."

"And what good will that do? I have tried to find you a match for years, but I have gotten nowhere! Are not my skills just as valuable? If you only knew how many letters I have written on your behalf, Gavin, inventing ways for you to meet eligible ladies."

Grace eyed Gavin knowingly and said, "Speaking of which, I believe Gavin has a few burning questions for you on that subject."

"I do?"

"You do?" His mother echoed. "On the subject of meeting eligible young ladies? Well, it is about time."

He was perplexed. What did he need to ask his mother? And why was Grace acting like he should know what it was about?

"Well, ask her, Gavin. Ask her what we have meant to ask her for the last few days."

He tried to read what Grace was playing at. She was teasing him, obviously, but what question was she suggesting? He stared at her and said, "Yes, well . . . there are several questions that we have . . . but I will let Gigi begin. Ladies first."

Grace smirked at his ploy to not play the fool and turned to face the duchess. "Actually, Your Grace," she said calmly as she could, "we recently discovered that someone intercepted the letters Gavin and I wrote to each other while he was at Eton. We were wondering if you were aware of it."

His mother took a deep breath. It was clear she was indeed aware of it. "Mother," Gavin asked, "did you know about this?"

"I . . ." The duchess seemed at a loss for words. *Well, that's a first*, thought Gavin. "This is not an appropriate discussion for the foyer," she eventually stammered. "And I am feeling unwell. I may need a minute to compose myself."

"Of course, Mother," Gavin soothed. "Perhaps we can meet in my study when you are ready."

The duchess agreed, and Gavin ordered tea, cucumber sandwiches, and biscuits to be brought in. As Grace followed him to the study, he whispered, "Could you not have given me a little hint about what my burning question was?"

"How could I? You do not know yourself well enough to ask the right questions."

He opened the study door and motioned her in. "And what are the right questions, Gigi? Has Harrison enlightened you so much that you have all the answers?"

"I received some answers, but I still have a few more questions. However, I believe that will be quickly remedied," she teased. But her smile soon turned into a worried frown. "Your poor mother, Gavin! I think we can assume that she knows something from her response."

"Yes. She knows something, and I am anxious to hear about it."

They spoke for a few more minutes, and then Gavin ushered her to the sofa near the fire. He stoked the fire a bit and was soon graced with his mother's presence.

The duchess chose the high-back chair instead of the sofa by Grace, which pleased him greatly since that meant he could sit next to Grace. He flipped his tailcoat out and sat down dramatically. "So, tell me, Mother, what secrets do you keep?"

Grace was a little more diplomatic and added, "It was probably wrong of us to use Eliza to traffic our letters to each other. I hope she did not get into trouble."

"Well, it is a rather complicated story. Perhaps now that my husband has passed, there is no reason for secrecy. Corbin was a better man than you thought he was, Gavin. He had some unbalanced priorities, but overall he had a good heart. He wanted what was best for his children. Unfortunately he thought gaining money, influence, and status was the best way to give you everything you needed."

Gavin frowned. "What I needed was my best friend," he said. "And Grace needed me too, especially when her father died."

"I know, but so much happened in such a short amount of time. I will start by saying that Mr. Moser felt obligated to reveal what happened at the dance lesson. Forgive me, Grace. I see you are getting flushed."

"It is the heat from the fire," Grace faltered.

"Yes, I suppose so," the duchess said graciously. "If Mr. Moser had come to me directly, I might have been able to dissuade Corbin from acting so heavy-handedly. I am sorry, Grace, but you were around our family often enough to know how much my husband valued his title. As much as it pains me to say it, he did not wish for any kind of alliance with your family.

"As the years went by, your close friendship became an issue. I saw nothing wrong with it. You both brought out the best in each other. Grace kept Gavin's head from exceeding its capacity, and Gavin helped Grace to stand and fight for what was important. Grace, my dear, you always seemed so hesitant to trust anyone. Whenever someone tried to get close to you, you put up a wall. Gavin was the only one you let in. I saw a relationship that produced good things.

"But because Mr. Moser went to your father first, I had little influence with what happened. My husband wasted no time in accelerating Gavin's travel arrangements."

Gavin said, "But, Mother, we never got to say goodbye."

"It was planned that way, my dear. Your father insisted upon it. He also overheard you asking Eliza to forward all of Grace's letters to you at school. This is where I agree with Corbin. You two should not have been writing to each other."

Gavin thought it was rather odd that she did not mention how they should not have been *kissing* each other either but thought better of mentioning it.

"At that point, it was fairly simple to intercept the letters. Do not put any blame on Eliza. She never knew. Your father gave instructions that no letters were to be posted or delivered without his inspection. Then Grace's father got influenza and died so suddenly. It was a busy three weeks for your mother, Grace. She had less than a month to get her house in order; your cousin was insistent that he inherit immediately. I met with her a few times during that period, and she hardly stopped writing directions to the solicitor in order to take tea with me. She was also determined to find positions for those servants that did not wish to serve under the new owner, and that took a great deal of time as well.

"The woman hardly grieved for her husband, but she was committed to not let her new station in life affect her three daughters. We appealed to Corbin to help set up a coming out for her daughters through me but . . ."

Gavin felt his heart lurch. There was obviously more to the story. "What happened? What did Father say?"

His mother looked at her hands, which she was wringing furiously. "I am afraid that Grace will be hurt by what I have to say."

"Please do not distress yourself," Grace said. "I already know that your husband did not approve of my friendship with Gavin." Gavin couldn't help but be amazed at her strength. While his mother was not looking, he put his hand on Grace's and gave it a reassuring squeeze and then returned it to his own lap just as his mother looked up.

"I had already told your mother that I would be happy to sponsor you and your sisters," the duchess continued. "She knew I had many more connections, especially now that she was a widow, and I did not think for one moment that Corbin would disapprove. We decided to unite and approach him together, but I soon saw that was a terrible decision.

"My husband was very vocal about how he would not take on any 'charity cases'." Gavin saw Grace flinch slightly out of the corner of his eye. "Not only did he refuse to let me sponsor her girls, but he told her that if any Iverson ever contacted our family again, then he would ensure that every family in the county knew that Grace had . . ."

"That Grace had what?" Gavin asked.

"Oh dear, I shall not ever find the strength to say it!"

Grace walked over to the duchess's chair, knelt down, and wrapped her arms around her. Gavin hadn't noticed that his mother had started to cry. After a minute, Grace pulled back slightly, put her hands on either side of the old woman's face, and brushed away the old woman's tears with her thumbs. "I do not blame you,

Your Grace. And I am stronger than you might think. I will not wilt from the poor opinion of a single man."

His mother reached up and covered Grace's hand with her own. "You are such a good girl. You did not deserve it."

Grace's voice was calm and reassuring. "Most people do not deserve the ill treatment they receive from others. I will be well, no matter what your husband said about me."

"I am so ashamed to say it! My own husband was so cruel!"

"Mother, what did Father threaten to say Grace had done?"

"He said that he would tell everyone of our friends in society that Grace—this is harder than I thought—that Grace had seduced you."

The silence in the air rolled in like an impending storm. So many thoughts were flooding him at once.

How could he have kissed her back then? He had risked her reputation and her sisters' as well. If word had gotten out, none of them would ever have found a match. His father could have destroyed their entire future. Anger started to build. He stood and walked to the fireplace and leaned against the mantle to give himself more time to think before responding.

He heard his mother apologize profusely, and Grace readily forgave her and her husband, but he could not do so—not so easily. He tuned out for a few minutes to try to get ahold of his reaction. Not only was he angry at his father, but he was angry with himself. *She was only fourteen! I could have ruined her with my overzealous impulses!*

He heard Grace say something similar to the thoughts running through his mind. "He was only sixteen, Your Grace. He never intended to compromise me. The only people who know about that kiss are the three of us here, Mr. Moser, and your deceased husband. My sisters found matches without much difficulty, and I shall too."

"I know you shall. That is why I was so determined to sponsor you this season. I had to make up for my husband's harsh words to your dear mother. Oh, she was so strong! You would have been proud. When he threatened her, she very boldly said, 'Your Grace, I shall not encourage any communication, but nor will I prevent it. It pains me that our lands have neighbored one another for generations and that our relationship has ended in this manner. As you know, my daughters and I will have limited funds to travel. We will not return to Sussex. But if, by chance, your conscience allows regret for today's actions, we will always welcome our dear friends as guests.' My heart just broke as she proudly stood, curtsied, and walked out with her head held high. I never saw or heard from her again. Grace, how can you possibly forgive me?"

"You have nothing to forgive. I am so sorry you had to find out about the kiss from Mr. Moser. It was just—"

Gavin turned around to look at Grace. How would she explain it? She glanced up at him, pleading for him to help her. He had promised to be the friend she needed, and she needed him now. "I am sorry, Mother. I thought I loved Grace back then. But I should have considered the potential ripple effect of my actions. I am to blame, not Grace. Would you mind letting me talk to Gigi alone?"

"Certainly, but do not hold her too long, she needs to rest before the Comptons' ball tonight. Everyone we know will be there. And I also need to discuss next week's ball with her."

"Oh, I would never get in the way of the plans for her ball. And, Mother? Grace's mother was not the only one who performed with grace in impossible situations. You did the best you could."

His words brought fresh tears to his mother's face, and she stood and embraced him. He kissed her cheek, and his mother left.

Grace walked over to him, put her hand on his arm, and said, "Thank you."

"For what part? For nearly ruining your family ten years ago?"

She smiled at him. "You were young," she said.

He wasn't done castigating himself. "But what excuse do I have for kissing you a few days ago?"

She stepped closer and put her hand on his shoulder. It was the opposite of what he expected. He wanted her to be upset with him, to blame him like he blamed himself. But instead he looked down into her eyes and felt an overwhelming urge to kiss her again. "Grace, you must know by now what you do to me."

"I think I have a pretty good idea." She stepped even closer and the hand on his shoulder slid down to his chest which made him nearly dizzy with confusion. *Didn't she just say this morning that said she wanted to be friends? Am I imagining things?*

Gavin's voice broke. "I should warn you, if you do not step away, I cannot be accountable for my actions."

"Is that so?" She brought her other hand to the back of his neck where her fingers started twirling his hair. Every sense was piqued. Her cinnamon scent was engulfing him, and he could almost count her eyelashes they were so close. Her blue eyes were mesmerizing. It was too much to ask of any man. He reached his hand to the back of her head and gently guided it toward his.

"All you have to do is say no," he whispered, almost fearful of her response. He wished to kiss her with every fiber of his being. The last hour had been so trying. He needed her. He needed his best friend. Her eyes danced from his eyes to his lips and back up to his eyes.

"Last chance, Grace. The time to fight me is now." He studied her a moment longer. Their lips were an inch or two apart, and he could nearly taste her sweet breath, but she did not pull away. "If I did not know better, I would think you wanted me to kiss you." He paused once more. "You pick now to show no resistance? Very well. You always have to win." He leaned forward, kissed her, and felt her melt into his arms immediately.

He enjoyed the moment for a minute. Then he pulled away and smiled at her glassy eyes. "Grace," he whispered, "I do not want you to find me a wife."

Her eyes flashed a look of fear. "You really do not wish to marry?"

He smiled at her and kissed her again but this time more passionately. When he pulled away he put his finger on her lips and said, "No, Gigi. You will not get the last word this time. When you were ripped from me, a part of me went dormant—the very best part of me. Perhaps that was why I felt so at home on the ship that thrashed one way and then another. It mirrored what I felt inside without you."

He continued, "I cannot be content to just be your friend. I wish to never say goodbye. Not then, not now, not ever. I love you, Grace Ingrid Genevieve Iverson, and I want to marry my best friend."

She smiled at him mischievously but said nothing.

"Grace, I asked you to marry me. Are you not going to answer me?"

"You said I could not have the last word this time."

He burst out laughing, which made her laugh too. He picked her up and twirled her around. He set her down and took both hands and brought her face to his again for another kiss. Between kisses he said, "Just. Say. Yes. Gigi. Or. I. Will. Keep. Kissing. You. Until. You. Do."

He felt her shoulders shake and knew she was giggling again, which made it very difficult to kiss her. He pulled away, and Grace said, "You never did know the right way to win an argument."

CHAPTER 13

"I knew it!" The duchess's voice startled them, and they jumped apart. Grace was mortified that she had been found kissing her son—again. She looked down at her fumbling hands as her face burned red hot. "Just as I suspected!" his mother cried. "I knew that if I gave you enough time, you would realize you love each other. All you needed was a little time together!" The duchess ran across the room and wrapped her arms around Grace. "I knew you could do it, my dear!"

"Then, you approve?" Grace asked in awe.

"Of course, I approve! All that nonsense about finding you a husband—it was all rubbish! And look! It only took a few days for you to work it out!"

"Mother, were you listening at the door?"

"Of course! How else was I to know what was happening? Now, let us settle this right away. Say 'yes', Grace."

Gavin chuckled and wrapped his arms around Grace again. "Yes, Grace, say 'yes'!"

Grace smiled broadly. Everything she had hoped for over the last ten years was all coming true! Her smile could not have been broader or more genuine. "Yes! Yes! A hundred times yes!"

Gavin had never looked happier than at that moment. In his eyes, she saw the schoolboy charm and contentment that was in his very nature. He reached his hand up to her cheek and caressed her face. "You have made me the happiest man," he whispered.

Gavin went in for another kiss, but his mother quickly pushed her way between them. "Oh no, Gavin," she said sternly, "this is no time to forget your manners. I allowed for the other kisses, but now there will be rules. Or Grace will have to return to her sister's house immediately."

"Yes, ma'am," Grace said obediently.

Gavin chuckled. "That is the quickest and shortest concession speech I have ever heard from you, Gigi," he said over his mother's shoulder. "You are supposed to argue with her! You always argue! Or do you not want to be kissed?" His eyes sparkled with a daring flirtation which made her giggle.

She could not believe he was being so bold in front of his mother. Grace tried to hold in her laughter as she replied, "There is great wisdom to knowing which arguments can never be won. I think we would be wise to concede defeat to your mother on this point."

The duchess said, "I always knew I liked you, Grace. Gavin cannot be trusted, you know."

"Mother!"

"But, it is true! Think of all those ladies—"

Gavin cleared his throat loudly and interrupted her. "Mother, please!"

Grace felt a twinge of sadness at the duchess's warning. Gavin had always been a ladies' man. She knew he had received his fair share of kisses. It wasn't new knowledge, but it pained her all the same.

"Do not listen to her, Gigi," Gavin insisted. "None of those other ladies mattered. Besides, the rumors have been greatly exaggerated." Then he gave the duchess a piercing glare. "Are you trying to sabotage my marriage before it even begins? Grace will think I am a rake!"

"I do not think you are a rake," Grace said hesitantly. "I think I know who you really are deep down."

Gavin stepped around his mother. He held Grace's hands and looked deeply into her eyes. "Grace, listen to me. I may have a reputation, but only one woman has ever captured my heart. Several ladies tried their hardest, and a few were quite persistent, but I have done little I could not detail to you right here and now in front of my mother."

He kissed her hand and held it up against his face. "You can trust me," he whispered.

116

His words were so poignant. Grace knew he was telling the truth, and her sadness turned to relief in a matter of seconds.

So many people had let her down before. But if she trusted anyone, it was Gavin. She had prayed all those years to find him. Deep down, she had always known he had not abandoned her. Not Gavin, not her best friend.

"Gavin, I do trust you," she told him, and she knew it was true. "I know you would never hurt me. You need not disclose any of your private moments with any other lady. Now, if you ask me, this conversation took a wrong turn. Were we not trying to celebrate our upcoming marriage?"

Gavin smiled at her and said, "Of course. I may be the Duke of Huntsman, but I know who makes those kinds of decisions. I will readily agree to whatever you and my mother decide."

His mother laughed lightly and said, "Such freedom! How shall we embarrass him? Shall we plan the grandest wedding in all of London?"

But Grace was not one for the public limelight. "Oh no, please, no," she begged the duchess. "I just want a small wedding. Perhaps it can happen sooner rather than later."

"Very well, Grace, but only because I like you so well. And I know you would fret about all the spectators eager to see the elusive Duke of Huntsman finally wedded. But I must insist on one detail. We must delay announcing your engagement for a few days."

Gavin and Grace simultaneously began to protest, but the duchess continued undeterred. "No, you must listen. We will all go to the Comptons' ball tonight as if Grace were still unattached," she said. "I will introduce her to everyone as a family friend. Grace will return to her sister's house in a few days, and then we will announce the engagement at Grace's ball next week. It will not do to have your betrothed living under the same roof."

Gavin frowned. He looked at Grace and then at the duchess. "Grace, I am sorry to admit it, but I have to agree with Mother. As much as I enjoy seeing you all day, I would hate to have you enter society under questionable pretenses."

Grace knew they were right, but it didn't make the news any more desirable. "Will I still be able to dance with Gavin tonight?"

Gavin's mother was about to speak, and Gavin shushed her with finesse. "Mother, I shall not hear of any other reply but in the affirmative. I will dance with Grace, and I shall even claim two dances. After all, I am commanding of my person when I dance, right, Gigi?"

"Yes, Your Grace, you are very graceful." She saw him smile for the first time at being called by his title, and she grinned back at him.

"That is enough for one day, I think," the duchess announced. She started tugging on Grace's elbow. "Come, Grace, we have much to prepare."

With one last wink from Gavin, Grace let the duchess guide her from the room. On their way out, Grace and the duchess happened upon Mr. Silence in the foyer.

"Greetings, Silence!" Grace called out cheerfully.

He bowed to her and replied, "Marvelous! When you address me, it sounds as if you are welcoming some peace and quiet!"

"With you around, I highly suspect that will not be the case. It is good to see you."

"It is always a pleasure, Miss Iverson. I look forward to the ball tonight. I hope you will save a set for me."

"I would be honored. Are you here to see Gavin?"

"I am. I have some news to share with him."

"Nothing too serious, I hope."

Mr. Silence looked briefly at the duchess and then back to Grace. He seemed a little hesitant to divulge anything further in front of Gavin's mother. "It regards a matter that he asked me to look into a few months back. Nothing that will keep him from the ball tonight."

"I hope it is good news," Grace speculated.

"Yes. Potentially, it is very good news."

"Then I shall leave you to him." Grace found Silence's responses somewhat mysterious, but she was in too good of a mood to be concerned. She was going to marry her best friend! Nothing could dampen her spirits.

*****

Gavin was sitting in his chair behind his desk with his arms behind his head and his feet propped up on his desk when Silence came in. "Ah, Silence! Good to see you! It is a beautiful day!"

"I can see the glint in your eye, Kingston. You know something I do not know." Silence had a knack for reading subtle signs in others. People often revealed things to him that they hadn't intended to share. He made quick judgments about people, and he was nearly always right.

Gavin just smiled. He had to hold his news until the time was right, but he was already counting down the hours until he could hold Grace in his arms again. "Just in a good mood for once."

"Seems to be happening a lot this last week."

"Indeed."

Silence paused and stared at him curiously, but Gavin was determined to keep his secret. "Well," Silence began, "I have news that might make your day even better."

Gavin wasn't sure anything could make his day better. "Really?"

"I shall get right to the point," Silence began. "I have news about Whitmore."

Gavin ears perked up. He put his feet on the ground and leaned forward. "Have you found the Earl of Longmont?"

"Not exactly. My man intercepted a letter from Whitmore to his nephew, the heir to his title."

"Who is the nephew?"

"A Mr. Broadbent. He resides here in London."

"I do not think I know him. We should track him down and arrange a meeting."

"No need. He will be at the ball tonight. We can question him there."

"That is good news," Gavin replied. "What did the letter say?"

"Whitmore is very sick," Silence explained. "He has apoplexy. He is hardly able to talk and cannot move his right arm at all. The letter was written by his solicitor. Apparently he is unable to eat without choking and is now having difficulty breathing. He can only last a few more days."

"Even better news. Did the letter say where to find the earl?"

"Unfortunately not. But it directed Mr. Broadbent to come right away."

Gavin pursed his lips in concentration. "Where is the letter now?" he asked.

"We put it in a new outer paper with a slightly inaccurate address, sealed it, then hand delivered it to his house yesterday under the guise that it was misdirected to his neighbor to the west, Heath Hansen, a good friend of mine."

Gavin stood and began to pace, carefully considering this new development. "How do you know he will be at the ball tonight?" he asked.

"Mr. Compton himself told me that Mr. Broadbent and his wife confirmed the invitation. They are very eager to attend."

"What do we know about Mr. Broadbent?" Gavin asked. "You say he is married?"

"Yes, but I do not know much more than that," Silence replied. "He has one sister and has been married for just under three years. No children. Financially he appears to live frugally with only a handful of servants, none of whom have loose tongues. But we will keep trying."

Gavin walked around the desk and clapped him on the shoulder. "Silence, you really are something!" he exclaimed. "Any more news about the earl's daughter?"

"Just that she delivered a baby girl two months ago. The footman we planted at her country home, a man named Littleton, regularly checks the mail. He had not seen any correspondence from Whitmore or the child's father. It seems they both have written her off."

Gavin digested the information. If the letter to Broadbent was a summons, Broadbent must know where The Earl of Longmont was hiding. "Very well. Tonight we shall seek an introduction with Mr. Broadbent. But we should be careful not to raise his suspicions. I do not want to scare him off. Besides, I intend to have a little fun at the ball tonight."

"Might a spitfire redhead have anything to do with those intentions?"

Gavin smiled and relished the memory of her sweet kisses. He could still taste her lips on his. It seemed nothing could restrain him from his happiness. He looked at Silence and said, "When she wants something, she knows how to get it."

Silence raised an eyebrow and said, "Is that so? And her getting what she wanted makes you this happy?"

"Indeed it does."

"Really? Tell me, will it be orchids or lilies for the wedding?"

"Blast it, Silence!" Gavin laughed. "How did you know?"

"You are an easy read, Kinston," Silence chuckled. "Why did you not tell me right away?"

Gavin shrugged his shoulders. "My mother thinks it unwise to announce the engagement until Grace has left Willsing Manor."

"Your mother is right. It would not look good to have her under your roof. If you remember, I told you the same thing the first day I met her. She has already been here for . . . what, five days?"

"Yes. And?"

"And?" Silence prodded. "And a lot can happen in five days, Kingston."

"Silence, you cannot believe everything you read about me. I may have kissed her a time or two, but that is all. She is perfectly safe."

"Good. So, the Duke of Huntsman has found a wife! Congratulations! I suppose I will have to refrain from collecting my wagers at White's until it is official."

Gavin was confused. "What wager?"

"Well, as it turns out, your engagement date has become a very popular bet in the last six months. I stayed out of it until I met Miss Iverson. But when I saw the way you looked at her during our game of charades, I went straight to White's and put in my wager that same day."

"Dare I ask what your wager was for?"

"Three hundred pounds that you would be engaged in two weeks."

Gavin chuckled. "Two weeks? You knew how dead set against marrying I was, and yet after an hour with us, you inferred that my entire philosophy about tying the knot was going to change?"

"Yes, and according to my calculations, you have ten days to announce your engagement or you owe me three hundred pounds. I will not lose a bet simply because you want a pretty little face to greet you at the breakfast table instead of a proper courtship of boring walks, chaperoned teas, and the occasional stolen moment at a ball. You should have limited access to the object of your desire, just like the rest of us."

"Indeed, I think I shall push for a quick wedding. From the way you make it sound, I just had my last kiss until I get hitched."

Now it was Silence's turn to chuckle. "It is the way of the world, Kingston," he explained. "You have to play by the rules."

"I never had to play by the rules before," Gavin sighed. "That was the best part of having Grace as a best friend. We could do whatever we wanted."

"Not anymore," Silence warned. "Now she has a reputation to uphold. I know you do not like it, but you need to behave like a gentleman. Bat your eyes at each other if you must, but your entire goal from here on out must be to safely usher her into society. Now I must be going. I am expecting a package soon for tonight's ball."

"A package?"

"New Hessian boots. And do not think I will not use them to kick you in the behind if you make a wrong step tonight."

CHAPTER 14

After Silence departed, they all took tea together, and the duchess started laying down the law. Grace tried to stay out of the crossfire as his mother dictated numberless rules of behavior. Gavin agreed to only three. The others, he said, would drive him to Bedlam.

"Mother, I shall behave as a gentleman. You have my word. But if you try to put any more restrictions on us, we might just disappear to Scotland."

The duchess gasped in disapproval, and Gavin winked at Grace, who couldn't completely stifle a giggle. They both knew the duchess had her heart set on a beautiful church wedding. "Dukes do not elope, Gavin!" his mother shuddered.

When his mother wasn't looking, Gavin snuck in one last kiss before releasing her to his mother for wedding preparations.

*****

Gavin only had a few hours before attending the ball, meeting Mr. Broadbent, and dancing with Grace. It would be a busy evening. But there was a pressing matter to attend to first.

He knew there was a Bible in the library somewhere among his grandfather's old journals. It took a few minutes to find it. The poor book probably had not been opened in years, and the dust on it showed. If he remembered right, his grandfather's collection contained a Bible dictionary too. After a little more searching, he found it.

He opened the dictionary and turned to 'G'. *"Goliath"*, *"Gomorrah"*, *"gopher wood"*. . . *ah, "grace"*. His head was filled with thoughts and visions of Grace. Her beautiful face swam in front of his eyes. But even after everything that had happened, he felt a quiet hunger in his soul to learn about spiritual grace. He began reading verses. As he studied, he made a few notes on a piece of paper.

A few hours later, Grace found him in his study. "Should you not be getting ready for the ball?" she asked. "What are you doing?"

"Reading the Bible," he replied as if he did it every day.

"Well, I would hate to interrupt such a worthwhile endeavor," she asserted. "I will leave you to it." As she turned to leave, Gavin jumped up from the desk and reached out for her elbow.

"No, do not go," he said mischievously.

"But this sounds like a personal quest," Grace teased. "And I believe I promised your mother that I would not to be alone with you anymore. Perhaps I could fetch you an archbishop."

He pulled her in for a kiss. "But I really do need your help," he whispered between kisses. "Could you not guide me a little?" he asked with a dazzling smile.

She nodded with a grin, surrendering remarkably quickly. He moved a second chair over to his desk and pulled out the list he had begun to make. "Well, I know that God loves us. He forgives us when we repent, but grace is somehow more than forgiveness, right?"

"True. God's grace applies to all of His children, no matter—"

"No matter how sinful?"

"Yes."

"Even if I kissed a few ladies?" he asked with a grimace.

She kissed his hand and laughed. "Of course. Gavin, there is not a human on the earth who has not sinned. God's grace is available for everyone."

He looked over at her, entranced by the angelic smile on her face and the way the afternoon sun illuminated her red hair. "Do you know how remarkable you are, Grace?"

"Enough puffing me up, Gavin," she teased him. "What was your question about grace? Or did you trick me into staying under false pretenses?"

"Actually, I would like your insight on 2 Corinthians 12:9. Paul writes, 'My grace is sufficient for thee: for my strength is made perfect in weakness.' I do not understand."

"Well, I think Paul is encouraging us to acknowledge our own weakness and lean on the Lord. When we do so, the Lord's grace will strengthen us. So our weakness becomes strength. God may not move the mountains in front of us, but He will give us the strength to climb them."

"So grace is what helps us make it from one day to the next?"

"Yes," Grace nodded. "It is an enabling power. It enables us to return to Him. What else?"

"Well, I understand that grace is a gift," Gavin continued, "but in order to use that gift, we have to live the best life we know how. For example, I know better than to lie and steal and cheat; if I do so anyway, I am basically rejecting the gift, right?" She nodded. He paused and a frown darkened his face. "It just seems like an impossible standard, Grace. By that standard, I have been rejecting the gift most of my life thus far."

"No, Gavin. None of us are perfect. We all make mistakes. All that matters is that we are trying, that we are improving. He only asks us to do our best," Grace assured him, "and that can change from day to day. Today my best may be to serve God, love my neighbor, and forgive my enemies. But perhaps tomorrow it may simply be to get out of bed. It does not matter. As long as we keep trying, the Lord will offer us His grace," she assured him. "How long have you been studying in here?"

He couldn't help but feel a bit of pride with the progress he had made. "About three hours. Ever since Mother left me with that laundry list of rules she thinks I will abide by," he grinned.

"Do you think you have a good understanding of God's grace now?"

"Hardly," he chuckled. "But I think I have made a good start. If I do all I can, be the very best I can be—then when I have exhausted all my efforts, God's grace will make up the difference."

"Precisely. When you have nothing left, grace will always be there as the precious gift that it is."

"Is that a promise?" he grinned. "Will Grace always be with me? Till death do us part?"

When she smiled again, he couldn't resist any longer. He glanced around the empty study and pulled her into his arms for another kiss. He held her tightly, breathing in her cinnamon scent.

"*You* are the precious gift, Grace. You strengthen me. You make me a better man." He felt a deep peace settle into his heart. "Thank you," he whispered.

*****

An hour later, Gavin was dressed and ready for the ball. He clippity-clopped into the foyer and met Grace by surprise.

"Ares's snake!" Grace blurted out before covering her mouth. "Forgive me," she mumbled. "You caught me off guard."

Grace felt her cheeks flush. He certainly cut a fine figure. Winston must have taken extra care with him tonight. His blonde curls were slicked back and plastered into place, exaggerating his finely chiseled cheekbones and jaw. His two-toned, tan-and-gold waistcoat fit him so well that she could nearly make out his chest muscles underneath. Over that, he wore a deep-blue, double-collared jacket that was flawlessly pressed. He was just beginning to button the jacket. She found herself disappointed that he was covering up such a handsome chest.

Gavin chuckled and asked, "Tell me, Grace, why was an oath to the Greek god of war the first thing that came to your mind when you saw me?"

Grace looked up from where his hands were buttoning the jacket and tried to meet his eyes. She lifted her chin and said, "Does it matter? My foul mouth never bothered you before."

"And it does not bother me now. I find your unique expressions rather humorous. But what is it that made you swear?"

"It was not a real swear word."

"I know. What exactly took those words right out of your mouth?"

"You are so arrogant." He waited expectantly but made no reply. "Very well, if you honestly want me to say it, I will."

He grinned widely. "I do."

"You look rather handsome tonight."

"Now I am graceful and handsome?" Before she could respond, he took her shoulders and pulled her into his arms. "What will I do with two compliments from you? I thought your goal in life was to keep the size of my head in check."

She didn't mind his teasing in the slightest tonight. She looked up at him and said, "Quite handsome, actually."

The humorous sparkle in his eyes turned into a more serious look, a look that told her what was coming. Sure enough, he leaned down and pressed his lips ever so lightly to hers. Her heart galloped away, and it felt as if lightning had struck her from her lips all the way to her dancing slippers. He reached his hand around to her lower back and pulled her in tighter, all the while caressing her lips with more fervor than he had yet used. As he pulled her closer, his lips became more urgent, and she lost all coherent thought. All she could think about was how delicious and tantalizing he tasted. Heat filled her bosom, and she wondered how much longer her knees would support her.

"Gavin Marcus Kingston, you release Grace this minute!" his mother shouted.

Gavin released her, grinned mischievously, and stepped away. "It was only a kiss, Mother."

"I do not care what you want to call it. You will behave. Do we need to go over the rules again?"

He sighed and repeated the rules. "No being in the same room together without a chaperone. No entering her bedchamber. No more kisses until we officially announce the engagement. I know, Mother, I know. But I believe you also have a rule about not being late, so unfortunately there is no time to spare for a lecture. Are you ready to depart?"

Grace couldn't help but giggle at his reluctance for the rules. It looked like they had just broken two out of the three with that kiss.

"Shall we?" Gavin held out his arms, one for his mother and one for Grace. Grace took his arm and looked up at him. She caught him looking sideways down at her, and he muttered under his breath, "I am sorry, Gigi. You are just so dazzling tonight. I thought I could get away with one more kiss."

"It is nothing I am not used to."

"You always have to have the last word."

"Always. Try not to forget it."

*****

Grace was ushered into the ballroom on Gavin's arm, but after a few introductions, Mr. Silence came up and begged Gavin's presence for a moment. In his absence, she looked around the room and felt slightly overwhelmed. She was wearing the ball gown that the duchess had rush-ordered for her. It was a silvery blue that reflected the candlelight and had a deeper neckline than she was used to.

The duchess must have noticed her discomfort, because she reached over and patted Grace's arm encouragingly. "He is right, my dear," she said. "You look dazzling in that dress. It really brings out your eyes."

"Thank you. I feel like a princess."

"Charlotte did a fine job with your hair as well. The braid around the crown of your head makes it look like you are wearing a tiara. In this light, you will capture everyone's attention. Remind Gavin to give Charlotte a raise."

"Thank you, Your Grace," Grace replied.

"It is time to make the rounds, my dear. Stay close. Gavin will find you before the first set; have no fear."

As they moved around the room, Grace was indeed grateful for the duchess's ability to maintain the conversation and make the introductions. Many people were curious, some were forward enough to ask direct questions, and others just examined her from head to toe. It was nerve-racking. She kept a close eye on Gavin across the room. He was in the corner with Silence and had a severe look on his face whenever he looked in her direction. She wasn't sure what to make of it.

She tried to refocus her attention to those she was meeting. With effort, she was able to recall several names and relationships. She was pleased when Mr. Harrison came up and greeted her.

"Good evening to you too, Mr. Harrison. It is nice to see a friendly face."

The duchess asked Mr. Harrison if he wouldn't mind occupying Grace for a few minutes and then excused herself.

Mr. Harrison took her arm and whispered, "If you stick with me, I may yet win the title of 'the Shiner'. I will outshine every man in the ballroom with you as my adornment."

Grace noticed that he did not stutter at all in that statement. "Thank you. It feels different this time."

"This time?"

"I had nearly a full season three years ago when I was one-and-twenty. But back then I had no one to usher me into the *ton.* I attended several balls where I did not dance even once."

"What a p-pity! Let me introduce you to a few p-p-people." They walked toward a small group that looked friendly. There were two ladies, each with impressive, ornately decorated gowns that put hers to shame. She particularly admired the brunette with the deep-burgundy chiffon dress held up with a single string of half-inch black lace ribbon on the shoulders. It was a dress to be admired, but never worn, in Grace's mind. There was far too much skin showing.

As they approached, she reminded herself to pay attention to the men as well. She was being introduced as a debutant, even though she was rather old in comparison to the seventeen- and eighteen-year-old ladies. Mr. Harrison greeted the women with a bow and started the introductions. If the tall man with his back to them hadn't turned around, it might have been possible to remember the ladies' names; but as the man turned, her breath caught in her throat.

At the same moment, she felt a hand on the small of her back that could only be Gavin's, but she did not dare turn to check, because there standing in front of her was Mr. Broadbent. She had not seen him since her first season, but there was no mistaking him. The moment was prolonged, as if in slow motion for dramatic effect. As he noticed her standing there, she saw awareness revealed in his face as Mr. Harrison gave her name to the group.

She felt a whirlwind of emotions. First was surprise. She had heard that he had moved to the country and given up his London townhouse, but there he was in front of her. The next was anger. As she took in the lady in the burgundy dress who was possessively hanging on his arm, she realized the woman must be

Mr. Broadbent's wife, the woman he secretly courted while he was lavishing attentions and promises on her. The next feeling was overwhelming jealousy; the woman was breathtaking. She had a flawless porcelain complexion with expressive brown eyes.

She then felt guilt for all of the above feelings. She told herself there was no reason to feel threatened. She was engaged to Gavin, the only man she had ever really loved. She had never had feelings for Mr. Broadbent. She had been flattered by his attention to her but felt nothing for him.

She finally returned her gaze back to Mr. Broadbent. He unabashedly looked her up and down from head to toe.

"Miss Iverson, what a pleasure it is to see you again. It has been far too long."

She felt the heat of anger rise up again, and pink infused her cheeks. She suddenly wished to be something other than a redhead; her emotions were all too readable. She found the strength to reply, "It has been nearly three years, Mr. Broadbent." It was not possible for Grace to return the compliment, to say that it was nice to see him again. She was far too honest to offer such a falsehood.

The moment seemed to stretch as Mr. Harrison realized that Grace knew Mr. Broadbent. The tension between them was not difficult to detect. The hand on the small of her back pressed firmer, and she turned to verify that it was indeed Gavin. He was looking between her and Mr. Broadbent in a rather curious way. It seemed he wanted an explanation—or at least an introduction.

Grace swallowed her pride and said, "Mr. Broadbent, may I introduce my friend, His Grace, the Duke of Huntsman."

They bowed to each other, and Gavin was his usual cordial self. He smiled politely and began innocuous pleasantries, asking Mr. Broadbent about his family and where he hailed from, acting as if he were completely ignorant of their history together. Then she realized he was. She had never told Gavin the name of the suitor who had deserted her for another woman three years ago. Grace realized she was staring again at the woman in the burgundy dress. She looked away just as the woman noticed.

Deciding that conversing with the woman would be far easier than addressing Mr. Broadbent, Grace put on her best smile and spoke as if nothing had ever occurred between the woman's husband and herself.

The woman, whom she now recalled from the introduction was Lady Monique Pinnock, replied, "I had heard that the Duchess of Huntsman had a pupil. What a beautiful woman you are! My father had red hair, and yet none of my brothers or sisters were blessed with such unique coloring."

Grace had always been proud of her red hair, regardless of the fact that many did not appreciate the color. "Yes, few possess it."

"And fewer radiate it as flawlessly as you do. I have missed you, Grace," Broadbent said. She willed herself not to flinch at his use of her Christian name.

She could not even say thank you, nor did she wish to acknowledge such a compliment from someone who had once unabashedly asked how many of her family were redheads and what was the likelihood that the coloring would be passed onto her children. And now he was pretending to admire it! It left her completely speechless.

Gavin stepped in and said, "Indeed. No redhead possesses finer features. If you will excuse us, our dance is starting." Gavin led her away, and they took their positions.

They were in the middle of the dance by the time she realized that Gavin had not said a single word to her. She was still in shock from seeing Mr. Broadbent again.

"Forgive me, Your Grace," she said, feeling the need to address him formally in public. "I was not prepared to see Mr. Broadbent again."

Gavin seemed to be pensive for a moment and then said, "Is there something I should know?"

Grace felt heat rise in her cheeks again but couldn't look him in the eye. It was far too embarrassing to admit that she had once hoped to marry the man and that he had rejected her in favor of someone else. It had been a dark time in her life. And though Grace no longer possessed money, or parents, or status, but she still had her pride. "No, sir," she replied. "There is nothing to tell."

*****

Nothing to tell? I'd wager otherwise by the look of those scarlet cheeks! Gavin wasn't ready to admit that he was jealous, but there was a familiarity in Mr. Broadbent's look, nay, even in his very words. He had seen Broadbent openly devouring her with his eyes. He had even called her by her Christian name. Gavin had been around enough degenerates to recognize desire when he saw it.

And to think Grace had been upset about the women he had kissed during the ten years they were apart. *A man does not look at a woman that way unless he has tasted of her sweetness.* He felt fury building in his chest that rivaled the anger he had felt toward the Earl of Longmont. At least that fury could be acted upon! He was so close to finding the earl through the very man that Grace knew . . . *intimately? Please let me be wrong.*

Their dance ended, and he had still not obtained control over his emotions. He stiffly escorted her back to the side of the room and turned to leave. He had to find Silence, but before he had gotten two paces away, he heard Mr. Broadbent ask Grace for the next set. Gavin glanced over his shoulder masochistically to witness her consent.

She was not looking at Mr. Broadbent; she was looking straight at Gavin as if asking his permission. He flicked his hand toward the man as if he didn't care one way or the other. His mother, who had just rejoined the group, eagerly accepted for Grace and thanked Mr. Broadbent for his attentions.

The next dance was the quadrille. Gavin was going to have to find a partner. Immediately.

He found the first lady in his path. "Miss Woods, might I have this dance?" At this point, he did not care whom he encouraged or whom he offended. He needed to be in that quadrille set with Grace and Broadbent.

"I would be honored to take the third set, Your Grace, but this set has already been requested."

He had hardly registered her answer when he saw Grace being escorted toward the dance floor. He muttered his apologies and took two steps to the left and bowed deeply to a somewhat robust woman wearing last season's gown. "Dance with me," he said. He did not pose it as a question. How many ladies would refuse the command of a duke?

"Of course, Your Grace," the woman flustered.

It was the first time he had ever abused his power. Perhaps he had more of his father in him than he was willing to admit. Nevertheless, the deed was done; he couldn't back out now.

In a pace that was perhaps a little urgent, he guided the nameless woman to the other couples that were forming the dancing group. He made it in just before the set was full; he maneuvered himself to the position on Grace's right.

As the opening notes were beginning to play, he realized he did not even know his dance partner's name. She was not an unfamiliar face. If he focused, surely it would come to him; but he found himself unable to think of anything but Grace and Mr. Broadbent.

He smiled at his partner as she curtsied and the dance began. It was a familiar dance, so he did not have to concentrate on the steps. He endeavored to keep his outward attention fixed on his partner but found himself hanging on every word of the conversation that was occurring on his right.

Broadbent purred suggestively, "I rarely get to dance with such a beautiful partner. In fact, it has been some time."

Grace cleared her throat. "How unfortunate for you that Mrs. Broadbent does not enjoy dancing. She is very beautiful."

"Monique?" He replied slyly. "She is not my wife."

"Forgive me. She seemed very familiar with you."

"You are familiar with me, but that does not make you my wife."

"You forget yourself, sir," Grace hissed.

"Since you will not ask," Broadbent offered, "my wife is not here. She planned to come with me, however she developed a headache. A common malady these days."

"I did not ask."

"Still the debater, I see," Broadbent smiled.

"Yes, I will fight for that which I hold dear, no matter what challenges others may put in my way."

"Tsk, tsk. Careful with the barbs, Gracie. There are others around."

"I hold my tongue when I wish to, not because of what others will say."

"Yes," Broadbent smirked, "you always were free with your tongue."

"Mr. Broadbent!" Grace exclaimed.

"I see you have moved up in the world. A duke!" Grace made no reply. "Were you getting lonely again?" Broadbent quipped.

"I was not lonely."

"You did not miss me then? I missed you, Gracie. I live a very lonely life now. My wife refuses to—"

"Mr. Broadbent," Grace interrupted, "please do not address me so informally. It has been several years since I have seen you."

"You do not wish to rekindle our friendship? It was so dear to me. Very fond memories, indeed."

"No, sir," she insisted. "I only wish for this dance to end."

"I see you have hard feelings. You always were a sore loser."

"Listen closely. If I wish to obtain something, I know how to get it. You were never a prize to be won." For the moment, it seemed that the conversation next to Gavin had come to a close.

Gavin chanced a glance in their direction and watched as Mr. Broadbent winked at her suggestively. "Yes, you always were good at manipulating the suitor," Broadbent said, glancing toward Gavin.

Gavin waited for her response, but there was none. He couldn't quite understand Grace's responses, but the innuendoes from Mr. Broadbent could not be denied. Something had happened between them. He could tell she was hiding something, something that made her defensive and hostile.

Part of him wished to end the misery and walk away from the dance. Another part wished to rush to her defense. But what if Mr. Broadbent's suggestions were true?

Was Grace manipulating her current suitor? Him? Was he just a prize to be won? *Did she seek me out because I am the Duke of Huntsman?* His stomach dropped at the thought. Was she just like every other lady he had met since his brother and father died?

The dance ended, and he could not have been more relieved. He turned and left his partner without so much as a farewell. Silence followed him to the refreshment table.

Gavin saw his stern look but ignored it.

"What has gotten into you?" Silence whispered.

"Silence, Silence! I need to think."

"About what?"

Gavin said nothing and started walking away through the crowd.

Silence hurried after him and grabbed his arm. "Kingston, what is going on?"

"Things are not going as planned. Grace knows Broadbent. I mean she *knows* him," Gavin hissed. "She is after my title, just like all those other ladies."

Gavin heard a gasp behind him and turned around to see Grace hurrying away. Silence quickly strong-armed him outside into the garden.

"Kingston," he snapped, "I did not plan to use these new boots for anything but dancing tonight, but you need a good kick in the pants."

CHAPTER 15

"I do not need a good kick in the pants!" Gavin grumbled, struggling to control his emotions. A few people looked over at him in puzzlement and began whispering to one another.

Silence took his elbow and led him deeper into the garden, away from prying eyes. "Kingston, what possessed you to say such things about Grace? And within earshot! Start talking, or I might just go after her myself."

Gavin slowly realized what he had done. "Do you think she heard me?" His stomach dropped at the thought. As angry as he was, he hadn't meant to hurt her.

"Of course she heard you!" Silence chided. "We will be lucky if she was the only one who did! Now, take a deep breath and start from the beginning. Clearly something happened to get your knickers in a twist. What was it?"

Gavin struggled to compose his thoughts. He was so angry he couldn't make heads or tails of anything. "Well, you saw that I was introduced to Broadbent."

"Yes, I believe Harrison did the honors. I did not know he knew him."

"Wrong. It was Grace. *She* knows him. She knows him very well."

"How well? Could she extract information from him?"

"Is that all you think about? There are more important things than finding the Earl of Longmont!"

Silence gave him a grave look. The cool night air stood thick between them.

Silence finally broke the stillness. "Love," he sighed.

"What?"

"At first I did not understand what could be more important than finding the Earl of Longmont. Now I know. It is love. It has finally happened, Kingston. You found something to fill the hole in your heart."

"Oh, do not lecture me now!"

"I will lecture," Silence insisted, "and you will listen! For six months, I have been the guy for all your dirty work. I chased, spied, lied, and cheated for you, just so you could get out of the black hole you have been wallowing in since Spencer's death. Nothing was more important to you than finding Whitmore and extracting your revenge. You were obsessed."

"That is not true," Gavin protested. But he could see Silence was right. "Very well, perhaps I was. But I deserved to be."

"That comment is as insightful as a thirty-year-old penny is bright," Silence chided."

"He took away everything I loved!"

"Then why let him take even more? You have given him a certain power over you. He has been at the heart of every motivation for the last six months. You are so consumed by this that you refuse to call him anything but his title. And yet you complain that others only see you for your title. Call him Whitmore, for heaven's sake!"

Silence wasn't done yet. "I have observed something from watching all of our friends find matches, Kingston: those who marry for convenience use their heads but are very unhappy; those who follow their hearts lose both their hearts and their heads, but they are happy. They become happy, irrational people, and you definitely qualify."

"What are you saying?"

"That is exactly what I am talking about. A week ago, you would have caught on, but now you are nothing short of a dimwit."

Gavin gave him a stern look. "No need to resort to name-calling, Silence."

"You fell in love, Kingston! It is the only thing that accounts for this irrationality, and it is the only thing that will pull you out of it too. After everything we have been through, you have pushed aside the one person you loved. You are letting your hatred and jealousy and desire for revenge destroy what you have with Grace." Silence sighed and took a deep breath. "Now, tell me exactly what Grace said that turned you against her so quickly. Why do you think she is conspiring against you?"

Gavin tried to remember. Was it the part where Broadbent said she was free with her tongue? No, she had seemed very upset about that. Was it the part where Broadbent called her beautiful? Certainly not. Grace's response had been a spiteful comment about his wife not wanting to dance with him. Was it his compliment about her red hair? No, she had seemed irritated by it.

He knitted his brows together in concentration. "I am afraid all I know is that they knew each other three years ago," he conceded.

"Perhaps they met when she had her first season," Silence suggested.

The answer suddenly dawned on Gavin. "Oh no," he groaned. "I think Mr. Broadbent was an old suitor who got her hopes up three years ago. Grace never talks about her first season with me. I only overheard her say something to my mother."

Silence confirmed, "He did get married almost three years ago."

"It must be him. What if she still has feelings for him?"

"Have you asked her?"

"No."

"Well, did she seem brokenhearted or angry?"

Gavin tried to separate his jealousy from his memories. He reexamined her body language and tone of voice. She had held her head high, and her shoulders had been pushed back. She had touched his hands as little as possible while they danced. Her tone had been cold and calculated. "Looking back, I think it was very clear . . ."

"What was clear?" Silence coaxed.

"Oh, Silence, I made a mess of things. She detests the man! It is so clear now. She is not after my title, is she? And I just abandoned her. I have to find her." Gavin patted Silence's shoulder and said, "Thanks for the kick. It hurt like the dickens, but it was well deserved."

"I will do it again if you do not make things right."

As he ran back to the ballroom, Gavin called out behind him, "Silence, Silence!"

*****

Grace hardly had time to consider what Gavin had said before someone asked her to dance.

She was mad at Mr. Broadbent, fuming even. But it was nothing compared to the pain and sorrow she felt over Gavin's words. How could he have believed Mr. Broadbent's lies so easily? He thought she was after his money? The pain stung so deeply that she nearly cried out in agony.

It seemed everything she held dear was going to be taken from her, and there was nothing she could do about it. She had trusted Gavin, had risked loving him, even convinced herself that they could be happy together. But he didn't trust her. At the first sign of trouble, he had abandoned her, just like before. She had been careless. She wouldn't make the same mistake again.

The gentleman she was dancing with asked, "Miss Iverson, you seem distracted, are you well?"

"I am afraid that I am feeling lightheaded. I do hate to end our dance early, but I think I should probably sit down."

"Certainly. Take my arm." He led her to the refreshment table and offered her some wine, which she declined. They awkwardly passed a few minutes in silence, watching the other dancers on the floor.

"Would you like anything else?" he asked.

"No, I will be fine," Grace said and shook her head. "I think I would just like to go home now."

"Then allow me to call your carriage for you."

"No need, sir," another gentleman responded. "Miss Iverson is welcome to use my carriage. I am confident that it has hardly been put away as I just barely arrived. You do look rather pallid, Miss Iverson. The sooner you get home, the better."

Sooner sounded much better than later. Grace nodded, and her partner bowed and disappeared into the crowd. The gentleman offering to take her home was familiar, but she couldn't remember his name. She hardly remembered her own after all of the night's introductions.

She allowed herself to be led toward the front door. Grace barely heard him order the carriage before the room started to spin. She quickly found a place to sit as they waited.

Her thoughts returned to Gavin. *Where could he be? Should I have gone after him? Did he really believe all those things?* The pain threatened to escape her eyes, but she resisted it with all her might. She was a strong woman, and tears were for those who were weak.

She heard the butler announce, "Lord Randall, your carriage is ready."

Lord Randall Fresden! Earl of somewhere . . . That was his name! He helped her to a standing position and ushered her down the Comptons' steps. "May I escort you home?" he asked.

Grace was surprised he would even suggest such a thing, as the offer was highly improper. A lady would never ride unchaperoned with a gentleman. "Thank you, but no. I shall be fine on my own," she replied. "Please let the duchess know I was not feeling well." Her chest felt tight, and she hoped she could get home in time before the tears came. She turned to step into the carriage and caught her slipper on the step, losing her footing. Lord Randall caught her in his arms and steadied her. Her heart lurched for a moment when he did not release her immediately.

"I think I am well now," she assured him.

"I must insist on escorting you home, Miss Iverson. On my gentleman's honor, you must not be left alone. You can hardly stand."

Her overwrought mind struggled to compose another polite refusal. But then she noticed a man dressed in dirty, ratty clothes leaning against the gate, eying her rakishly. Late as it was, and alone in a strange city, perhaps having Lord Randall accompany her would not be so terrible. She hesitated for a second before forming a reply.

"Very well," Grace conceded, desperate to get home as quickly as possible. "I will not be good company, I am afraid. Talking seems to make me even more lightheaded." *And it will just make me cry.*

"We need not converse." There was an air of authority in his voice, but she was glad he was in agreement. She stepped into the carriage. He quickly gave directions to his driver and followed her in, taking the seat across from her.

They rode for a few minutes. Cold, dark thoughts about her broken hopes soon returned, making her shiver.

Lord Randall reached under the seat and pulled out a lap blanket and moved to the seat next to her. He draped the blanket on her knees. She was shocked to feel his hand remain on her leg.

She sat up straighter and removed his hand with authority. "Lord Randall! I assure you, I can adjust the blanket on my own!"

He placed his finger on her lips and shushed her, but she shook her head to remove it.

"Shhh, Miss Iverson. I told you, we need not converse."

*****

Gavin could not find Grace anywhere. He asked Eliza if she had seen her; she only remembered that Grace had been dancing with Lord Carter. He headed over to Lord Carter and tried to find a polite way to interrupt a conversation about a bill in the House of Lords.

"Pardon me, but I believe Miss Iverson reserved the next dance for me. Have you seen her?" In truth, he had probably missed the waltz that he had promised her. His self-castigation was at its worst.

"I was dancing with her, but then I escorted her to the refreshment table as she was feeling unwell. I believe Lord Randall Fresden offered her his carriage."

"Thank you."

Gavin made quick progress around the room, scanning furiously for Grace. She was definitely not in the ballroom. Neither was Lord Randall.

Gavin felt a twinge of anxiety creep down his spine. Fresden was the last man he wanted enjoying Grace's company. He had a less-than-stellar reputation. He regularly kept a mistress or two, and Gavin personally knew of two ladies who had mysteriously disappeared from society after being courted by him. Rumors were that he had convinced them to run away with him, promising an elopement to Gretna Green, but yet he remained a bachelor. The girls were shunned from society, of course, but

Fresden seemed unbothered by their plight. He often made bets at White's on how fast he could ruin a new debutante.

Gavin tried not to panic, but he couldn't shake the feeling that Grace was in danger. He walked toward the entrance to speak with the footman. "Have you seen a beautiful redhead in a blue-and-silver gown? Her hair was braided around the crown with ringlets."

"Yes, sir. She left about ten minutes ago. She looked a little pale, and a gentleman helped her into the carriage."

"Which gentleman? What carriage?"

"I am not sure. I can ask Mr. Hershey. He was the one who ordered the carriage."

"Yes, please get him right away. A lady may be in danger." *Maybe he really did only offer his carriage*, Gavin tried to tell himself.

The minute it took to retrieve the butler was excruciating. In the meantime, he asked the other footman, who was eyeing his pacing with pity, to get the Kingston carriage ready. "On second thought, just saddle Harrison's horse." He knew that Harrison rarely took his phaeton or carriage when he could ride, and he undoubtedly had the fastest horse there.

"Yes, Your Grace."

Another minute went by, and finally the butler came from the ballroom. "Mr. Hershey," Gavin stated, "it is paramount that you tell me where Miss Iverson went."

"I believe Lord Randall offered his carriage to escort her back to Willsing Manor. She left about ten minutes ago. Is there a problem?"

"Where is Lord Randall now?"

"I do not recall him coming back inside. Perhaps he went for a stroll in the garden?"

"I highly doubt that," Gavin muttered under his breath.

Mr. Hershey led the way outside to speak with the grooms. "Which way did Lord Randall's carriage go?" Mr. Hershey asked.

"That way, sir," the groom pointed. "Toward Mayfair. Willsing Manor, I believe."

"Was she alone?" Gavin asked desperately.

"No, sir," the groom replied. "It looked that way at first, but then at the last minute, a gentleman got into the carriage with her." Fear coursed through Gavin's body like a tidal wave. *Why is Grace in a carriage with Fresden?*

Mr. Hershey stepped closer and asked, "Is Miss Iverson in trouble, Your Grace?"

"I do not know. As privately as possible, please let my mother know that I have escorted Miss Iverson home. And get Harrison's horse ready immediately." The groom was dispatched to see to the horse, and Mr. Hershey left to inform his mother.

Gavin quickly reentered the ballroom, spied Silence and Harrison from across the room, and motioned to each of them. Silence excused himself from his group and made his way over. Harrison quickly cut his way through the crowd, and they both arrived at Gavin's side at the same time.

"What is it?" Harrison asked.

In low tones, Gavin said, "Miss Iverson left fifteen minutes ago with Lord Randall, in his carriage."

Silence asked, "While we were in the garden?"

"I believe so."

"Th-this is n-not g-good."

"Kingston," Silence muttered, "if she knew his reputation, she would never willingly ride in a carriage with him—"

"I know," Gavin said. "I do not have a good feeling about this."

Silence frowned, deep in thought. "I think it is time to summon the magistrate, Kingston."

CHAPTER 16

"You must know how much I admire you."

"Lord Randall, kindly remove your hand." *You have to be brave*, she told herself. *Do not be afraid. He can sense fear.*

"Miss Iverson, may I call you Grace?"

"Absolutely not! We have only just met! You, sir, can have no reason to admire me. You know nothing about me."

"Ah, but I do!" He brushed his fingers against her cheek, but it was not tender like Gavin's touch. His fingers were rough as if he did manual labor.

Keep him talking. "What do you know about me?"

"For starters, I know that I will be paid handsomely to escort you home."

"Who has paid you handsomely?"

"A mutual friend of ours."

As soon as he said it, she remembered seeing them together. "Mr. Broadbent," she whispered automatically. Why had she not remembered this fact before entering the carriage? *Stupid girl!*

"Beautiful and intelligent. Yes, Broadbent said that about you. He needed a little help tonight. It seems he has plans to evade a certain friend of yours who has been inquiring about his personal affairs."

"What friend of mine? I had not seen Mr. Broadbent for three years until tonight."

"Ah, but your new friend, the Duke of Huntsman, is rather too curious about Broadbent's immediate future. Broadbent is about to inherit a fortune when his uncle passes, and he cannot have any interference right now."

"His uncle? But Broadbent has only one uncle, and they were not close. Whitmore, I believe his name was."

"He goes by many names."

He was beginning to slide closer. She turned on the bench and faced him, putting her hand on his chest to stop him. "What other names?"

"When his estranged uncle Whitmore takes his last breath, Broadbent will become the Earl of Longmont."

She couldn't help but gasp! Broadbent's uncle was the man responsible for the death of Spencer and Gavin's father! But before she could process the information further, Fresden leapt forward with such speed and force that she was pressed against the side of the carriage. It took all her might to push back. She had spent many years wrestling Gavin and Spencer as a girl, and she knew how to defend herself. She had to get out of the corner. She used the heel of her hand to hit him in the neck. Her blow left him coughing and gasping for breath.

In the moment she had bought herself, she threw aside the blanket, freeing up her legs, and scrambled to the other side of the carriage. All she had with her was a handkerchief, a bottle of her cinnamon toilette water, and a small sewing kit—a necessity, according to Charlotte, in case she had a "fashion emergency". The man kept coughing, but she knew she was running out of time. She quickly reached into her reticule and pulled out the small pointed scissors. They would have to do.

"You wretched thing!" he sputtered. "I never have qualms about sullying a woman, but you have just made this a sport!" He reached across the carriage and grabbed her arm. His grip was tight and desperate.

She said, "I warn you, Lord Randall, leave me be. I will not speak of this to anyone."

"Who would even believe you?" he sneered. "Everyone saw how you let me take you home without so much as a farewell. I could not have planned it better if I tried." His other hand gripped her dress sleeve, and in one lightning-fast move, he ripped it off her shoulder. His grin widened, but she dared not adjust her dress for fear of revealing the hidden scissors tightly gripped in her fist.

He hissed, "Now there is not a person alive who will not know you are a ruined woman."

Just as he sprang at her again, the carriage lurched to a halt, and the sound of the wheels grinding against gravel pierced her ears. Her back slammed against the front of the carriage, and Lord Randall landed in her lap. She immediately felt warmth on her hand and thighs, but the night was dark, and she was not sure what happened.

Fresden started coughing and sputtering. He made an awful, high-pitched noise and slid to his knees. She screamed and tried to extricate herself, but his weight was too heavy. She pushed and pulled and managed to get a knee up high enough to push him with her foot. The man was making the most terrible gasping noise. As she kicked him off, she remembered the scissors in her fist. They must have pierced his throat as he fell. His ghastly coughing continued. She realized it was the choking sound of a man drowning in his own blood.

The door of the carriage swung open just as Fresden collapsed with a gasp onto the carriage floor. It should have been too dark to tell who was at the door, but she would know those broad shoulders anywhere.

"Gavin!"

*****

"Are you all right? Did he hurt you?" Gavin could only see that the man was on the floor and struggling for breath. Grace was hunched in the far corner, but the moonlight from the window allowed him to see her silhouette showing the rapid rise and fall of her shoulders.

"I am well, but I think I may have killed him."

Relief rushed through him. Her voice quivered slightly, and he wished only to comfort her.

Gavin grabbed the man's collar and tried to pull him out. Fresden was no small man, and the angle of being halfway in the carriage made leverage slightly complicated. Gavin finally dragged him out by the shoulders, not caring a bit when his legs thudded lifelessly to the ground. Even in the faint moonlight, he could see the man had a gaping wound in his neck. Blood was still gushing from it. From the amount on his clothes, Fresden didn't stand a chance. Gavin had seen enough bloodshed in the navy to know that.

He climbed into the carriage to assess Grace. "Gigi, I am so sorry. What happened? Are you all right? Do you need anything? Harrison is right behind me with the carriage, and he is bringing Silence."

She did not say anything right away. Finally she replied, "Silence will be nice."

"Of course he will be nice. What do you mean?"

"You said Harrison will be bringing silence. I hope I never hear another sound again. Oh, I will never forget the sound of him choking!"

All of a sudden she burst out in tears. The sound of Grace crying was something that he would never forget. It was heart wrenching and morose. Her sobs came from some place deep and protected, an area of Grace's heart that she never let anyone see, not even him.

Gavin sat down next to her, pulled her to his chest, and held her. He rocked her as her body heaved with the force of grief. It was as if she were feeling everything she had ever held back during her entire life. Very brief gasps of breath only resulted in another audible moan that spoke of pain and anguish. His eyes filled with tears as he rocked her. She clung to him as if he were life itself, and he promised he would never let anything happen to her again.

He heard a carriage pull up beside them. Apparently so did Grace, because she quickly pulled away and started fumbling around in the darkness.

"It is just Silence and Harrison. Do not fret." He still hadn't fully released her, but she began pushing on him, and he gave way. She rummaged in the darkness on the floor and picked up a blanket. "Are you chilled?" he asked.

"I am indecent," she sniffed, panic in her voice.

"Here, take my coat." He removed his garment and placed it around her shoulders. It was then that he noticed her dress was torn. *What happened? Did Fresden do that?* By this time, he heard both Harrison and Silence outside. He exited the carriage.

"Grace is well, but she is in a state of shock."

"Wh-what happened? Fresden is d-de-dead."

Behind him, he heard Grace exiting the carriage as well, and he turned around when she spoke, "I . . . I do not fully know. The carriage stopped suddenly and he fell . . . It all happened so fast. But then it was all in slow motion. I must have. . . no . . . I . . . Did I kill him? Oh dear!"

Her voice shook as she sobbed, "There is so much . . . I cannot go to prison! Oh, that sound!" Grace put her hands up by her ears as if the noise was still occurring, and that was when Gavin noticed the bloody pair of scissors in her hand. She swayed forward then backwards, one way and then another, as if rocking herself.

Silence said, "Miss Iverson, even in this darkness, I can see you are about to faint."

Gavin stepped forward, putting one hand under Grace's arm, offering support. She shrunk back a bit from his touch, but it did not deter him. He placed another hand on the small of her back and started guiding her toward Silence's carriage.

"Grace, there is no reason to make sense of it now," Gavin reassured her. "Let me take you home and get you cleaned up."

"Yes, Miss Iverson," Silence added, "Let me handle this. Of course we know it was an accident. Perhaps you could give me those scissors in your hand."

Grace's eyes bulged out of her head in panic. Gavin could see that it was mere minutes before she would collapse. It was a very good thing that Willsing Manor was less than half a mile away.

She looked down at the scissors in her hand in disbelief. She quickly dropped them and began wiping her bloody hand on her dress. But Fresden's blood had seeped into the delicate creases of her skin and would not wipe away. Her sobbing began anew, but there was something ghostly about her wails this time.

Gavin hurried her into the carriage just as the magistrate arrived. As they passed his carriage, Grace's screams could be heard clearly and distinctly: "I killed a man! I am a murderer!"

*****

Gavin had ordered a bath and hot tea for Grace and gave explicit instructions for Charlotte to return and report her condition. His heart ached for her. And he knew the cascade of the evening's events had all started with his own stupidity. She only left the ball early because of his careless words.

How could he have imagined that Grace was ensnaring him for his title? She had not brought up money, not once, the entire week. And how could he have believed she had been intimate with Broadbent? *What was I thinking?* Jealousy was truly a cardinal sin. Its repercussions rippled through his aching heart.

And now Grace was tangled up in this mess. Why had Lord Randall targeted her? What was her history with him? Was there a connection to Broadbent, her former suitor, hidden in all this? *Surely she knew nothing of Fresden's reputation or of Broadbent's connection to the earl,* he reasoned, but he knew he was only trying to convince himself— like a monk who tries to talk himself out of admiring a beautiful woman.

Gavin was still in the habit of doubting a lady's loyalty. There had been too many women who presented false fronts, all eager to earn the title of duchess. But he tried to push away his suspicions. He couldn't doubt Grace's loyalty again. Not now, not when she needed him.

*****

About half an hour later, Robison entered to notify him that Mr. Cornwall, the magistrate, was here to see him. Gavin pushed the heel of his palms against his eyes as counter pressure against the building tension.

"Show him in," he instructed.

Gavin adjusted his cravat and tried to shake the unease he felt in meeting with a magistrate at such a late hour. He stood as Silence led Mr. Cornwall into the study.

"Please, have a seat. I have been expecting you. Would you like a drink?"

"Thank you, Your Grace. A glass of port would be welcome about now."

Silence cleared his throat. Gavin awkwardly clarified, "Unfortunately I cannot offer you port. I can summon a fresh pot of tea."

Mr. Cornwall seemed confused. Gavin watched his eyes glance around the room at all the typical bachelor's study tokens— the chess game, the well-stocked library, and a beautiful painting of the sea, but no decanter of amber liquid. Gavin could see Cornwall's mind silently piecing the clues together.

"My cook works miracles with hot chocolate. No liquid offers more fortification than hot chocolate," Gavin weakly offered. Mr. Cornwall brows furrowed together slightly. "And we keep a wide range of teas."

Mr. Cornwall finally broke his silence. "Tea," he grumbled. "A strong tea."

Gavin nodded his head to Robison, who had been waiting patiently for the command. He turned back to Mr. Cornwall and again offered him a seat.

Gavin watched the magistrate take out a pencil and a sheet of paper as he sat down. "I was hoping to speak with Miss Iverson. Will she be joining us?"

"No," Gavin replied. "I am afraid she is indisposed. No doubt you heard her hysterics as we passed your carriage. Her lady's maid is attending to her now. But I can assure you of her innocence. I have known Grace all my life, and she has never lost control like that before."

The magistrate's eyebrow rose slightly, and he jotted something down.

Silence scooted forward in his chair and said, "What the duke is trying to say is that Miss Iverson is distraught about the accident." Silence gave Gavin a pointed look.

"You say she lost control?" the magistrate inquired, eyeing Gavin.

Gavin finally understood the implication of what he had said. "No. I mean only that tonight's events have been very trying, and she is overwhelmed at present. A good night's sleep will help her sort things out."

"Pardon me, Your Grace, but I do not wish her to 'sort things out' as you say," Mr. Cornwall protested. "I want the truth, not whatever story she is concocting to ease her guilt. A man has been murdered. It is my duty to seek justice."

Silence was much better at this than Gavin was. Gavin gave him the subtlest of looks that indicated that he wished him to take over. Silence cleared his throat and said, "Absolutely, Mr. Cornwall. But as a gentleman, I am sure you agree that the fairer sex must sometimes be handled delicately in such matters, no?"

Cornwall hesitated before making his reply. "Of course. But I am sure you agree that key facts are sometimes confused when investigations are not executed in a timely manner."

"Absolutely. I only wish she could speak to you now. But truthfully, she is still hysterical. It would be a waste of your time. Surely it can wait until morning, first light even. Besides, the light of a candle offers only the meekest of assistance to see into the carriage. It may assist your investigation to gather evidence from the scene of the accident before questioning the victim."

"Mr. Silence, I am mystified as to why you refer to Miss Iverson as the victim in this matter. It is not her body that is being transported by the undertaker at this moment. She is, at the very least, a witness. She may even be a cold-blooded murderer. I have nothing to investigate until I can question the sole surviving passenger of that carriage!"

Gavin began to worry in earnest. But then he saw Silence's lip turn up slightly, and he knew Silence was about to seal Grace's safety for the night. "You are a intelligent man, Mr. Cornwall," Silence soothed. "You originally were summoned to Willsing Manor to ensure Miss Iverson's safety, were you not?"

"Yes, I was told the lady's reputation and physical well-being were in jeopardy."

"And why would I have summoned you to follow someone who was set on committing murder? This was not premeditated. This was nothing more than an accident. I recommend we all go to our respective homes, and when we have the light of day and a bit of rest, we will investigate this case as diligently and thoroughly as you please."

Gavin could see the logic in Silence's words. "I promise to let you speak to Miss Iverson at first light," he vowed. "But there is a whole ballroom of people to interview who are beginning to scatter even as we speak, while Miss Iverson is not yet fit to be seen. Should you not investigate why she left the ball in the first place? Or how she knew Lord Randall? Surely someone at the ball must have seen something."

Mr. Cornwall silently debated their suggestions. He glanced up as the chime of the clock struck midnight. "I suppose her interview can wait until morning," he concluded. "I will start inquiries at the Comptons' before the ball breaks up. But I expect to see her at eight o'clock tomorrow morning."

Gavin let out a breath he had not realized he was holding. "You have my word. Let me show you out," he offered.

As they walked toward the front door, he caught sight of Charlotte coming down the stairs. He quickly bid Cornwall farewell and rushed Charlotte into his study.

He searched her face for any news, but all he could see was her panic. Hoping to calm her, he offered a cup of tea. She took it with shaky hands.

"How is Grace?" he finally asked.

"I am afraid she has not said much, Your Grace," Charlotte confessed. "She became quite distraught during her bath when I tried to clean the blood from under her nails. What happened to her, sir?"

Gavin's heart dropped in disappointment. "I was hoping you could tell me. Did she not say anything? Did she try to explain what happened?"

"No, Your Grace. She has not said a word."

Gavin frowned and furrowed his brows. "How is she?" he probed.

"She is resting right now. Well, she is in bed in her nightclothes. But she is staring at the ceiling as if it were likely to fall in on her. It gives me goose bumps, I tell you."

"Did she drink the chamomile tea?"

"Yes, sir, she drank all of it. Did not even need coaxing. She wouldn't touch the toast though."

"Thank you, Charlotte. She will have a very early visitor tomorrow at eight o'clock. Please see that she is ready, but let her sleep as long as possible."

Charlotte rung her hands and knitted her brows together. "Your Grace?"

"Yes?"

"She did say one thing. It may not be my place to tell you, but since you seem so anxious about her, I thought I should mention it."

"What is it?"

Charlotte bit her lip and looked down at the floor. "She said, 'Now Gavin will not wish to marry me. I am ruined.'" Charlotte looked back up at Gavin's face. "The sleeve of the dress, sir . . ." Her words hung in the air.

Silence answered for him. "That will be all, Charlotte. Thank you." She put down her tea and left the room.

Gavin's heart sputtered at Charlotte's revelation. Had more happened than simply a torn dress? Had Lord Randall taken more than the light in her eye or the skip in her step? His heart lurched once again, and he was suddenly weak in the knees. He found solace in the sofa by the window and put his head in his hands. The weight on his shoulders was too much.

"I failed her, Silence. She was under my roof, under my protection, and I failed her in every way. My jealousy blinded me, and I doubted her. I thought she had aligned herself with someone like Broadbent, and I chose to pull away at the moment she needed me the most."

Silence came and sat next to him. "Why *did* you think the worst, Kingston?" he asked. "I hardly know Miss Iverson, but she is the last person I would ever suspect of duplicity."

Gavin closed his eyes and tried to remember the events at the ball. "When Broadbent implied all those intimacies, I became so jealous. I . . ."

"But why? You have had many women in your life. If anything, you strayed farther from propriety than she did. How many ladies' hearts did you break between voyages?"

"This is hardly helpful, Silence," he muttered, his head in his hands again. Then he looked up and whispered, "Do you think she will ever forgive me?"

Silence put a hand on his shoulder. "I think so. She loves you, Gavin," he reassured him. "Unfortunately, that is the least of our problems right now."

*****

153

Gavin and Silence quickly went to work. They began by sketching a timeline of the evening's events. Then they began making a list of everything they knew about Broadbent and Fresden.

"We must be missing something, Silence," Gavin mused. He tapped his fingers on the desk and reviewed their notes again. "Why did Fresden target Grace? Her dowry is too small to be the aim. Was it just opportunity knocking? Simply a chance to get what he could when the moment presented itself?"

"No, I think we can safely assume that this was no coincidence," Silence replied. "Harrison and I had a few minutes to talk when you took Grace home. He told me that Lord Randall was very hard up on money. So strapped that he offered to sell Harrison his last horse, Impetus."

"The black stallion? The one he won in a card game?"

"Yes. It seems his luck has turned on him. He was asking Harrison for an outrageous amount. He is a fine horse for sure, but Harrison turned him down. If Fresden was hurting badly enough, he would have been an easy target for just about anyone."

Gavin pondered this for a moment. "Is there any connection between Broadbent and Lord Randall?" Silence murmured incoherently. "Well, is there?"

"I cannot say. I only just met Broadbent tonight. Harrison remembers seeing Broadbent and Fresden together a time or two— he even played at the same table once where Broadbent lost terribly to Fresden—but he has never seen anything to indicate a deep connection between them. I have sent him a note to my informant asking for anything he might have on them, but I doubt I will hear back before Cornwall's visit tomorrow morning."

"Then there is nothing else to do," Gavin sighed. "I just wish I knew more."

"Try to get some sleep, Kingston," Silence suggested.

I doubt I will be able to. He put his head back in his hands and rubbed his forehead as if doing so would massage out the anxiety and turmoil that was brewing. The pressure he felt was building, and none of his sources offered any relief. Charlotte had no secondhand information about what happened in the carriage. Silence knew only enough about Fresden and Broadbent to create further questions. And Grace was still beside herself—apparently lying in her bed, staring blankly at the ceiling. No one could settle his anxiety.

For the first time in months, his mouth burned with the desire to drown himself with drink. He had always known it wouldn't be easy to turn away from drink after being so dependent on it for years and years—but tonight was especially hard.

He methodically poured himself a cup of tea and drank every last drop. Silence held his tongue, but Gavin could see him watching him like a hawk.

"Will you be all right?" Silence finally asked. Gavin nodded after a moment.

"Just thirsty." Gavin knew that Silence would understand what he meant.

"Do you need me to stay?" Silence had stayed with him for a solid week when Gavin decided to give up alcohol. It was miserable. He had vacillated between fits of rage and weeping. He could hardly feed himself with all the shaking. But once the week was over, it was simply a matter of ridding the house of all alcohol and being well hydrated before going out. And he never, ever, went out when he felt the urge to drink. Like he felt now. It would be too easy to find himself walking into White's and ordering a scotch.

"I do not know," Gavin admitted. "I need to know Grace will be well."

"Now is not the time to cross boundaries," Silence warned. "You have no idea what could be going on in her mind. It might be perceived as opportunistic."

Gavin glanced at Silence. He had an unnerving knack for reading Gavin's mind. He had been contemplating checking on Grace in her chambers. "I suppose not. But maybe if I just—"

"Kinston, I would not do it I were you."

"I know her better than anyone. She needs me right now. I already let her down once. I cannot just sit here, knowing she is in there helplessly staring at the ceiling."

They sat in silence for a few minutes. "Do you want me to stay up with you?" Silence offered.

"No," Gavin replied. He was touched by Silence's offer. For all his teasing and sly comments, Gavin knew he was lucky to have such a good friend. "Get some sleep. At least one of us should."

Finally Silence stood and headed for the door of the study. "Try to get some rest, Kingston." With one hand on the door, he looked over his shoulder and added, "Think about what was not said between us. You do not want to hear it, but there will be gossip. She needs no more scandal tonight."

He was right, but so wrong at the same time.

*****

Grace closed her eyes again, but as soon as she did, she heard Lord Randall's god-awful cries as he gurgled on his own blood. She sucked in a breath and looked up again at the ceiling. Pushing the blankets off her legs, she tried to sit up, her arms still shaking against the weight of her body. She did not know which felt more unsteady—her head or her heart.

She stood and wrapped her dressing gown around her and walked to the window, tightly folding her arms in front of her. She heard a light tapping on her door. It wasn't Charlotte's knock, so she ignored it, assuming whoever it was would leave. But the knocking came again, a bit louder this time.

With effort, she found her voice. "Come in."

She continued to look out the window as she heard the door open behind her. Slow, steady steps let her know that someone had entered the room. The steps stopped, and she knew it was Gavin.

He had come.

She took a deep breath and held it in as if doing so would also prevent her from dissolving into a puddle of tears. She had endured terrible losses in her life, but she doubted she would be able to survive losing Gavin again.

Slowly and deliberately, he placed his hands on her shoulders. She could feel the tenderness in his touch, and she felt something shift inside. All her life she had hoped to be considered a strong and confident woman, someone who endured and excelled no matter what trials came. She wanted to live up to her name. She wanted to be full of grace.

But she didn't want to be strong right now. She wanted to need someone. She let out her breath and leaned backwards into his chest.

Gavin welcomed her into his arms and buried his head in her hair. He whispered, "It will be all right, Grace."

He took her shoulders and ever so gently turned her around and pulled her closer into his embrace. She felt the heat of his chest on her now-wet cheeks, and she feasted on his strength. His hands caressed her back as her tears continued to run unleashed. For the first time in her life, she admitted she needed someone.

It was entirely inappropriate for him to be in her chambers, even against the duchess's rules, however they had never truly kept to the rules of propriety. She was never the demure lady who was afraid of getting her petticoat dirty. He was never the calm and collected lad who coddled her. What had started as friendship had evolved into something quite tangible. They may have been apart these last ten years, but neither of their hearts had ever really moved away. The thought tortured her to no end. She knew what she had to do. It was a basic survival instinct. But the fear of doing it sent chills up and down her spine.

"You are shaking. Here, sit down." He guided her to the window seat, and she laid her head on his chest, her arms wrapping around him.

She did not know how long he held her. Seconds turned into minutes, and minutes turned into moments, and moments turned into memories. She noticed that his breathing seemed to be synchronized with hers. Every breath she took was easier knowing that he was breathing with her.

She lifted her head a bit only to have him kiss her forehead.

"Let me hold you a bit longer," he whispered as he guided her head to his chest again. "Can you tell me what happened?"

She closed her eyes tighter, hoping it would make the metallic smell of the blood disappear. Having him hold her was like putting salve on a fresh wound. It took the sting out, but she knew applying it would be painful.

"Lord Randall offered his carriage to take me home. I was not feeling well after . . . I must have looked unsteady, because he said he would escort me to Willsing Manor. I refused him, but he insisted. I was so desperate to leave, and I did not want to argue with him. There was a man on the street looking at me in such a way . . . I do not know what came over me. I was not thinking clearly."

"Grace, I am so sorry for what I said. This is all my fault. Can you ever forgive me?"

She stiffened slightly. She sat up; this time he let her. With all the events of what happened in the carriage, there had been little time to fully comprehend what Gavin had said at the ball. She refused to open that wound also. She was a strong woman, but she could not afford to evaluate his actions at the moment.

She took a deep breath and tried to suppress the hurt he had inflicted. Suddenly the pain of his betrayal far exceeded the traumatic events in the carriage. She realized that she most definitely was not ready to talk about it quite yet. She stood and said coolly, "Gavin, thank you for coming to check on me. But you should go." He locked eyes with her, and she looked away.

He stood as well, and she felt him guide her chin to look at him. For a moment, panic shot through her. Was he going to kiss her? She had let him comfort her and hold her, but he had betrayed her earlier that night at the ball. He had assumed the worst with Mr. Broadbent. He had thought she was a fortune-hunter.

She pulled away and walked toward the door. "Please leave." She put her hand on the doorknob.

"The magistrate will be here at eight o'clock." Hurt was apparent in his voice as he repeated his apology, "I am so sorry, Gigi." It was an apology that Grace was not ready to receive. She wasn't sure if she could trust it. She just couldn't ponder it at the moment.

He leaned in to kiss her, but she quickly opened the door, nearly hitting his head with it. He muttered his farewell and looked at her one last time. She lifted her chin and tried to keep a blank expression on her face.

She closed the door, pleased that she had not betrayed her emotions in front of him. She would have to find the strength to resist him. It would be a fight, but she could win this war over her heart.

She turned around and leaned against the door. For a moment she thought she heard him say "I love you, Gigi" through the door. Then the sound of footsteps walking away dissipated until she was left with only a deafening silence.

You may not win this one, Grace, she told herself. And she knew it was true. She would have to leave. But how could she battle her deepest feelings when the war on her heart's loyalty had already surrendered to him.

Her knees could no longer hold her weight, and she slipped down to the floor.

CHAPTER 17

Gavin's fears had proven true—he had not slept well.

All night he had tossed and turned as his mind reviewed again and again the scene in Grace's chambers. She had seemed so fragile as she wept in his arms. It had felt so right to comfort her, and at first she had seemed to accept his arms around her. But later, when he leaned in to kiss her, she had pulled away.

She is still angry with me. And my apologies are only making her angrier. The coolness in her speech and demeanor when she closed the door on him had been truly terrifying.

His head ached with tension. The only way he could think to solve the misunderstanding with Grace was to resolve the Fresden issue. Once that was out of the way, he would focus on seeking Grace's forgiveness.

He knew Grace was forgiving in nature. After all, how many times had he seen her wrestling Spencer to the ground over some offense, only to see them laughing together ten minutes later? More times than he could count, Gavin had quarreled with her over something ridiculous. He had always apologized immediately and tried to talk it over with her. But she seemed more content to wait out the storm. It wasn't simply that she was too proud to apologize. It was more than that. He had learned over the years that Grace was not interested in discussing a problem until she had worked out the solution. After a while, her joyful and playful self returned without the ceremony of an apology.

This thought lifted his spirits a little. Perhaps it would be like it used to be. Perhaps if he just gave her enough time, they could put this in the past and move on. Perhaps she would walk right back into his arms.

But Gavin knew this was more grave than some schoolyard quarrel. He hadn't just pulled her ringlet one too many times. He hadn't called her "just a girl" or accused her of being stubborn. Those offenses could be easily dismissed as immaturity. This time his jealousy had made him behave downright stupidly.

The door to his study flew open. He heard Robison trying to inform him that Silence had arrived, but his friend was already three strides into the room. "Thank you, Robison," Gavin chuckled. "That will be all."

Robison bowed and left the room. Less than a second lapsed before Silence said, "You survived. I am proud of you."

"Barely. I would not count it a success yet. We still have to meet with Cornwall." Gavin turned away and walked toward the window. "Did you hear back from your man?" he asked.

"Yes. Broadbent and Fresden did know each other." Silence continued, "Broadbent's wife is Fresden's cousin. Mrs. Broadbent and Lord Randall grew up as close as siblings. In fact, Fresden has spent his winters at Broadbent's country home for the last three years. I have no doubt that given Fresden's reputation for ruining women and his need for money, that Broadbent paid him to—" He suddenly stopped.

Gavin looked over his shoulder to see why Silence had stopped mid-sentence and saw that Grace had entered the room. He cautiously walked toward her, but she circumvented his approach and took a seat in the nearest hardback chair.

"Good morning, Miss Iverson," Silence began. "How are you feeling?"

Grace looked down at her shaking hands and then back up at Silence before replying. "I am fine, thank you. Please do not let me interrupt your conversation. What have you discovered?" Her eyes pointedly avoided Gavin.

Silence looked over at Gavin before answering, "Not much, actually. We still do not understand why Fresden targeted you."

She took a deep breath and swallowed before speaking. Her voice was distant and controlled. "All I know is that Broadbent hired Lord Randall to attack me. He told me so in the carriage." An uncomfortable silence filled the room.

"I am sorry to ask so bluntly," Silence hesitated, "but why would Broadbent pay Fresden to harm you, Miss Iverson?"

Grace glanced at Gavin before replying. "Gavin was sniffing too close to home," she stammered. "Lord Randall said he was interfering with Broadbent's inheriting everything from the Earl of Longmont."

Silence raised his eyebrows and took a deep breath. "Yes, I think I see," Silence murmured.

"I still do not," Gavin said. He looked to Silence for an explanation.

"Well, Whitmore is wanted for murdering your father, right? That is why he went into hiding. What would happen if the earl were to be captured and imprisoned?"

"I do not know. I suppose I would do everything in my power to see the earl hang."

"Yes, but an earl hanging for murder? I doubt the Prince Regent would stand for it. I am not suggesting he would interfere in the case, of course, but he would certainly strip the man of his title to avoid a scandal. The earldom has not even passed a generation yet."

"Hmm," Gavin mused. "And I bet a good deal of the estate was entailed away with the title."

"Exactly," Silence agreed. "Revoking the Earl of Longmont's title would significantly reduce Broadbent's inheritance. Now, that is motive."

They all jumped at the sound of Robison clearing his throat in the doorway. "Mr. Cornwall, Your Grace," he announced.

"Thank you, Robison. Will you bring in refreshment and strong tea for the magistrate?"

Robison bowed and closed the door behind him.

Gavin nervously glanced at Grace. Her face paled as she saw the magistrate. She looked like a lamb going to the slaughter.

*****

Grace felt the walls crumble around her. It was time to disclose everything. The aftermath would have to speak for itself.

Gavin took a step closer to her and made the introductions. She stood and was pleased to discover that, at the moment, her legs still had the strength to curtsy. "How do you do, Mr. Cornwall?"

"I have been better. Investigating a murder is not one of my favorite activities."

She sucked in a breath. Silence quickly interjected, "Unfortunate accident, you mean."

"We shall see." Mr. Cornwall turned back to Grace and asked, "Can you tell me what happened last night?"

She took her seat, and the men found chairs as well. She folded her shaking hands in her lap. *I can do this!* "What would you like to know?" The quiver in her voice was probably apparent only to Gavin; she avoided looking at him.

"Let us start with the reason you left the ball early," Mr. Cornwall suggested. "Surely you must have known that Lord Randall has a blemished reputation among the ladies of the *ton*."

"No. I was only introduced to Lord Randall last night. I had never even heard of him until then."

"Who introduced you?"

"I believe it was Lady Cornelia Grisham and her friend, Monique . . . I do not remember her last name."

Silence added, "That would be Lady Monique Pinnock, a favorite of Mr. Broadbent."

"Yes," Grace agreed. "We were introduced by Lady Monique."

Mr. Cornwall wrote down a few things and then looked back up to her and asked, "And did you dance with him?"

"He asked, and I told him I would reserve the fourth set for him. Unfortunately I fell ill while I was dancing with Lord Carter Kissinger." She glanced briefly at Gavin and then looked away. The concern on his face was unnerving. "Lord Carter escorted me to the refreshment table, where Lord Randall observed my condition. It was then that Lord Randall offered me his carriage, which he stated had not even been put away yet. I was quite lightheaded. His carriage was brought round within a few minutes."

"When did you press him to join you in the carriage?"

She was shocked at the question. "Pardon me?"

"At what point did you make plans against Lord Randall?"

"I had never made any plans against Lord Randall. What are you implying?"

Mr. Cornwall wrote a few things down and said, "We will come back to that question. So, you both got into the carriage. The driver mentioned you appeared out of sorts, perhaps even tipsy."

"Certainly not," Grace corrected him. "I only had half a glass of punch. What did the driver say?"

"This is my interrogation, miss. I will be asking the questions. What happened once you entered the carriage?"

Her palms were moist from being clenched so tightly. She held back her retort with sheer determination. She did not like having the event referred to as a murder or hearing herself described as "tipsy". Nor did she like learning that Lord Randall had a poor reputation with ladies. She closed her eyes and bowed her head.

After a prolonged breath, she began the story, "We had hardly left the party before he placed a blanket upon my legs, depositing his hand where a gentleman's hand should not be. When I removed his hand, he forced himself on me. I was trapped in a moving carriage with no one to help me. The noise of the wheels on the cobblestones made it unlikely the driver would hear me. And I was not sure Fresden's driver would lend any assistance even if he did hear me. I kept him talking while I made my plan."

"So you admit you had a plan? Was that why you coerced him into accompanying you?"

"Please, Mr. Cornwall," Gavin interrupted sternly, "let Miss Iverson tell her story."

The magistrate made no apology. "Go on, Miss Iverson," he retorted.

She took a deep breath and continued, "My only *plan* was to ward off his advances. It was clear that he intended to ruin me. He informed me that Mr. Broadbent had paid him a large sum of money to do so. It was not until then that I recalled seeing them together at the ball. That is when I knew I was on my own. No one was going to save me but myself."

"That is quite an allegation, Miss Iverson," Mr. Cornwall mused. "Highly unusual for a woman to fight off a man and escape without so much as a bruise—"

"Enough, Mr. Cornwall," Gavin interrupted. "I will not stand for this. Miss Iverson, you are free to go."

"Do not leave, Miss Iverson," Mr. Cornwall replied. He peered at Gavin with look of determination on his face. "Your Grace, I can understand how a man in your position is used to getting his own way, so I will forgive your interference. But this is my investigation. I will decide when I have enough information," he declared. "Now, Miss Iverson, what happened next? How did you subdue a man twice your size?"

Grace tried to hide her trembling hands in her skirt. "I slammed him in the neck with the heel of my hand," she said in an unsteady voice. "That bought me a few seconds to move to the other side of the carriage while he caught his breath. I took the scissors out of my reticule while he was coughing. Then he became very angry at me and attacked me."

"How did he attack you?" Gavin asked gently.

Mr. Cornwall threw him an irritated look and repeated, "How did he attack you, Miss Iverson?" He scribbled a few things on his paper, and when she didn't respond right away, the magistrate looked up at her. "Would you like me to ask these men to step out?"

"No, sir. This is just something I do not wish to recall."

The tea came in, and she was grateful for the distraction. Her mouth was suddenly dry. She knew it was the context of the conversation, not the number of words, that had left her feeling desiccated. Silence stood and distributed the tea to everyone. She took hers gratefully, but she noticed that Gavin simply placed his aside on the desk. His intense gaze disquieted her resolve. Even though she looked away from him, she felt his eyes on her while she drank her tea.

It seemed the whole room was waiting with baited breath for the most important part of the story. She put down her cup and smoothed her skirts. Her courage trembled inside, wavering when she caught a glimpse of Gavin walking toward her. He stopped behind her chair and stood there, close enough that she could smell his cologne. Her heart galloped, remembering how he had held her last night.

She closed her eyes and finished the story. "Lord Randall was irate. He grabbed my arm and threatened me again, laughing about how he would enjoy ruining me. Then he ripped the sleeve of my dress. I dared not move. Suddenly the carriage lurched to a stop, and he fell forward onto my lap. I do not quite know how it happened, but he must have fallen right onto my scissors."

When she opened her eyes Mr. Cornwall asked, "You were going to attack him with the scissors?"

"No, sir," she answered icily. "I was going to *defend* myself. It is quite different." He wrote a few things down.

"So the injury to his neck was because the carriage stopped suddenly?"

"Yes, sir. He began to make the most horrific choking sound. It has haunted me all night; it is something I never wish to hear again. It was clear he could not breathe due to the amount of blood pooling in his throat."

"Why did the carriage stop?" the magistrate asked.

Gavin spoke up from behind her. "I stopped the carriage with Harrison's horse. I was trying to help Miss Iverson." She could hear the pain in his voice.

"Then what happened, miss?"

"Then Gavin was at the carriage door, pulling him out. It was all over before I realized what had happened."

Mr. Cornwall looked up at Gavin. "And was he dead when you got to him?"

"Very nearly so. I could tell by the amount of blood that there was no hope in saving him. And after what I just heard, I cannot say that I regret my inaction."

Mr. Cornwall wrote a few things down and then asked to no one in particular, "What I do not understand is motive. Why would Lord Randall attack her? Excuse me for being so bold, Miss Iverson, but there is little monetary reward for marrying you. So why ruin you?"

Silence raised his hand and suggested, "His Grace and I were just discussing that before you arrived. We have a working theory, although I admit there is no real proof."

"And what exactly is this theory of yours?" Mr. Cornwall grunted.

"You have probably heard rumors of why the Earl of Longmont suddenly vanished."

"Yes, he fled after supposedly shooting the former Duke of Huntsman in a duel."

"Not 'supposedly'," Gavin quickly corrected. "It was murder."

Silence continued. "Well, Mr. Broadbent is Whitmore's sole heir. I intercepted a correspondence a few days ago that indicated that the earl has suffered an apoplexy and is not expected to survive the week. If he were to die before his whereabouts were discovered, then Broadbent inherits all. But if Whitmore is found and charged with murder in the next few days, his earldom will most likely be revoked so as not to cause scandal. Broadbent stands to inherit everything so long as the earl dies in hiding."

"So, Broadbent has ulterior motive for keeping Whitmore's location secret. Very well. But how does this involve Miss Iverson?" Cornwall asked. "Why attack her?"

"Because I love her," Gavin answered. "And I have devoted the last six months to finding the earl. He knew he only needed a few more days to claim his inheritance. I was getting close. Broadbent orchestrated this attack to distract me. Miss Iverson is not to blame for any of it." His deep voice shook with the power of his words. For the first time in the interview, Grace was forced to suppress tears from escaping. She was successful until Gavin placed his hands on her shoulders. His thumbs, concealed from Mr. Cornwall, were caressing the tender part of her neck where it was exposed. Her lip shook, refusing to heed her efforts to control it.

Mr. Cornwall looked at her sympathetically for the first time. He closed his book and put his pencil in his jacket. "I have what I need for now," he announced. "There are, however, some inconsistencies between Miss Iverson's story and what I have already discovered. I will need to make further inquiries."

Silence asked, "May I assist you?"

"No. I will try to call again this afternoon when I have more information. Do not go anywhere, Miss Iverson." He stood and bowed to Grace and then shook both the gentlemen's hands before departing.

Besides lifting his hand to shake Mr. Cornwall's hand, Gavin hadn't removed his hands from her neck. As soon as Silence escorted Mr. Cornwall from the room, Grace recoiled from Gavin's hands and stood up.

"Excuse me," she sniffed.

"Grace," he pleaded. She turned her treacherous heart toward his kind voice and looked at him. "I am so sorry for what happened in the carriage. Fresden was a detestable man. I should have protected you instead of abandoning you. Please forgive me."

"There is nothing to discuss here."

"For once in your life, just accept that people are human and make mistakes! Please! I sincerely regret that I allowed myself to be jealous of Mr. Broadbent. You have always been my Gigi. It never occurred to me that your heart might have been touched by someone else. But I was wrong, and I am deeply sorry. I should never have said those things at the ball. It is entirely my fault that you left early. It is my fault that I was not there to escort you home. It is my fault that I stopped the carriage so abruptly. I killed him."

Grace deliberated for an extended moment. Could she trust him? He certainly sounded sincere, but actions spoke louder than words. "I have already endured a great deal this morning," she announced. "Please excuse me, Your Grace. I would like to return to my chambers."

"Gigi, please—" But she did not wait to hear his plea. She had heard enough to know her heart was far too fragile to look at the situation logically. She could not let her emotions lead her into trouble again. As she hurried up the stairs, she thought, *I love you too, Gavin. But I cannot entrust my heart to you again, even if it still beats only for you.*

CHAPTER 18

The rest of the day was torture for Gavin. Several guests from last night's ball tried to call on Grace—some only eager, no doubt, to hear what had happened. He was sorely tempted to remove the knocker and barricade himself inside, but he had to be available for Mr. Cornwall. He put up with the first two calls, but after that, he simply told Robison to tell everyone he was unavailable. It wouldn't look good, but he didn't really care anymore. Grace took luncheon in her room. His mother had heard of the scandal, of course. But when she saw the misery in Gavin's eyes, she had blessedly little to say on the matter. "Do not lose her again, Gavin," she warned.

Cornwall finally called just before six o'clock.

"Come in, Mr. Cornwall," Gavin replied. "Robison, take his hat and coat."

"I tried, Your Grace. He says he does not intend to stay. He only has a few questions for Miss Iverson."

Gavin did not like the sound of that. Perhaps he was being paranoid, but the magistrate didn't look like he had good news to report. He dispatched Robison to fetch Grace and then turned to Mr. Cornwall. "Did you speak with Broadbent?" Gavin asked.

"I would prefer to wait for Miss Iverson, sir. No sense in repeating myself."

A quiet engulfed the room. Mr. Cornwall took off his hat and seemed to give the rim of it a great deal of attention. He kept glancing at the door of the study as if the Prince Regent were expected to walk in at any moment and Cornwall did not wish to miss the grand entrance.

Gavin sat at his desk and spent a few minutes shuffling papers and rearranging his paperweights. The tick of the clock began to irritate him. After a few minutes, he finally asked, "Are you sure there is nothing I can get you? Some tea perhaps?"

"No, Your Grace," Cornwall replied brusquely.

"Well, perhaps I should go and check on Miss Iverson." He stood and took three steps toward the door just as a groggy, starry-eyed Grace walked in, still fixing the pins in her hair.

"Forgive me, sir," she addressed the magistrate. "I was resting when you called." She brought her hands back down at her sides and curtsied.

Mr. Cornwall made a slight bow, and Gavin motioned for everyone to sit down. They all took their seats. Mr. Cornwall began, "Miss Iverson, did Mr. Broadbent give you any money in the time that he courted you?"

A strange look flashed in her eyes, and she tilted her head to the side. "I fail to see your meaning, sir," she responded.

"I see," Cornwall muttered. He looked down to make some notes on his paper. "He claims you conned him out of a thousand pounds over the course of several months. Do you deny it?"

"Did he say why I would do such a thing?"

Gavin couldn't help but notice that Grace hadn't directly refuted the statement.

Mr. Cornwall frowned. "Apparently you were in dire financial straits and could not access your dowry until after your marriage."

"Well, the same could be said for many debutantes," Grace replied. "Why on earth would I take money from him? And what would I spend it on? A few dresses? A thousand pounds would buy dozens of wardrobes. I had no need for a thousand pounds. He is lying." Just hearing her say it was a relief. Gavin sighed quietly, but apparently not quietly enough, because it drew her attention, and he was the recipient of a very dark look.

Cornwall turned to Gavin and asked, "Have you provided any financial support to Miss Iverson?"

"No," Gavin insisted.

"And have you given things to her? Supplied her wardrobe perhaps?"

"Certainly not. My mother has purchased some dresses for her, but I have never given Miss Iverson so much as a farthing. And she has never asked me for one. How do these questions pertain to Lord Randall's death?"

"Well, it seems that Miss Iverson is a swindler," Cornwall announced. Gavin heard Grace gasp beside him. "Three years ago she conned Broadbent out of a thousand pounds. When he confronted her about it, she ran away to Sussex. He never saw her nor his money again—not until last night, that is. And Lady Monique claims to have heard Miss Iverson attempting to blackmail Lord Randall to the tune of five hundred pounds. It appears that is why she joined him in the carriage last night. I am afraid to tell you, Your Grace, but Miss Iverson has probably been playing on your sympathies to pad her pocketbook."

Grace jumped up from her chair, her face turning an immediate deep red. "Blackmail Lord Randall? How? I hardly knew the man! When he offered me his carriage, I could not even recall his full name! This is preposterous! Gavin, it is a lie. I swear it."

Gavin stood as well and walked toward her. "I know, Grace. Sit down. I do not doubt you in any way."

"Yes, you do! You doubted me at the ball. And you doubted me again just now. I heard you sigh!"

"Please, sit down, Gigi." Gavin guided her to the sofa, and he sat beside her and took her hand in his. He gave her a reassuring look and then turned to Cornwall and stiffly said, "This is unbelievable. How can you make such an accusation?"

Cornwall pulled out his notebook. "Your Grace, I have confirmed it with both Mr. Broadbent and Lady Monique," he explained, "as well as a Timothy Gardner."

"Tim?" Gavin asked in surprise. "My footman? Where does he come in to all this?"

Cornwall began to read from his notes. "Let me see, 'I have seen Miss Iverson in private company with the duke on more than one occasion.' He agrees she has used her womanly arts and allurements to entrap you into proposing." Cornwall looked up and added, "He says he discovered the two of you in, shall we say, improper circumstances in the music room a few days ago. Is that true?"

"This is outrageous! How can—" Grace began, but Gavin's eyes pleaded with her to stop.

"Yes," Gavin admitted, "I admit he walked in on something a few days ago, but Miss Iverson did not entrap me. I have known her for years. I love her, and I cannot imagine a life without her by my side. She has accepted my suit regardless of my being a bacon-brained ninny. I will give you my word as a duke that she is no swindler. Is that clear?"

Mr. Cornwall seemed unconvinced. "If that were all the evidence, Your Grace," he continued, "then I would dismiss Broadbent's claims. But you should know, Your Grace, that Mr. Gardner produced bank notes signed by Lord Randall in the amounts of—let me see—three hundred forty pounds. He says he found these notes in Miss Iverson's chambers early this morning."

Gavin's face paled. *But how can that be true? Why would she have Fresden's bank notes in her room?* He turned to look at her, trying to hide his confusion. "Grace?" he whispered.

Grace's eyes filled with tears. She stared at Gavin as they spilled onto her cheeks, her pain written on her face. Then she ripped her hand away from his. "I see," she muttered. Gavin felt panic rise in him. She stood up and wiped away her tears and turned to face Mr. Cornwall. "Sir, I swear to you, I had nothing to do with those bank notes," she declared icily. "Have you checked the signatures?"

Cornwall flustered a bit. "No, not yet," he said. "It was my intent to see how you reacted to the facts—"

"How I reacted to the facts? What facts are you speaking of, Mr. Cornwall? All you have is the word of a meddling footman, a lying suitor, and a mistress! And based on that, you have accused me of murder, blackmail, and theft!"

Cornwall sputtered, "I was not accusing you, madam."

"By gads! Yes, you most certainly were!" She cursed under her breath. "I will not submit myself to this scrutiny a moment longer," she protested. "If either of you wish to doubt my integrity further, you can find me at my sister's house."

"Grace!" Gavin ran after her, but she kept up her pace and walked right out the front door. He had no choice; he quickly found Robison and asked for her pelisse and bonnet. He caught up to her two blocks down the street.

Her hair had fallen down around her face, and she held her arms tightly to block out the chill from the October wind. The skies threatened a drenching at any moment. He already felt a few drops on his face. He gently draped the pelisse around her shoulders, and she slowed her stride and then came to a complete stop. Wordlessly, she put on her pelisse and bonnet, shoving the loose hair in.

A burst of lightening reminded them of the storm's impending arrival. He could literally see the sheets of rain moving toward them. He took her hand and pulled her into the nearest store. It was a bakery, and it smelled like cinnamon. It smelled like Grace.

He guided her toward the back, where there was an empty table. "Sit down, Grace."

She was obedient but refused to look at him. He took her chin in his hand and guided her face in his direction. Their eyes locked, and he looked in her eyes. There was every kind of pain imaginable in their blue depths.

"Blue as bluebells in rain or shine."

"Stop it, Gavin."

"I love you, Grace. I swear to you that I know you are innocent. I know that you are no mercenary. I am sorry." She pulled away from his reach but made no reply. "I will prove that those bank notes were forged," he continued. "Timothy was about to be let go, and he knew it. A few days after you arrived, he was found in a compromising position with a housemaid. I thought I had fixed the situation. But a real duke would have fired him on the spot. My mother was right; I have done nothing worthy of a duke's title." He was so ashamed that he wanted to look away, but he was a weak man. Her glossed-over eyes turned back to him, filled to the brim with unshed tears. They were searching his for something. Whatever she was looking for, he would give.

*****

Grace listened to his impassioned self-depreciating speech. This was not the overly confident man-boy she had always known.

He seemed to ache with grief over his brother's and father's deaths. It was just how she ached when she thought of her mother and father. As she looked in his eyes, she saw a glimpse of the suffering he endured over the last six months. She recognized an element of desperation.

"Please, Grace. Give me another chance." He stopped talking and just looked at her. How could she deny him the deepest desire of her heart? The ache inside grew until she could hold her tongue no more.

"Do not fail me this time, Gavin. I cannot endure it again."

"And if I can prove you innocent?"

She owed him honesty. "I still do not know if I can marry you. You must understand that."

"Thank you. I do understand. But come back to the house with me. Please do not go. Do not leave me like this."

She took a deep breath and nodded. He possessively took her arm in his and covered her hand with his other hand. His grip was strong and confident. They hurried toward Willsing Manor but did not beat the rain, which quickly turned into sleet. He tried to shield her from the worst of it, but it was coming in sideways, and Grace could have sworn it was seeping into every crease of her gown. Her slippers were soaked through.

She had not realized how far she had walked. By the time they reached Willsing Manor, there was not a dry bone in her body. Her nose was icy, and she could not feel her toes.

They entered, and a sneeze suddenly snuck up on her; she couldn't hold it back.

"Bless you. You should have a warm bath." He helped her remove her saturated pelisse and bonnet, and she sneezed again.

Robison announced, "Mr. Silence is waiting for you, sir." Gavin nodded and then informed the housemaid that Grace would need Charlotte and hot water for a bath immediately. As Grace started to head upstairs, Gavin put his hand on her arm. "Thank you for giving me another chance. I will not let you down. Not this time."

We shall see.

*****

Gavin watched her walk upstairs. Robison handed him a hand towel, and he dried his face and hair. "Send my man up to my chambers. Tell Silence to meet me there too."

"Yes, Your Grace." Robison motioned to one of the footman, who went directly to the servants' quarters.

He turned back around to Robison. "And I wish to speak with Tim in the library. Tell him I will see him when I see him; he is to wait there, and not leave, until I come. Is that clear?"

"Of course, sir."

As he was heading upstairs, Silence caught up and said, "Good, you are home. I caught Cornwall on his way out. He told me everything." He then seemed to take in his saturated appearance and added, "Should I wait outside while you change?"

"I am not shy if you are not."

Silence snickered a little and followed him up to his chambers. Gavin struggled with the wet cravat. Silence took a position at the window and said, "Your man will not appreciate the state of that knot in your cravat. Silks have a tendency to be devilishly stubborn."

Gavin pulled harder in frustration.

"I take it Grace is the source of your dispute with that garment. Perhaps you should leave that particular entanglement to Winston and tell me what has you all tied up."

Gavin rolled his eyes and started pulling off his jacket. "I will lose her if I cannot prove her innocence. How much did Cornwall tell you?"

"About Broadbent's accusation that she was mercenary. And about how your man supposedly found bank notes in her chambers."

"Yes, but I do not see how Tim could have found them. He is never supposed to be in that part of the house. He is only a footman." He threw his jacket on the bed and then thought better of it and moved it to the ottoman. Winston would not appreciate wet clothing on the bed.

Gavin continued talking while he worked on his boots. "Besides, a few days ago, Tim was found cavorting with a housemaid. I reprimanded him and put him on probation. Since then he has done nothing more than serve meals and haul dishes to the kitchen. Mrs. Bearl and Robison have made sure of it."

"So then the bank notes were falsified."

"There is no doubt about it. We just need a way to prove it. Do we have Fresden's signature or Broadbent's handwriting anywhere?"

"Both regularly placed bets at White's. His name would be sprawled all over the books. Cornwall and I could verify it within a half hour. He was headed in that direction. What else?"

Winston's knock was heard, and Gavin gave the command to enter. "Winston, you tied a devilishly tight knot, and I am in a hurry."

He lifted his chin while Winston went to work. He turned his head toward Silence. "If I can get Tim to admit he planted those bank notes, and you can prove that Broadbent forged Fresden's signature, I might have a chance of winning Grace back." Gavin paused. "She withdrew her consent."

"Really?"

"More or less. I really made a mess of things at the ball. I have always been too hasty to follow my emotions. But she is different. She uses her head. She is probably drafting a pro and con list about me as we speak. If I cannot make her think with her heart, and quickly, I might lose her," he sighed. "I can see what she is planning. As soon as I sort out this murder charge, she intends to walk right out that door and leave me forever." Winston removed the last of the confining garment, and Gavin pulled his shirt up over his head. Avoiding looking at Silence, he added, "She thought I believed Cornwall's accusations."

Silence walked around into his line of sight, tilted his head to the side, and then dropped his jaw. "Kingston! Do not bother defending yourself," he reprimanded. "I can see the guilt in your eyes!"

Winston gasped and froze. Gavin took the new shirt from Winston's out-stretched hand and hastily threw it over his head, if for nothing else but to break the accusatory glares Silence and Winston were giving him.

"You are done for now," Silence warned.

Gavin turned to Winston and said, "Hurry please. I have a great deal of work to do." Then turning toward Silence he said, "Perhaps I let out my breath a little too loudly when she finally denied the accusations."

Silence whistled. "Well, I have work to do as well. And you might consider practicing your groveling."

*****

Part of Grace was grateful to be back at Willsing Manor. But the last twenty-four hours had been so demanding. She feared the stress of it was wearing down on her, even making her ill.

She and Gavin had come to a compromise of sorts. Along the freezing walk back, he had begged her to stay one more night. He said that all he needed was another day to clear her name and prove he was trustworthy. He had again tried to apologize, but she would not have it. It only confused her more to hear him try to explain it away. She was torn. Her heart felt as fragile as ice upon a lake after the first hard freeze. It was so much safer to hope for an undeniable freeze, to break things off irrevocably with Gavin, rather than risk falling through into the freezing water.

As Charlotte helped her into the bathwater, she pondered her predicament. Trusting Gavin again went against every instinct. All her life, she had never depended on anyone but herself. She was a strong woman who never so much as wanted a lady's maid. And look at what she had become in such a short time. *After one week at Willsing Manor, I can't even dress myself anymore.*

How could she have let down her guard so willingly? And she had to admit that she had done it willingly. She always loved Gavin, but she had let her love for him change from childhood friendship into a desperate longing, an overwhelming need.

The thought struck her with such power. She needed Gavin! She was not the kind of woman who needed anyone! She was not some simpering female who measured her self-worth by whose arm she was on at the moment.

She shook her head. There was no way she would ever need a man. It was too much risk. She had risked giving her heart to Gavin, and he had assumed the worst. He had assumed that she had not kept her virtue with Mr. Broadbent. He had thought her a fortune-hunter.

And when Cornwell had accused her of trying to blackmail Broadbent and Lord Randall, he had held his breath as if his very life hung on her answer. His relieved sigh had destroyed her last bit of hope for their happily-ever-after. It hurt her deeply. And that kind of pain she could do without! Lord Randall and Broadbent were both sinister, greedy men. But what they did to her was nothing compared to the pain she felt when she remembered how Gavin had doubted her, not once, but multiple times.

And now he knew what had happened in the carriage. She wondered if he only apologized for what he said at the ball out of guilt. *Does he pity me now? Does he feel guilty his angry words pushed me into that carriage? Is that the extent of his love—pity and guilt?*

It certainly felt like it. And she was not going to start a marriage based on that.

I love him too much to let him do that. He deserves better. He deserves someone who is not bathed in scandal. By now all of London probably knew of the incident with Lord Randall. And from the sounds of Mr. Cornwall's questioning, more lies were being added to the story every hour. How could she bind herself to the Duke of Huntsman and tarnish his reputation like that? Even if he was sincere and had only acted stupidly out of jealousy, his life could be ruined by her scandal.

As she stepped out of the bathwater, she saw that Charlotte had laid out another fine dress, one she had not worn yet. She looked at the pale ivory muslin with the silk forest-green ribbon at its waist, and she knew she could not wear it.

"No, Charlotte. I want to wear the dress I came here in." She had made her decision. She would leave.

"The gray one? But I could not remove all of the dirt from your fall."

"Yes. That is what I came here in; that is what I will leave here in. I shall not be taking those new dresses with me."

"You are leaving, miss?"

"Yes. Please start packing my trunk with the things I brought from my sister's house. Everything that the duchess bought me may be sent to charity."

"Oh, no, Miss Iverson! Please do not go—"

"The gray dress, Charlotte."

"Yes, ma'am."

Charlotte did not say another word. It was rare that Grace set boundaries with Charlotte. She had been a most loyal servant, and it had been so nice to have her own personal maid. Charlotte finished buttoning the back of the dress and then set to do her hair.

"No, I will fix my hair myself." Grace could see the displeasure on Charlotte's face.

There was nothing more to say. Goodbyes were not Grace's strength. She would not waste her efforts in saying goodbye to Charlotte when she would need every bit of her fortitude to say goodbye to Gavin.

When she was finished, Grace looked in the mirror. She felt ten years older than she was, but at the same time, she felt like a little girl again, with all the pain of ten years ago. Her thoughts returned to those first few months when she had waited by the window, eagerly watching the road for a message from him. When she wasn't digging for potatoes in the cold ground, she would write long letters to Gavin telling him how much she missed him. She would have to be stronger this time. She could not return to that same lost, lonely soul.

Enough of that! You survived before; you will survive again. At least this time you will be able to say goodbye. But she wasn't sure that would make it any easier.

With new determination, she fortified herself and walked out of her chambers. At the top of the stairs, she paused to look down at the enormous marble entryway. Gavin was right; the stairs were very tightly wound and did not make good use of the space. There were two tables with fresh flowers along the sides, but other than that, the room was empty. Sconces were lit on the walls, giving it a soft, welcoming look. She was surprised how quickly Willsing Manor had begun to feel like home. She would miss it.

She began her descent. With each step, she hardened her heart to what she would be facing. He might care for her, but that didn't mean she could trust him. Another step.

It could be as simple as telling him she did not want to ruin his reputation. He could hardly afford another scandal. Another two steps.

Besides, it would be too painful for him to align himself with any woman who had nearly married the future Earl of Longmont. One more.

He probably wished to be released from the engagement now anyway. She was doing him a favor. Two more steps.

Informing him of her decision would just save him the discomfort of asking her to leave. Another step.

He might inquire as to her purity. She knew he was jealous of her relationship with Broadbent. She still hadn't disclosed the truth, as chaste as it was. That took three steps and stole her breath, because if he asked that, it would confirm that he did not trust her. She would have to be strong. Stronger than she had ever been.

Even if he still felt obligated to marry her, she couldn't let that happen. Two more steps.

There were just a few more steps to go. She paused, closed her eyes, and prayed.

Give me the grace to handle this. Help me to do what is right. Help me to free him from the only thing I ever wanted. She took a deep breath and stepped down to the landing. She was ready.

"Do you feel better, Gigi?" She was startled to hear Gavin's voice behind her. Twirling around, she saw him under the stairs. He stepped into the candlelight. "Come, sit with me," he coaxed. He took her arm and led her to a small sofa under the stairs that she had never noticed was there. Perhaps he had just moved it there. She took a seat and braced herself. Should she start, or should she let him ask the questions?

Their silence filled the small, dark corner. She could read each and every curve of his face in this soft candlelight. He was incredibly handsome. He smelled heavenly. This was going to be the hardest thing she had ever done.

"You used to wear your hair like this when we were children," he observed. "Do you usually do it this way?"

"Yes," she admitted. "I do not have Charlotte's skill for embellishment."

He leaned in and smelled her tresses. "Mmm . . . cinnamon. Such a relaxing and comforting smell. The cook cannot understand why I suddenly want cinnamon desserts every day. I just cannot get enough of the smell."

"Gavin, please do not make this harder than it is."

"Make what harder? I am just saying that I adore the way you smell."

"We both know that we can never be."

"Hmm . . . Is that so?" Gavin murmured.

"Yes."

"Why is that, Gigi?"

"Do not call me that."

"Why not? You never cared before."

Grace stood and said, "I cannot do this. I cannot sit here and listen to you say sweet things only to break my heart. I know you think I was improper with Mr. Broadbent. And Fresden has ruined my reputation. You could never bind yourself with me now. So, let us say it plainly."

"And how would you say it, Grace?" his voice was soft and velvety in the darkness.

She stepped away and turned to leave, but he restrained her arm. She pleaded, "Please . . . just allow me the chance to say goodbye this time. Let me have a little dignity."

"Is that what you want? To say goodbye?"

She wanted to shake her head violently, but all she could do was blink back tears. She had lost herself in his arms twice already, once in the carriage and once again in her chambers. She was not sure she was strong enough to endure his kindnesses a third time. "I am sorry, I cannot do this. Goodbye, Gavin." She shook off his arm and walked toward the stairs to do one last sweep of her room.

"To the death!"

She froze with one foot on the first stair. "What did you say?" she whispered.

"I challenge you to the death." His voice was stern and commanded her attention. For the first time, he sounded like a duke.

"You cannot be serious."

"I am more serious than I have ever been. But instead of climbing the ladder to the treehouse, we will use these stairs. You know the rules, Gigi. You must be honest with me. Every. Single. Step. If I suspect you are hiding something or not being honest, you must let go and *fall to your death*." The last part was said with emphasis.

Yes, she remembered the rules. She knew that it was a game that he had invented to make her confide in him, to make them trust each other. If she were dishonest, then she had to let go and hope that he would catch her. "I know the rules."

"And I know you never back down from a challenge."

"Of course not, but, Gavin, this is a childhood game. We are adults now."

"Adults who have had far too many missed opportunities. Ten years' worth. So I challenge you to the death."

"If I reach the top, will you let me go?"

He paused. "If that is what you want," he replied. It wasn't what she wanted, but it had to be done.

She turned her back to him and took a step. "I accept," she said over her shoulder. It was easier not to look at his face.

There was a prolonged moment before he began. "Did you truly sing *The True Lover's Farewell* during those ten years when you missed me?"

"Yes. I always thought of you when I sang that song."

"You may step up." She did so. "If you had known I was the Duke of Huntsman, would you have sought me out sooner?"

She swallowed her pride and answered as honestly as possible. "I always hoped I would find you again, and I wish I had sought you out—but not because of your title. That means nothing to me."

"I believe you. Step up." He stepped onto the step behind her. She could feel the heat from his body, and it stirred her. Tiny sparks surged between them.

"What are you doing, Gavin?"

"I am just getting ready to catch you."

"Are you afraid I will be dishonest?"

"I think you are afraid to be honest with yourself."

"Continue with the challenge. I never back down."

"Very well. Before I ask this next question, let me preface it by saying that I did more research on the biblical definition of grace."

She spun around in surprise only to find she was nearly lip to lip with him. She quickly turned her back to him again. "You mean you studied it more since we talked before the ball?"

"Yes. I even had a discussion with Winston. But this was my challenge, so I get to ask the questions. Are you ready?"

"Yes." She put one foot on the next stair, making a slightly larger gap between them.

"Not so fast. I have not asked my question yet. According to the Bible, the grace of God is something that can never be taken away, no matter how grievously one sins. In fact, it is the very thing that saves us. Regardless of whether I have lived a perfect life or sinned every sin known to mankind, I would still need and qualify for God's grace. Do you believe that?"

"Yes."

"Take a step." She did so, and he followed with one of his own. His breath was warm on her neck. She involuntarily shivered. "Grace, I am not perfect. I failed you. It was wrong of me not to trust you."

"Yes, it was."

"That deserves a step," he chuckled, and she stepped up. His tone became more serious again. "But are you really so afraid to forgive me that you are willing to say goodbye forever?"

It was the moment she dreaded. He had asked for honesty—it was the very rules of the game—and she had to decide what to do. Did she trust him? She put a hand on the rail, and he put his hand right over hers, making their entire arms brush up against each other. She closed her eyes and spoke. "Everyone in my life has failed me. I always told myself that you were the exception, that you had not really abandoned me. But you chose to think the worst about me. I do not know what hurt worse—wondering if you ever loved me, or realizing that your love was not strong enough."

There was silence for a full half a minute. His hand squeezed hers, and she felt a pressure on her back encouraging another step so she stepped up, and he followed. He moved his other hand down to her waist. It was as if they were dancing the waltz with her turned the wrong way.

"Do you love me?"

She did not hesitate on this question. "I will never love another more." The honesty was getting easier. She was nearly half way to the top now. Freedom was a few questions away.

"You may step up two steps because I like that answer so much."

Did he wish her to reach the top?

Gavin squeezed her hand and asked, "Is there any hope for you to forgive me?"

This question was a hard one. "Gavin, I know my limits. I must depend on my own strength."

"That was not entirely forthcoming. I will give you one more try."

"Very well. It would take some time, but yes, I could forgive you."

He squeezed her hand again, and she took that as an indicator to step up. When he followed this time he moved his hand on her waist around to her front and pulled her up against his chest. She resisted the urge to melt into the curves of his body. He whispered into her ear, sending tingles and goose bumps up and down her body, "Grace."

"Yes?" she managed to breathlessly whisper.

"I was not calling your name. I am begging you for grace. Grace is when you have done all you can do and someone else makes up the difference. I know I failed you. I am so sorry. I have apologized for being a muttonhead. I have done all I can to seek your forgiveness. Now I need your grace, Gigi. Please."

"I will never hurt you again," he vowed. "I swear it made me more unhappy than I have ever been. Now that I have had a week with you under my roof, there will be nothing to live for without you. We belong together. I need you. And needing someone is loving someone. Please tell me you need me too. I need my best friend to hold me when I am sad, to challenge me when I am bacon-brained, to correct me when I am in error, to give me confidence when I am in doubt. I have done all I can do, but now I need *your* grace."

Slowly her body relaxed at his tender words. He nestled his face in her neck, placing tantalizing kisses on it. The heat from his lips purged her of all the fear she ever had. "I need you too. I love you, Gavin."

He took their hands off the rail and wrapped them around her front, clasping her tightly. He gently squeezed her hands and said, "I am afraid to tell you to step up, but I know that to be an honest answer."

Together they stepped up, their bodies as one.

His lips traveled up to her ear, and he nibbled on the lobe. Gavin paused momentarily and said, "I love you too. You are so very dear to me. Please say you will not leave me again. I cannot endure another goodbye. I shall fight for your heart every day. I will be worthy of your trust. I will never fail you again. Will you,

Grace Ingrid Genevieve Iverson, marry me? Please, Gigi. What can I say to make you stay? Tell me what you want, anything, and I will deliver it to your hands."

She stepped up two steps, extracting herself from his arms, leaving only one stair left before the top. She turned toward him. Every sense was piqued. She knew she owed him full honesty for her two premature steps. "Kiss me. Kiss me, Your Grace, and I will marry you."

His voice was deep and husky as he murmured, "I cannot deliver that to your hands."

He reached toward her face and, as smoothly and gracefully as she had ever seen him move, he glided the last two steps between them. Their chests were nearly touching, and he gazed so lovingly in her eyes that fire surged through her as she prepared for what was coming. He tilted her head, and their lips met. They merged together so well that they could not decipher where one began and the other ended. They were one, as it should be. They both took the last step and reached the top.

Suddenly every vacant, lonely part of her heart disappeared, and she was filled with his grace. He had saved her in every way.

CHAPTER 19

Gavin kissed her with all the passion he had held back for ten years. He had known she would try to leave. But despite everything that had happened in the last two days—and despite the lonely years apart, the drinking, and the foreign ladies—she had forgiven him. She loved him like he had always loved her. It seemed inconceivable that he deserved someone so brave and valiant.

He heard a ruckus down the hall but decided that claiming her lips a half a second longer was worth the risk of being seen. When he did pull away, the shadows on her face gave her an angelic glow. He smirked and rubbed his fingers across her cheek, which prompted her to open her groggy eyes. He was struck with the vision in front of him, but the ruckus was getting louder.

He turned to look down the hall and saw her trunks being hauled out of her chambers. Grace noticed it as well, and if her cheeks were not rosy from the kisses, they were now aglow with mortification.

"I suppose we have several things to discuss," Grace said.

"There is nothing to discuss." Gavin took her hand, and together they walked down the hall. "If those are Grace's trunks, you may unpack them. She is not leaving," he instructed Charlotte.

Grace pulled on his hand, "Gavin, I cannot stay here if we are engaged."

"You most certainly can! My mother is a fine chaperone; if you have any doubt, I am sure she would be eager to review the rules again." Grace looked unswayed by his reasoning. "Gigi, I do not care if I have to hire a dozen armed nuns to chaperone you day and night, but I have no intention of letting you out of my sight. Perhaps I could rent an entire convent. Would you feel better if I invited the Archbishop of Canterbury to stay?"

Grace rolled her eyes at him. "Gavin, are you familiar with the legal definition of 'imprisonment'?" she giggled. "I cannot stay here!"

He ignored her and turned again toward the servant. "Grace and I would like tea in the library. Please inform my mother that she is welcome to come scrutinize us. And do unpack that thing and take it all the way up to the attic. I do not wish to see it again for many months."

"Yes, Your Grace."

"Come," he informed Grace, "we can discuss the details of your nunnery guard tomorrow. Right now we have a footman to interview."

They walked together back to the narrow, tightly wound staircase. Gavin graciously let her go first.

She paused halfway down and put her hand to her nose. The daintiest sneeze escaped. "Pardon me. I fear I may be catching a cold."

"You should drink peppermint tea. It clears the sinuses."

She giggled and replied, "Thank you, doctor."

He chuckled. "Could you not let me feel for just a moment longer that I had the world by the tail? Must you always measure, weigh, and dissect my ego?"

Giggling, she looked over her shoulder and said, "What kind of wife would be if I did that?" They reached the bottom of the stairs, and she turned and put her hands on her hips. "You love that about me."

He tried not to smile. He took the very hips she was using to make her point, and pulling them toward to him, he smothered her with kisses again. He gave her hips a squeeze and said, "I love everything about you. Do not ever forget it."

Her eyes smiled back at him, and he guided her the rest of the way to the library. As they entered, Tim jumped up from his sitting position and bowed stiffly.

"Your Grace, Miss Iverson, forgive me," he stammered. "I was summoned to the library an hour ago and was told to wait until you arrived."

Gavin did not acknowledge his tardiness nor Tim's apology, but Grace did. "Hello, Timothy," she said kindly. "I am sorry to have kept you waiting. Have a seat." The tea was brought in, and Grace poured some tea for Tim, who took it warily.

"Thank you," he replied.

Gavin wanted to demand answers, but something told him to let Grace guide this interrogation. She started by asking about Tim's family. Her words were considerate and attentive, as if she truly cared about them. Tim's tone soon softened to match hers.

"My ma is all alone now," Tim confided. "My pa took an early grave a few months back. My younger sister is hoping to find a place to offer her services. She is a fine seamstress."

"What is your sister's name?"

"Alice."

"What a beautiful name! I suppose your mother and sister must be very proud of you and your position here."

"Very much so. When I visit on Sundays, they drill me with questions about what it is like to work for a duke."

"I am sure you bring home a few entertaining stories."

"No, ma'am," Tim insisted. "I am very careful with what I share. My job is very important to me."

Gavin tried not to scoff and managed, through sheer willpower, to keep a straight face. Apparently he made some slight sound, because Grace flashed him a look to silence him.

"I can see that," Grace replied to Tim. "Would you like a biscuit? They are delightful. Or perhaps you prefer scones?"

"Cook's scones are unbeatable. Thank you."

Grace allowed him a moment to eat. Gavin leaned back, marveling. *She is handling him with all the grace of a duchess.* She seemed to know intuitively what to do. It couldn't be easy for her, Gavin knew, facing the man who had framed her for blackmail. If she couldn't get Tim's confession, she might be brought up on charges, or even go to prison. And yet she was as confident and polite as ever.

They chatted a bit more about inconsequential things until Grace said, "Thank you for meeting with us. I wanted to get to know you a bit. I do not know whether you have heard, but His Grace has made me an offer. We are to be married," she smiled.

Tim face was a mixture of fear and surprise. "I had not heard that. Congratulations are in order."

"Do you know what this means, Tim?"

He at least had the humility to flush crimson. "I believe so. You shall be mistress."

"It is hard for me to imagine such a thing, but yes. I shall be the one making decisions from day to day within the household. I am sure I could find a position for your sister Alice. Would you like that?"

Tim put his cup down and slowly raised his eyes to meet hers. "Miss Iverson, your kindness is surprising. When I saw you walk in here with the duke, I was fairly sure you had come to dismiss me. I do not think I would have been so forgiving."

"What is there to forgive?" Tim flushed again but made no reply. "Are you referring to the banknotes that you supposedly found in my chambers?"

Gavin sat up a little straighter, earning Tim's attention momentarily.

"I never said I found them in your chambers," Tim stammered. "A gentleman told me you dropped them as you were leaving the ball. He said that unless I wanted to get caught up in a murder investigation, I would turn them over to the magistrate as evidence. But when I did, Mr. Cornwall asked all sorts of questions about how I found them. He assumed they were from your chambers—it was like he already knew all about them—and I didn't dare correct him. I was afraid that if I told the truth, he would get suspicious. I can't afford to get mixed up in a murder investigation, Miss Iverson. I swear I had nothing to do with Lord Randall's death."

"I believe you, Tim. What happened next?" Her voice was smooth and reassuring. Gavin knew he wouldn't have been able to speak so calmly in her place.

"Well, Mr. Cornwall asked if I had ever seen you and the duke together. I told him you were alone together all the time. I'm sorry to say this, but he asked if I had ever seen you and the duke together in a romantic way. I had to tell him about the time I walked in on you in the music room. He is a law man after all."

"It is all right, Tim. You were just answering his questions. It sounds as if Mr. Cornwall had his suspicions already. Do you think someone told him about the banknotes before you turned them in?"

"It sure seemed like it." Tim looked to Gavin. "Am I going to be dismissed?"

Grace answered for him. "No, Tim. But I need you to go with the duke and tell the truth to Mr. Cornwall right away."

Gavin was in awe of the way Grace had pulled the truth from Tim without ever accusing him or putting him on the defensive.

Gavin stood and shook Tim's hand. "We have work to do. Grab your coat."

"Yes, Your Grace." He turned to Grace and asked her, "Were they not your banknotes?"

"No, Tim, they were not. But I think I know who gave them to you."

*****

Gavin watched Tim wrap his light coat tighter around himself. Gavin asked, "Do not have a warmer coat?"

"No, sir. I have been saving up for one. I was hoping for another month's wages before winter set in. But it's no matter, sir. My shaking has more to do with my nerves than the weather. Where are we going?"

"Mr. Broadbent's townhouse. I sent word for the magistrate to meet us there. I want you to go to the servants' entrance, and when the time is right, I will have you summoned. I am fairly confident that the man who gave you the notes will be there. All you have to do is identify him before the magistrate, and I will handle the rest." Gavin didn't come out and say whom he suspected. He did not wish to plant any assumptions in Tim's mind. If Tim identified Mr. Broadbent on his own, then the case against him would be irrefutable.

Tim's eyes widened. "I will do my best."

"That is all anyone could ask of you."

They pulled up to the townhouse, and Tim raked his hat into his hands and said, "Thank you, Your Grace, for giving me this chance to help Miss Iverson. I didn't realize how much trouble those banknotes would cause."

"You can thank Miss Iverson for believing in you. I cannot say I would have been so generous in her place. Have you been staying away from Helena like you promised?"

"Yes, sir. I haven't even looked her in the eye since we talked. I haven't been alone in the same room as her either. You were right. She is mighty beautiful, but a gentleman would never have done what I did. She is safe from me."

"Good. Go in through the servant's entrance, and if anyone asks, just tell them you are with me and that it was too cold to wait in the carriage. Do not say anything else about why you are here. Do you understand?"

"Of course."

They exited and went their separate ways. Just as Gavin was about to knock, another carriage pulled up. Silence and Cornwall stepped out. The magistrate was carrying a heavy black valise and did not look pleased. Gavin took off his hat and bowed as they came up the steps.

Silence announced, "We just came from White's."

"And did you find anything?" he asked.

Cornwall cleared his throat and said, "Your theory was correct. The handwriting on the notes is quite similar to Mr. Broadbent's hand. The f is identical, and the slant is telling. Mr. Silence told me that you spoke with Timothy Gardner as well."

"Indeed," Gavin said. "He came here with me. He is waiting in the servants' quarters, ready to identify the man who gave him the banknotes." Gavin cleared his throat and added, "Tim also said he never told you that the notes were in Miss Iverson's chambers."

"Yes," Mr. Cornwall admitted. "It seems I owe you and Miss Iverson an apology. Mr. Broadbent told me that Mr. Gardner had found some damning evidence in Miss Iverson's room. When I questioned Mr. Gardner, I jumped to the wrong conclusion. Be assured I will not make the same mistake again."

Silence chuckled, "Well, I suspect the next few minutes will be rather entertaining."

"Shall we?" Gavin asked.

Cornwall said, "Allow me. I am rather anxious to get to the bottom of this." Cornwall knocked loudly. The butler showed them in and took their hats. They were led into a small parlor, but they did not have to wait long.

Mr. Broadbent greeted them a few minutes later. "Good evening," he purred. "I hope this will not take much time; I have dinner guests waiting to be served. What can I do for you, gentlemen?"

Cornwall said, "I just have a few more questions for you, sir, if you do not mind."

"Of course. I take it this is about the murder?"

Gavin bristled at his word choice. He schooled his features to a cold indifference. Cornwall did not hesitate to begin. "Mr. Broadbent, you do know that lying to a government official is a crime?"

"Of course. Do you have reason to believe that I have misled you?"

Cornwall took out the forged banknotes and showed them to him. "Have you seen these before?"

Broadbent appeared to study them for a moment. "That is quite a bit of money. Is that what the servant found in Miss Iverson's chambers? I must admit I am shocked."

"Are you denying that you have ever seen these notes?"

"Why would I have seen them? They are written in Lord Randall's hand to Miss Iverson."

"And you have never seen them?"

Broadbent shifted his weight and looked at Silence and Gavin for a moment before returning his gaze to Cornwall. He appeared to be weighing the consequences of answering. He cleared his throat and announced, "Actually, yes. Lord Randall came to see me a few days ago. He stated that Miss Iverson was threatening to blackmail him, and he asked for my advice on how best to dismiss her. I advised him to go to the police, but he decided the only way to solve the problem was to pay her. He wrote those notes right here in my study. I watched him do it."

Cornwall said, "You are sure about that?"

"Very sure."

"Excellent. Could you write a statement to that effect for me? To help explain it to the courts?"

"If you think it will help." Relief seemed to flood Broadbent's face; Gavin tried not to gloat in the trap that Cornwall had placed.

"It will. It most definitely will."

Broadbent walked to the writing desk and sat down. He pulled out the paper and dipped a pen in the inkwell.

Cornwall stepped a little closer and watched him write. After a few minutes, he added, "Be sure to write how you directed Fresden to seek the help of the police. You would not want anyone to think that you omitted any facts." While Broadbent was scribbling away on the paper, Cornwall looked at Gavin and subtly nodded.

Broadbent finished and dusted the paper, handing it to Cornwall. Now was the moment of truth. Cornwall took the paper and compared it to the banknotes. Then he folded both papers neatly and methodically and put them in his pocket. "Thank you, sir. Before I go, is Lady Monique Pinnock here tonight? I have one last question for her."

"Yes, she is," Broadbent flustered.

Gavin asked, "And would you be so kind as to send for my footman? He should be in the servants' quarters."

Broadbent looked confused, but he nodded and pulled the bell. When a servant came to the door, he instructed him to bring Lady Monique and Gavin's footman to the study. Tension started to build as the minutes passed in silence. Broadbent seemed to sense something was amiss.

Gavin took the opportunity to tell him, "I am to marry Grace."

"Is that so?"

"Yes, I hope to make her my wife before the month is over."

"Well, I know better than anyone how charming Grace can be when it suits her," he smirked. "At times, one could almost forget her humble circumstances. I would keep an eye on your banknotes, though."

Gavin bit his tongue and tried to remain calm. "I admit that she may not have much in the way of money or status," he responded, "but she is far richer in spirit than anyone I have ever met. She has the strength of David. And she has slayed many

193

Goliaths over the years. Do you know what I find interesting about the story of David and Goliath?"

"No, Your Grace," Broadbent snickered. "But I suspect you are going to enlighten me."

"Yes. It reminds me of a saying that I have always loved: 'No one ever trips over mountains. It is the small pebble that causes you to stumble. But pass all the pebbles in your path, and you will find you have crossed the mountain.'"

"Forgive me, Your Grace, but I do not see where you are going with this."

"I shall explain. It was a single pebble that took down the mighty Goliath. It was not brute strength or an army of men. In fact, brute strength failed rather spectacularly. No, the giant was defeated by an obscure shepherd blessed with intelligence, strategy, fortitude, and a bit of skill. Would you not say that Grace possesses those same qualities?"

"I would not know," Broadbent sneered. "I have not seen her for three years. I did not even know she was in London."

Really? So Fresden didn't come to you for advice about Grace's attempts to blackmail him? Gavin threw Cornwall a look to see if he had heard Broadbent's accidental revelation. Cornwall had a small smile on his face and gave the subtlest of nods.

Gavin continued talking to Broadbent. "Of course she has these qualities; they are her strongest gifts, as you well know. It is too bad you underestimated her three years ago. If you had seen her true worth as I do, you would never have let her go. She is your David, Broadbent. And with ease, she has knocked you from your throne. In so doing, she has fully earned the title of the Duchess of Huntsman, and you shall never have the title of earl."

Anger and fear were mixing in Broadbent's eyes, each fighting for dominance. A storm was brewing. Gavin had always enjoyed the toss and turn of the waves at sea. On a ship, one always had to be ready to readjust balance. Just when you thought you would be tossed right, a wave knocked you forward. And when you were expecting to pitch forward, the waves hit you on the side. It was an exciting game. One had to know when to batten down the hatches, to stand and fight—and when to abandon ship. Broadbent might not have realized it yet, but his ship was going down.

Lady Monique came in and assessed the occupants of the room. As her gaze rested on Broadbent, she seemed to sense his unease.

Cornwall stepped forward and said, "Lady Monique, I have nearly finished my investigation of Lord Randall's death. Mr. Broadbent has been very helpful these last few minutes. But I am sure the judge sentencing him will want to know whether or not to charge you as well."

"What?" Broadbent sputtered. "I had nothing to do with Fresden's murder! It was Miss Iverson! Witnesses can testify I was at the Comptons' ball!"

"Oh, I do not plan on charging you with Lord Randall Fresden's death," Cornwall assured him.

"Then I demand to know what charge I am accused of!"

"*Charges*, sir. Let me see—harboring a fugitive, providing false information to a magistrate, and forging these banknotes."

Broadbent stuttered, "I only . . . you cannot prove . . ." Then he looked to Lady Monique, who slowly took a step away from him. "Do not say anything, Monique."

Cornwall was quick. "On the contrary, Lady Monique, now is the time to talk. I do not give second chances. You see, Mr. Broadbent here has just written me a letter detailing how he and Lord Randall discussed Miss Iverson's alleged blackmailing scheme. His letter confirmed two suspicions. First, his handwriting is identical to the banknotes, proving that he was the one who wrote the notes. Second, his statement is entirely false, and now it is in writing. He has indisputably lied to an officer of the law. Any minute now, a footman will walk in here and confirm that those banknotes came from Broadbent and were never in Miss Iverson's chambers. He has little foundation to stand on."

Gavin smiled slightly and said, "Yes, one might say his ship is sinking. The only question that remains now is who will go down with him."

"Indeed," Mr. Cornwall agreed. "What say you, Lady Monique?"

"Monique, keep quiet," Broadbent warned. "They have no real proof. Many people have similar handwriting."

At that moment, there was a knock on the door, and the butler brought in Tim. Gavin watched Broadbent for his reaction.

The color quickly drained from the scoundrel's face. The moment should not have been so rewarding, but it was. Broadbent knew now that he would spend the rest of his life in prison.

Cornwall directed his question to Tim. "Mr. Gardner, can you identify the man who gave you the banknotes and told you they were Miss Iverson's?"

"Yes, sir," Tim answered, pointing to Broadbent. "It was him."

"Are you sure?"

"Most definitely."

"Were the bank notes ever in Miss Iverson's chambers?"

"No, sir."

"So you see, Lady Monique, there is little more that Broadbent can do but bring others down with him. Would you like to amend your previous statement that you overheard Miss Iverson threaten Fresden at the ball?"

She looked around the room with wide, desperate eyes. "Oh, please, Mr. Cornwall! Do not send me back to prison! I nearly died there! All I ever did was steal food to keep from starving. I cannot go back! I never saw Lord Randall with Miss Iverson. He told me to say that."

"Who told you?"

"Mr. Broadbent."

"You wretched woman!" Broadbent hissed. "After all I have done for you! How could you betray me like this?"

"Me? I betrayed you? You lied to me! You had me lie to the police! You used me to frame an innocent woman! I may have been a desperate convict with an ancient, flimsy family title when you found me, but I still have some of my integrity left. I am done lying for you. We dance around your wife as if she does not know about us. But you continue to hurt her just so you can gratify your desire for a second course! It is over, Broadbent!"

Broadbent drew back his hand to hit her, but Gavin and Silence quickly restrained him arms. Instead, he cursed Lady Monique and spit at her, staining her dress. Gavin and Silence pushed him back, pinning him against the wall.

Lady Monique hissed, "May you rot in hell!" Then she turned on her heel and left the room.

Cornwall calmly pulled a pair of shackles out of his heavy black valise and attached them to Broadbent's hands. "Mr. Broadbent, it seems your dinner plans have been altered."

Broadbent soon gave up resisting, and Silence and Cornwall escorted him toward the door. "Lady Monique's comment may prove prophetic, you know," Silence added. "Far too many men really do rot in jail."

"Yes," Cornwall agreed. "I once knew a prisoner whose death went unnoticed for three days. The rats had eaten his toes and ears." Then Silence and Cornwall began discussing the need to talk to a judge about searching Broadbent's house for evidence on Whitmore's whereabouts. In a few more days, it seemed the earl would be brought to justice, either by the courts or by God Himself.

Gavin only partially listened to their exchange. *The earl might already be dead by now*, he realized. For some reason, this comprehension was not disappointing in any way. Maybe knowing Grace had helped him come to terms with his brother's and father's death. Maybe he did not actually have to see Whitmore hang to find peace. It was strange that after spending just a week with Grace, he felt comfortable abandoning a course of revenge that he had devoted his last six months to.

Gavin motioned for Tim. "Thank you for your help, Tim. You are a good man. Helena should be proud that you have singled her out. Good luck to the two of you."

"So does that mean I have your permission to court her?"

"As long as you maintain propriety and treat her with respect, I see no reason not. In fact, how about I let you each have Sunday morning off?"

"That would be splendid, Your Grace!"

"Mrs. Bearl tells me that Helena is smitten. Treat her right. And do not try any more moves like the one Mrs. Bearl saw."

He blushed slightly. "Of course, Your Grace. It really was just a peck on the cheek, I swear. Nothing like what I saw you doing with . . ." Tim seemed to realize what he was saying and stopped himself. His face turned a deep scarlet.

Gavin chuckled and slapped him on the back. "Yes, that last dance step was rather bold. The dancing master at Eton never taught that one."

Tim smirked and added, "Well, I imagine no one needs to be taught *that* step, Your Grace."

This time Gavin laughed outright. "You are quite impertinent, Tim. Has anyone ever told you that?"

CHAPTER 20

As they pulled up to Willsing Manor, Gavin could hardly wait to see Grace again. It was getting late; the crisp, cool air made it difficult to concentrate. Tim had thanked him several times on the way home for giving him the opportunity to court Helena. But Gavin hardly listened to him.

It seemed that everything in his life that had caused him pain and sorrow was resolved now. He had been reunited with Grace; he had learned to accept his father's title; and he had abandoned his plans for revenge against the Earl of Longmont. He was even engaged to be married—which pleased his mother a great deal.

As soon as they walked in the door, Grace walked toward them. Tim bowed to her and excused himself, saying he had a very important person to go see downstairs. She wished him well, and he walked away like a man with a purpose.

Gavin relished the sight of Grace coming toward him. She had changed into a gown that he had not seen before. It was pale ivory with a green ribbon around the waist, accenting her narrow form. She walked toward him, and he saw how she carried herself gracefully, entirely congruent to her nature. There was nothing more attractive than a woman who knew who she was and carried no airs.

Of course, Grace had her weaknesses. She was sometimes a bit hot under the collar, but he could not imagine his life without her passion and devotion. Her eyes were as honest and loyal as any he ever had ever seen. It matched her deeply compassionate heart.

She was a prize that he was astounded he had won; he doubted he deserved her, but he would never take her for granted.

She smiled sweetly at him, igniting a warmth to counteract the chill that still lingered from the carriage ride. She glanced one way and then the other, and then went on her tiptoes and kissed him soundly.

She murmured softly, "I hope you have good news."

"Hmm . . . I might. I might not."

"Are you not going to tell me what happened?"

He smiled mischievously and tapped her nose with his finger. "I believe you must buy my secrets."

She raised her eyebrow at him so temptingly that he had to pull her into his arms. She rested her cinnamon-scented head of hair on his chest, and he took the moment to inhale deeply, which sent ripples of pleasure throughout his body. It was going to be painful to have her return to her sister's house. Painful, truly painful.

"And how shall I pay for such secrets?" she whispered. The flirtation in her voice was so thick he could touch it.

He lifted her chin toward his and with punctuated tender kisses said, "You. Must. Pay. For. Them. One. Kiss. At. A. Time." Then he let his lips linger. She reached her hands up to his face and pulled him down to her. Her lips found a rhythm that was entirely to Gavin's liking. A moment ago, in the carriage, he did not think he would ever be warm again; now he feared he would never be cool again.

He pulled away and consciously slowed his breathing, which had developed a life of its own. He could hear her doing the same thing. After a moment, they simultaneously each took a deep breath, realizing that they must reign it in.

"Gavin, I cannot stay here," Grace whispered. "Nuns or no nuns. You must see that."

"I know," Gavin grumbled. "I have never been a patient man, Gigi. I fear I cannot wait much longer for you."

"Nor I. Could we get a special license and marry as soon as possible?"

"My mother would shoot us both in our sleep if we do not give her a full three weeks to prepare."

"But there is not much difference between two weeks and three. She works well under pressure, Gavin. And I can help her. I doubt I can wait a day over two weeks."

"Then perhaps you should be the one to tell her. I think she likes you best."

She giggled a little bit. "Deal. Now tell me about what happened with Mr. Broadbent, for I believe I paid for your secrets sufficiently."

"What? No debating the issue? Oh, no, Gigi, do not ever lose your deep-rooted desire to win an argument. I love that about you."

She smiled at him and leaned in and offered three simple kisses, nothing like the moment before. "I will save my debate skills for a time when there is something to win. For now, the prize I want most is somewhat out of my reach."

Gavin wrapped her hand around his arm, and they began walking to his study. Along the way, he told her all about Cornwall's clever trap for Broadbent and Lady Monique's recanted testimony.

"Well, it seems the judge will have plenty of evidence to convict him," Grace replied.

"Yes, all thanks to you." He opened his study door and motioned her in. "Can I ask you something? How did you know to handle Tim like that? It was as if you knew he was innocent of malicious intent. He was putty in your hands."

Grace took a seat on the sofa, and Gavin sat down beside her. "At first, I was not sure what to do," she admitted. "But as soon as we entered the room, I could see it in his eyes. He was scared out of his mind. It was the same look I saw in your eyes when I told you I would not marry you."

"Oh, Gigi!" he laughed, "I was terrified when you came down those stairs in your old gray dress! I knew it meant that you had made up your mind to go." He stroked her cheek and whispered, "I was desperate not to lose you again; it crushed me the first time. Promise me you will never try to leave me again."

"I doubt I could survive another attempt. My heart is too fragile. It is hard to admit to needing you, Gavin, but I do. I gave my heart to you long ago without knowing it, and this week with you has proved that it shall never beat for another. The way you kick it into a gallop, beating to a new rhythm, is something I do not ever wish to lose. I do not want a predictable heartbeat."

"Then I shall make it dance every day," he murmured.

"Like you did with that last dance lesson."

"Like I will do right now."

Gavin devoured her lips once again. The pleasure was worth the pain of having to separate once again. But this time, there would not be ten years standing between them—only two weeks.

The next two weeks are going to feel like ten years.

EPILOGUE

"Winston, make haste! I cannot be late to my own wedding!"

Winston was tying the cravat as fast as he could. Despite Gavin's desperate tone, he was really only irritated with himself. He should have known better than to steal a raspberry tart from the wedding breakfast tray when he had only a few minutes to be at the chapel.

He heard a knock on the bedchamber door and assumed it was his mother. "There is no time for another lecture on clumsiness, Mother!"

The door opened, and Silence walked in the room. "Very well. I will save that lecture for another day. But do not call me Mother."

"Silence, Silence!" Gavin said smiling at him through the mirror. He dared not move for fear of impeding Winston's progress. "Welcome back."

"I see I arrived just in time."

"I do not know about that. I am actually fairly late." Winston finished and patted him on the shoulder. Gavin turned and led Silence down the corridor to the stairs and said, "Talk while we ride." Gavin clippity-clopped down the stairs and was reminded of that special moment two weeks earlier when he had held Grace right here on the stairs and heard her say those three wonderful words, "I love you". He would never rebuild the stairs now that it held such a special memory.

The very next day Grace moved to her sister's house, and they made their wedding announcement. He smiled, because with her sister still laid up in bed, there had been plenty of unchaperoned moments at Foxtail Lane. His mother would have been shocked. But neither of them were the kind to get carried away despite their strong love for each other. She had done more than forgive him in that moment. Grace had inspired him.

Silence started filling him in while they climbed into the carriage. "It is finished. The former Earl of Longmont has passed. He was in Scotland all this time, going by a different name. Broadbent has been charged with harboring a felon since it was clear from the letters found at his home that he knew all along where Whitmore was. Broadbent was offered prison or a chance to sail to Australia. He left port a few days ago. The magistrate had no other questions about how Fresden died and has closed the case. There is nothing else to report."

"Splendid news!"

They chatted a minute or two more until they rolled to the front of the chapel and he hurried out of the carriage. He took the steps into the church two at a time and rushed to the front. He was very pleased he did not fall on his face in his haste. He glanced at the bishop and gave him a look of both apology and embarrassment as he took his place. The music began immediately.

He turned to look for his bride. She was backlit by the morning sun coming through the windows. As she walked, his heart sped up. Every minute of the last ten years had been leading up to this moment.

The vows were said, and he placed a gentle kiss on her lips.

After the wedding breakfast and the best wishes, Gavin and Grace climbed back in the carriage to return to Willsing Manor. He handed Grace a box wrapped in brown paper and tied with a ribbon.

"What is this?" Grace asked.

"I do not know. My mother only said that we were to open it immediately after the wedding, the very first moment we were alone together. She made me vow that I would not delay even a second. You know how she is about rules."

"It is heavy." She shook it a bit. "Not quite as heavy as books."

"Yes, but too heavy for garments."

"And it does not rattle. What do you think it is?"

"All I know is that she said we both would appreciate it. She said she could not think of a better gift for our wedding."

Grace smiled at him and started unwrapping it. It was a plain wooden box with a single metal clasp. She carefully opened the lid, and Gavin saw what looked like a hundred envelopes. Grace gasped.

Grace's voice cracked as she murmured, "She kept them."

"What are they?"

Grace pulled out the first letter in the box, and showed it to him. "The letters I wrote to you when you were at Eton."

He riffled through the box and saw one in his own writing. "And my letters to you!"

There were no words to express his astonishment. His mother had saved all their letters over the years! He was not prone to tears, but moisture welled in his eyes as he looked at Grace, who also was tearing up.

"What wonderful entertainment for our honeymoon!" Grace exclaimed. "We shall read a few every night."

He cleared his throat, and his voice came out a bit huskily. "I had my own plans for our entertainment, Your Grace . . ."

"Oh, Gavin! You are such a flirt! There will be plenty of that too," she grinned. She placed her hand on his face. "You wrote," she murmured. "You really wrote, just like you said."

"Yes, and here is the proof of it. Now you must believe me. I loved you all that time, Grace," Gavin said. "You have inspired me in every way."

He kissed her gently, but soon he felt her lips turn up into a smile. Sure enough she was smirking.

Grace giggled and said, "Perhaps next time I can inspire you to be on time to your own wedding."

"You always have to have the last word."

"Dearest husband, do not forget it."

THE END

About the Author

Jeanna is a mother of three daughters, all whom are well versed in *Pride and Prejudice*; they are her best friends and the inspiration for her writing. She also proudly states she is the eighth of thirteen children. When she isn't blogging, gardening, cooking, or raising chickens— or more realistically, writing—she is thoroughly ignoring her house for a few hours at a time in order to read yet another romance novel. Somewhere between being a mom, sister, writer, and cook, she squeezes in three 12-hour shifts each week as a Registered Nurse in a Neurological ICU. She finds great joy in her writing and claims she has never been happier.

Jeanna fell in love again with Jane Austen when she was introduced to the incredible world of Jane Austen inspired fiction. She can never adequately thank the fellow authors who mentored her and encouraged her to write her first novel. Through writing, Jeanna has gained something that no one can take away from her: hope for her own Mr. Darcy. More than anything, she hopes to prepare her three best friends to look for their own Mr. Darcy and to settle for nothing less.

Jeanna's works include: *Mr. Darcy's Promise, Pride and Persistence, To Refine Like Silver, Hope For Mr. Darcy, Hope For Fitzwilliam, Hope For Georgiana*, and *Inspired By Grace*. For more information on these books, please visit her website, www.HeyLadyPublications.com

Praise for *Mr. Darcy's Promise*

"This is a superbly written, highly romantic (while staying completely clean), funny and clever exploration of an alternative path for the classic story of Pride and Prejudice which is so loved all around the world."—Sophie Andrews, Laughing with Lizzie

" . . . I found this to be a memorable, endearing, and poignant variation."— Meredith Esparza, Austenesque Reviews

"Not only was it lighthearted in places, fun, serious, upsetting and very touching, it told a great story with meaning. It made me think, laugh and cry."—Janet Taylor, More Agreeably Engaged

"Mr. Darcy's Promise is a charming novel about a promise that is made to be broken and being patient when it comes to matters of the heart."—Anna Horner, Indie Jane

"The all time best P&P variation I have read. Characters were more true to Austen's interpretation than other stories. The book was very chaste but still tantalizing leaving certain events to your imagination."—Austen Fan 49

"I loved every second of it!!! A book that I most definitely will read over and over again!" — Elizabeth Willey

Praise for *Pride and Persistence*

"The perfect book for curling up with after a trying day at work; brilliantly funny and wonderfully romantic, which will leave you feeling perfectly content and with a huge grin on your face." – Sophie Andrews, *Laughing with Lizzie*

"*Pride and Persistence* is such an adorable and admirable variation! Filled with recovery, reflection, romance, rejections, and a plethora of proposals, this novel will be sure to make you laugh, smile, and sigh with delight. I highly recommend!" – Meredith Esparza, *Austenesque Reviews*

"Thank you, Jeanna Ellsworth, for a lovely book. I enjoyed every minute of it and didn't want to put it down." – Janet Taylor, *More Agreeably Engaged*

"*Pride and Persistence* brings us the same characters that we know and love from the original classic, but a brilliant twist adds more to the story than even Jane gave us all those years ago." – Alice, *Reading with Alice*

"I absolutely loved this book! Jeanna Ellsworth knows how to awaken the spirit of *Pride and Prejudice* and Darcy and Elizabeth's growing love—and we get to watch it all through words, and those words certainly came to life." — Elizabeth Cohan

Praise for *To Refine Like Silver*

"It is emotionally very touching and I was completely drawn into it as I read. It was a book where reaching the 'happy ending' - and not just for Lizzy and Darcy - has never felt more satisfying!" — Sophie Andrews, *Laughing with Lizzie*

"Ms. Ellsworth uses a bit of impertinence, love, laughter and spirituality to take us on a journey through the darkest days of our favorite characters right to the heart of Pemberley bringing with it new life." —Elizabeth Cohen

"Regency and Inspirational Romance fans do not want to miss this work of literary art! Jeanna has a vibrant and vivid way of capturing the English countryside and sophisticated Regency era, customs, and manners that would make Jane Austen proud." — Alice, *Reading with Alice*

"*To Refine Like Silver* is a story of surviving the worst that life throws at us, feeling the pain but not letting it consume us, trusting that happiness and joy will come again, and learning to forgive (but not forget) in order to find peace within ourselves. Regardless of one's faith, I think the words of wisdom from Elizabeth's prayer journal could be helpful to all." —Anna Horner, *Diary of an Eccentric*

"*To Refine Like Silver* is an inspiring and thought-provoking tale of three *Pride and Prejudice* characters and their walks of faith. This story is filled with difficult trials, inspiring words, heart-fluttering romance, and an uplifting message that brings peace. For fans of Christian Fiction and Inspirational Romance this is not one to you will want to miss!" —Meredith Esparza, *Austenesque Reviews*

www.ingramcontent.com/pod-product-compliance
Lightning Source LLC
Chambersburg PA
CBHW020410210626
46816CB00006BB/2204